Praise for

DEVIL IN THE GRASS

"A fast paced, action-packed thriller that is, at the same time, warm and exciting in a uniquely positive way. The somewhat unusual setting for a thriller-suspense novel—The Everglades—will provide particular entertainment for readers who have visited Florida. The novel is further enriched by the wide range of interesting and provocative characters and the cleverly intertwined plotlines involving romance, good vs. evil, southern politics, and regional issues. Highly recommended!"

—THE COLUMBIA REVIEW

"*Devil in the Grass* is a brilliantly plotted and chilling read! With characters that you don't want to meet in dark places, those that you won't forget in a hurry popping off the pages. The book just grabs hold of you and does not let go until you reach the climax and hopefully remember to breathe. Highly recommended for lovers of fiction that has a darker edge to it, this entertains all the way."

—BOOKLOVER CATLADY,
TOP RANKED REVIEWER & BOOK PUBLICIST.

"Woah, what a crazy book! I'm not one for rehashing the plot (that's what the summary is for on the book description page), but trust me when I say you've never read anything like this before! It starts off with some considerable backstory to set up the scene and ground the reader in the world-building, which the author Christopher Bowron does a wonderfully convincing job of creating a believable backdrop for Jack to meet his new 'friends'. The story progresses when he meets Sarah, and continues to get creepier and more disturbing, but in the best way… Bowron has a great "voice" in spinning these complex and intelligent plotlines all together, and if you like thrillers with and edge, you'll enjoy this one. It's a pretty fast read and has some interesting philosophical discussion, something I wasn't expecting. Would love to read more from Bowron in the future." (5 stars)

—NICOLA FLOOD – BOUNDLESS BOOK REVIEWS

"WOW—I couldn't stop reading this book once I started, and I'm still haunted by the McFaddens, some of the best and most frightening bad guys I've ever encountered in a book. Bowron had me from the very beginning, and I turned many pages with a kind of horrified expression, fearing and eager to see what happens next. The book fit in well with my experiences of the Florida swamp, although it expanded and illuminated them in a way that will make me watch over my shoulder the next time I'm there. Highly recommended! Five STARS!"

—LORI STONE, GOODREADS – AMAZON REVIEWER

"Devil in the Grass is an intense thriller filled with riveting suspense and chilling characters which quickly capture and a hold a readers attention from beginning to end.

Jackson "Jack" Walker, is an ex-NFL player who, after a disgraceful fall from glory, is set on turning his life around. After landing a job with a prominent Republican Senator, Jack thinks he's done just that however things aren't always what they seem. Shortly after meeting Sarah, Jack's life begins to spiral out of control. He tries to overlook her membership with The Brotherhood of the Set, but soon feels himself getting pulled into the satanic cult. Just when Jack decides enough is enough he wakes up in a pool of blood. It doesn't take a genius to realize he's been played, but for the life of him he doesn't have a clue why. Until he can sort things out Jack must lay low and rely on his family and their strong Seminole roots to clear his name. But, those loyal to The Brotherhood of the Set don't give up that easily and Jack finds himself in the fight of his life.

I found *Devil in the Grass* to be an absolutely gripping novel. The complex characters are well-developed and credible, aiding in bringing the shocking plot to life. The author artfully spins this sinister tale through his appealing writing style and rich detail making Devil in the Grass a story worth reading.

I highly recommend pre-ordering a copy." (5 Stars)

—STACIE, BEACH BOUND BOOK REVIEWS

"This book by Christopher Bowron was terrific! Once I started reading I didn't want to stop until I'd finished the whole thing. It pulls you in from the beginning, and I enjoyed the author's descriptive narrative and style of writing. The interweaving plotlines were well-developed and certainly not predictable, and the element of the Satan worshipping cult a new angle for me—never read any with this before and it was interesting how the author framed it as a "point of view" and made it feel authentic not come caricature-style plot device. The way this book was written grabbed me right from the beginning and kept my attention throughout. It was intelligent, weird, sad, dark, funny, deep, tragic . . . I thought the storyline and the character development to be very well done and thought out. I feel like this level of complexity could have easily ended up badly, but instead I darn near gobbled the whole book down in just a few evenings. There were some pretty shocking events that may upset some readers but I thought Bowron handled the sensitive subject matter well. This book will haunt me for a long time, but in a good way. I'd love to read more from this author in the future! Recommend for adults only." (5 stars)

—ANABELLA JOHNSON (BELLAREADZ)
GOODREADS; INDIE BOOK REVIEWERS

"*Devil in the Grass* by Christopher Bowron is one of the most original and well-crafted books I've read in a while, and I absolutely loved his descriptions of the different scenery and locales (felt like I was really there in Florida, gaters and all . . .), and his attention to character detail and their personalities through their actions and conversation. Great "bad guys" and Jackson made for a good, solid lead. The story itself was fairly even-paced, but I thought the beginning was a bit slow until things started to pick up as it begins with backstory on his character and situation (and then repeats as new characters come into play) to set up the scene and ground the reader in the various perspectives, which the author does a wonderfully convincing job of creating as believable background for the plot to unfold. Then the action begins as a slow simmer, then a rolling boil, finally to an exciting explosion. This book does touch on some pretty heavy subject matters and there are shocking events. A powerful, mind-bending read that kept me captivated. Liked the characters but the ending was a head scratcher . . . is there more? Recommend for mature readers." (4 stars)

—STEPH COLEMAN – GOODREADS; INDIE BOOK REVIEWERS

"Wow, *Devil in the grass* by Christopher Bowron was awesome! I haven't read anything like that in a long time, if ever. For once it seemed like the characters were anything but the stock, ordinary typical hero/protag guys, but instead all had demons (literally – ha!), motivations, secrets, and I don't want to focus too much on it, but I thought the satanic aspect was pretty cool too. I loved the plot line, as it was really original and unlike anything I've read before. I was really invested in the character's fates, and was surprised more than once. I thought the ending was perfect, and overall it was a genuinely good book. All came together to create a fresh-feeling novel that was out of the ordinary and kept me hooked throughout. This was a standalone novel (not a part of any series, it appears), but I hope Mr. Bowron writes more like this in the future. I'd be reading it! A well-written and compelling read, and one that will definitely appeal to fans of thriller/mystery/suspense novels." (5 stars)

—DARLENE CUPP – GOODREADS; INDIE BOOK REVIEWERS

"This was the first book I've read by this author Christopher Bowron, but I certainly hope it's not the last. He has a gift for writing descriptive and life-like scenes that make us feel like we are really there inside the story, as opposed to it all just being "told" to us, as so many rookie authors make the mistake of doing. I like that this book didn't feel stale or derivative, but instead like a new niche of suspense that serves well to help diversify a somewhat cookie-cutter genre (in my opinion). Great editing (I notice things like that) but the frequent italics were a bit annoying. Started off a bit slow, and there was a lack of tension at times where I though could be more – things were just sort of glossed over on occasion, but overall the entire novel was one that I thought was nicely developed and delivered a wild ride of unexpected twists and turns. I like the darker element, and there were some pretty sexy scenes as well, but I wasn't sure about the ending. Best suited for mature fans of thriller/suspense who'd like a new twist." (4 stars)

—CORY BANYAN – GOODREADS; INDIE BOOK REVIEWERS

"From the opening pages of *Devil in the Grass* I knew it would be different from the books I've been reading lately and I was right! Christopher Bowron sets of the scene and characterizations in a skillful way that not only pulls us in, but creates great visualizations and elicits emotional investments. I truly cared about the characters' fates, and was shocked and saddened at certain things (no spoilers). I think Mr. Bowron writes very well . . . very descriptive and strong and we feel like we are there almost like watching a David Lynch movie or something. There were some slow parts where I thought there was too much dialogue and conversation that did little to advance the forward progression of the plot, and at times was bit too 'telling' when would have preferred more action. But it all came together in the end in a shocking way. Overall a unique, if not surreal novel that pushes the boundaries of typical suspense/thrillers. An interesting and diverse cast of characters, along with several intriguing plotlines interwoven against unique, diabolical setting makes this a memorable read for me. Highly recommend. Warning—only for mature readers as has some graphic subject matter and language." (4-5 stars)

—CARLA BIGGINS – GOODREADS; INDIE BOOK REVIEWERS

I love a well written mystery/thriller novel and this one fills the bill perfectly. Devil in the Grass by Christopher Bowron is a riveting book with a complex storyline and consistently excellent action.

The story's constant twists and turns engage the reader up to the end. Best of all, the book is so skillfully written that I felt I was there watching each event unfold.

Every character in Devil in the Grass has such depth and their quirks and agendas are so well described that they are no longer characters in a book, but real people. The good guys had my sympathy and the bad guys made me cringe. I wondered if I'd ever met anyone capable of doing the things that the bad guys in this book do. You may find yourself wondering the same thing, because really, who does these things? Devil in the Grass is an outstanding example of the mystery/thriller genre. It's definitely a 5 star read.

—SUSAN PHEND, GOODREADS – AMAZON REVIEWER

"Move over Randy Wayne White and Carl Hiaasen. Chris Bowron has arrived!"

—BETSY ASHTON,
AUTHOR OF *MAD MAX UNINTENDED CONSEQUENCES*

"A snappy, scary premise executed with skill against the backdrop of the Florida Everglades...Chris Bowron's debut novel is a gripping read that promises even better things to come."

—RON BASE – AUTHOR OF *THE SANIBEL SUNSET DETECTIVE SERIES*

Jack is a young man who used to be a football player. He gets mixed up with drugs and gets booted out. He soon finds a job and a woman. This woman is not who she seems to be and soon he is in a big downfall spiraling ever further down.

This book was really good. It had me on page one and kept me enthralled the entire book. You see a man with a promising future get sucked, unbeknownst to him, into a world full of cult magic.

This book was definitely different, but it was a great, fast paced, action filled read. I hated putting this book down.

—STORMI – BOUNDLESS BOOK REVIEWS

Satanic rituals, a beautiful young woman, and a former NFL quarterback all come together to form the heart of this sensational mystery, carved out of the Florida Everglades and woven tightly with spellbinding suspense. This is an exceptional piece of first-class fiction, with a strong dose of Stephen King horror thrown in for good measure.

Jack Walker is just looking for a quiet restart to his life when he meets Sarah, a petite twenty-something who promises Jack a very good time if he can just accept one little thing about her -- she's a devil worshipper, a devout member of the Brotherhood of Set.

Jack doesn't want to jeopardize his job working for a prominent state senator, but the flesh is oh-so-weak, and he winds up agreeing to deliver a packet stuffed with hundred-dollar bills to an old plantation house late one night.

What he finds there is a bloody knife, two dead bodies, and a frame-up custom-made to indict him. To make matters worse, his new girlfriend has disappeared, and he has to kill someone who is at her apartment waiting for him. The police quickly start pursuing Jack and, out of options, he flees to the Seminole reservation nearby, where he enlists the help of his family -- native Americans with the ability to hide him in the trackless swamps.

Meanwhile, Jack's luck is about to run out as both police and the Satanists begin closing in on him. The McFadden's -- deranged good old boys in deep with the Devil worshippers -- are seeking revenge for the brother who was killed when Jack fled Sarah's apartment. They are the creepiest characters in the book and if they don't produce at least one nightmare from you as you read this, you are either on high doses of Valium or not paying attention.

The author does an excellent job of ratcheting up the tension as one event after another spiral things out of control. A hundred-year-old witch named Henrietta LePley figures prominently in the growing and grisly death toll, and characters for whom you've developed a strong emotional attachment begin falling under her spell -- and worse. Much, much worse.

The story builds inexorably from its well-drawn beginning to its heart-stopping finish. Indeed, the entire last one-third of the novel will keep you riveted to the action as blood-thirsty gators and ten-foot-long bull sharks join in a feeding frenzy with one terrible objective -- the painful death of Jack Walker and anyone who helps him.

Five sterling stars to *Devil In the Grass,* a stunning debut novel by Christopher Bowron, a talented writer with tremendous authorial expertise. We look forward eagerly to the sequel, and perhaps an action-packed movie as well.

—PUBLISHERS DAILY REVIEWS

Devil in the Grass
by Christopher Bowron

ISBN 978-1-63393-206-7

This is a work of fiction. The characters are both actual and fictitious. With the exception of verified historical events and persons, all incidents, descriptions, dialogue and opinions expressed are the products of the author's imagination and are not to be construed as real.

Published by

köehlerbooks™

210 60th Street
Virginia Beach, VA 23451
212-574-7939
www.koehlerbooks.com

DEVIL IN THE GRASS

CHRISTOPHER BOWRON

VIRGINIA BEACH
CAPE CHARLES

DEDICATION

For Helen

Stands of trees, miles of cutting grass
Whispered stories in the wind too old to tell
Blue skies, the sun, blooms of billowing cloud
There is fear to be found in its vastness
If the ancient swamp could take its due
Like the devil she would . . . if she could
She sits and waits

1

PURGATORY

JACK THANKED THE STOCKY Seminole woman with a nod as she handed him his coffee in a tin can. She had been sent by his grandfather to look after him while he was in hiding. The can burned the tips of his fingers as he held it gingerly. *No coffee cups?* He reminded himself this was a hunt camp in the middle of nowhere. He stirred in some sugar and watched the woman as she left through a tattered drape that half-covered the only doorway. The room contained nothing more than a cot, a table, and two chairs. The plank-board floors and walls were a collage of warped paneling and narrow horizontal logs. The room smelled musty, with a slight undertone of rotting wood. The lone window looked out over the grass plain and wetlands of the Big Cyprus Swamp. A rusty piece of bug screen attached to the frame was covered with duct tape. The hot breeze did little to change the oppressive, stifling heat pressing down on Jack's already sagging shoulders.

Jack took a sip of the strong coffee, careful not to burn his lips on the hot tin. He set the drink down on the table and leaned forward, running his hands through his sweat-drenched hair, his mind churning. He'd become a shell of the man he had once been. Perhaps it was the fact that he was sober, or perhaps it was the reality of his dire situation, that allowed him to lay a finger on the truth for the first time in years. He breathed a heavy sigh. His mother's death during his senior year in college had hit him harder than he'd been willing to admit. He blamed himself in part, and had a hard time dealing with his guilt. He'd buried his emotions, trying his best to be the strong guy. But then he'd cracked. His fall from grace had been steady, including substance abuse and the demise of his professional football career. He'd allowed himself to slide into despair, to the point where he felt he didn't know himself anymore.

Jack stared at the ceiling, slowly shaking his head. He remembered idolizing great football players like Joe Montana and John Elway when he was a teenager, trying to emulate the way they played the game. He appreciated their skill, but it was the fearlessness with which they marched onto the field that had mattered to him; they seemed oblivious to the adversities they faced and allowed their abilities to produce great results, unhindered by doubt. Jack worked hard to exhibit many of the same characteristics during his high school football days, and then later at the University of Florida. He'd grown into a person that his teammates looked up to, the one who didn't back down. He was a gamer.

Jack had fallen a long way from that standard these past few years. He didn't blame anyone. He'd become soft and apathetic. He'd made a half-assed attempt to clean himself up after hitting what he thought was rock bottom. He realized now that he had never dealt with the root of his problems, he'd only masked the symptoms.

The magnitude of his situation and the possible consequences hit him like a slap to the forehead. He picked up the *Naples Daily News*, which lay at his feet. It was the third time he'd read the front page since waking an hour earlier. His picture was prominently displayed with the headline beneath it:

CULT LEADER SLAYS TWO IN CLEWISTON

A Fort Myers man in his mid-twenties is the subject of a massive manhunt in connection with the slaying of a man and woman in the small town of Clewiston, near Lake Okeechobee Tuesday night. The suspect, Jackson Walker, is described as 6-foot-2, with dark hair and athletic build. He was last seen in LaBelle, east of Fort Myers.

Walker, a local football star, played three years for the University of Florida Gators. Walker was later drafted by the Cincinnati Bengals and played three years in their system. He currently works as an intern for Sen. James Hunter.

Walker is believed to be connected with a local Satanic cult called The Brotherhood of Set, based in South Florida. Not much is known about the cult, or whether it is associated with other Satanic sects within the country.

Details and names of the deceased are being withheld pending further investigation. Anyone with information or knowledge of his whereabouts should call the Lee County Sheriff's hotline. Walker is considered armed and dangerous.

Jack threw the paper into the far corner of the room. "Fuckin' hell! . . . Cult leader, armed and dangerous? Come on." He shook his head. Jack possessed nothing more than the clothes on his back and a little cash in his wallet. Reading the newspaper again infuriated him.

The Naples Daily was a small rag, but by now his story could be on WINK news, maybe even Fox TV, his history dissected and the media hounding anyone closely associated with him. He shook his head once again. *This doesn't look good.* He stood up and paced the small room. He was not a devil worshiper, nor was he a cult leader; he needed to prove his accusers wrong.

He'd known that there were risks associated with his involvement with Satanists. He blamed his naiveté for becoming involved with Sarah. It could have happened to any red-blooded American male, and he was paying a massive price for chasing that woman. Now he was accused of murder, facing a long prison sentence, and perhaps the death penalty. He would not turn himself in—not yet. He couldn't get caught by the Satanists either; that would end badly. He shuddered.

He was stuck in the middle of the largest swamp in the United States, sweating profusely in a small, dismal hut. If he were to give up at this point, he wouldn't be able to prove his innocence. He owed that much to himself and his family. He needed time to figure things out. *Why me?* What were his assailants' motivations? He didn't think it a coincidence that the whole affair began shortly after he was hired by Senator Hunter. He had been drawn into some sort of conspiracy? To what end? Had he been preyed upon because of his apathetic state? He banged his fist on the table. Most importantly, he needed to become the Jack Walker he had once been. He could feel the fury building in him like he hadn't experienced in a long time. He would need this emotion to get out of the mess he was in.

Jack paced the room waiting for Janie to arrive. Janie worked for a Naples law firm, and had been hired by his Aunt Rebecca from Atlanta. Jack didn't think that the situation was going to be resolved with legalities, but for the time being, he was out of options and had to trust his aunt. He lay down on the rusty cot. *At least the bedsheets are clean,* he thought. *Aunt Rebecca took care of everything.* The smell of the freshly laundered bedding gave him some comfort. He put his hands behind his head and closed his eyes, thinking about the crazy events of the past few months.

2

THE INTERN

"TURN UP THE AIR, son, it's roasting back here."

Jack guided the car onto the ramp to I-75 South, toward Naples. He merged into the slow-moving rush hour traffic before adjusting the temperature. Florida Senator James Hunter sat in the back of the town car with his personal secretary, Phyllis, without whom he seldom went anywhere. Jack had begun his internship with the Republican senator two months earlier; it was one of those get-your-foot-in-the-door jobs. He was willing to start at the bottom in a state senator's office and work his way up. The position was a drastic step down from the professional football career he'd worked so hard for, but this was South Florida, smack in the middle of the worst recession since the Great Depression, and he was happy for the work. He missed the thrill of a big game, but it did him no good to lament the past. Hunter was a big Gators fan and felt sorry for Jack. He'd seen most of Jack's home games when he was in college and had wanted to give the young man a break. Jack was thankful.

The job varied from day to day and required many hats; today he was the driver.

Hunter was all business at work—always in a stylish suit, his salt-and-pepper hair never out of place. After hours, it was different. Jack was often invited to Hunter's home for a few drinks to talk sports, shoot the shit, and to watch that night's big game, whatever sport it might be. It wasn't a bad gig, but he wondered where it might lead. He figured his best bet was to work hard and move up through the ranks of the Republican Party. There were a few ex-athletes making it big in politics. Instant recognition fueled their political success. He would watch and learn the ropes. Hunter was a pro, and as long as he didn't patronize him, Jack would work hard for the man. There were people who got off on hanging out with pro athletes, even has-beens.

Jack picked up the senator and his assistant Phyllis at Punta Gorda Airport, a half hour north of Fort Myers. His boss's next appointment was in South Naples, followed by a late dinner in Miami. Jack sighed. *This is gonna be a long, boring night.*

The drive to Miami passed quickly with little traffic until they reached the downtown area. Halfway through the drive Jack saw out of the corner of his eye Hunter brush his hand along Phyllis' leg. Phyllis' eyes met Jack's through the rear-view mirror. Jack turned his eyes back to the road, not wanting them to know he'd seen their private moment.

His mind wandered as he settled into the drive. Jack had met Hunter's wife, Debra, at a barbecue a month earlier. She was attractive and in her late forties, slightly plump, but well-proportioned. The two of them had enjoyed the afternoon—Hunter's hand making a similar gesture on his wife's backside, her head turning to meet his gaze, a knowing smile. Jack shook his head to clear the image. *Who am I to judge?* Yet it left a bad taste in his mouth.

The evening in Miami was painfully long. The temptation of the South Beach strip was tantalizing, the art deco buildings and buzz of the street like a lodestone pulling at Jack. But he was no longer a celebrity, he was a normal guy now, a guy who needed to earn an honest living. He longingly remembered the many nights he'd spent in the chic nightclubs, being the playboy.

He tried to banish the thoughts. The high life had done him no favors, and had left him with an empty wallet and a substance-abuse problem.

His drug use had begun with weed in high school, but he'd cut back in college because it was frowned upon at the University of Florida. In his sophomore year, he suffered a separated shoulder, which fostered a new addiction—pharmaceutical painkillers. He continued to take them for the rest of his college career and into his early days with Cincinnati. His mother had warned him before her death that she was concerned about his health, having seen how booze had ruined his father and their marriage. But professional sports are ultra-competitive, and all about money. Jack was lucky enough to be counseled by the Bengals' team physician about the risks involved with painkillers and alcohol, and at the request of team officials, he was sent to drug rehab in his first professional off-season. It led to some bad press.

Then came performance-enhancing drugs. The doctors guaranteed that his shoulder would recover and there would be no issues with drug testing, but deep down Jack knew that something wasn't right. His instincts proved correct; indifferent play and substance abuse ended his short stay in the NFL.

The realization that his dream was over was too much for Jack to come to grips with. Coke and Jack Daniels came after he was released. He still had some cash and he needed to be numb. Within six months, he had blown five hundred grand partying in Dallas, New York, Miami, Los Angeles, Toronto—wherever there was a party, he was there. It was a free-for-all until the money ran out. Once he could no longer afford his binge lifestyle, Jack tried to clean himself up. Every now and then he would buy some cheap Florida-grown pot you could get nearly anywhere, if you knew where to look.

He stood in front of the Delano, a swanky restaurant one block from the water on Collins Avenue, where Hunter was dining. Jack made small talk with the front security for a bit, a large man with a good sense of humor who remembered him from his party days.

"Jack Walker. No shit. Wassup, bro?" The two men clasped hands. "You got a table?"

"No, man. I'm on the other side now."

The large man looked him up and down. "What you mean, bro? You are the shit!"

"Not anymore. I'm washed up, cut, lost all my cash. Earning an honest living like you now."

"Never woulda believed it. Read somewhere that you were having problems, figured you'd work it out. Catch on with another team. Real sorry, man."

"That's life, man. Here I am, no contract and working for a state senator, waiting for the man to finish dinner."

The security guard just shook his head. "I remember you draggin' two girls in on your arm in the day."

"Wasn't that long ago. Carter . . . right?"

"You got it. Your college days were your best. You were a cult hero. It was like a switch flipped and you took off. If you coulda done that at will, you'd still be the shit. Loved watching that, you were the king of the comeback."

"To tell you the truth, I was always a bag of nerves, worried about making mistakes. We'd either have to be down and out, nothing to lose, or someone would have to knock the shit out of me to wake me up, piss me off, and then it was academic. They didn't have the patience up in Cinci, or maybe I was just scared shitless most of the time."

Carter laughed. "Coulda paid me the big bucks. I'da knocked you upside the head."

Jack smiled, clapping the man on the shoulder. These conversations became tedious after a time, but Jack went along with them. He knew the day would come when the adoration ended.

After chatting for an hour, he shook Carter's hand and strolled across the street to grab a bite to eat on Lincoln Road. As he walked across the street, he received a text from Phyllis, asking him to have the car ready in fifteen minutes. He grabbed a couple slices of greasy pizza and a coffee, and retrieved the car.

The drive home across Alligator Alley was long, straight, and boring, and late at night. He'd made the drive dozens of times to take in a Miami Heat or Dolphins game, not to mention the odd night out on South Beach. The only difference now was that he was getting paid and didn't have a belly full of cheap beer. He closed the privacy panel that divided the front and back seats. The senator was asleep, and Phyllis was busy tapping away on her iPad. He anticipated that they might want some privacy. He downed the remainder of his coffee and tried to settle into a groove. His eyes were biting a bit, but he knew that would soon pass if he kept his mind occupied.

He smiled. Earlier in the day he'd met a young clerk named Sarah Courtney while waiting for the senator as he convened his Naples meeting. Sarah worked for the Republican Party and dealt with Hunter's office on a regular basis. The young woman was not beautiful in a conventional sense. She was petite and fairly short, with dark brown hair and Asian eyes. Jack couldn't figure out exactly what the attraction was; perhaps it was the way she carried herself, her confidence. He took a deep breath and focused on the road.

Jack had been sitting in the lobby reading a dated *TIME* magazine for the better part of an hour when Sarah walked into the room. He looked up over the corner of the magazine as she sauntered through, not giving her too much notice, but within a few seconds she was standing over him. He didn't really see her as much as he felt her presence, her closeness . . . no . . . it was more than that—he could smell her. Jack lowered the magazine slightly, feeling a little uncomfortable. He was getting tired and didn't really want to talk to anyone, but it felt like she willed him to raise his eyes and look at her.

He was about to glance down at the magazine again in a fit of shyness when she lightly grabbed the edge of it and pushed it to the side. Her voice was deep.

"You must be Jackson? The new guy . . . the football player?"

He raised his eyebrows.

"The girls in the office have been talking about you." She backed up a few steps, placing her hands on her hips. "I don't think you are as gorgeous as they say, but you certainly are cute."

Jack swallowed and muttered. "I *am* Jackson Walker, but I don't know about all that other stuff." He could feel his face getting warm."You are a bit forward if I might say so."

"Well . . . maybe, kinda." She eyed him for a moment, biting her bottom lip. "I'm new as well, maybe we'll see each other around, unless the senator has you working too much?"

"How busy do I look right now?"

"Good point. Look, I don't make a habit of asking guys out, but I'm new here and life's been boring as hell since I started this job. It would be great to have a coffee next time you're stopping by."

She's pretty aggressive, but what the hell. "Sure, why not."

She grinned. "Gimme a call, here's my cell." She wrote the number on a small piece of paper, then turned and walked back toward the office, taking one last sideways glance. Jack was speechless, his mouth dry. He'd been checked out before, but never so blatantly. He wasn't sure that he felt comfortable; actually, he didn't know what to think. She was more than forward, she was on a mission. He was somewhat turned on by her demeanor. It wasn't love at first sight, but it was clearly sexual, and undeniable, and strong. It stuck in his mind throughout the day.

He tried to think of something else as the car rolled smoothly along the highway. Fifteen minutes later he whispered, "Damn it." He hadn't been with a woman in some time and the thought of her, the smell of her, was too much to resist.

He picked up his iPhone and voice activated Sarah's number, which he'd programmed earlier in the day . . . just in case. "Call Sarah Courtney."

The phone rang five times. He was about to give up when Sarah answered. "Hello?"

"Hey, it's Jack, we met earlier . . . " There was a slight pause.

"I was disappointed . . . I didn't think it would take you this long."

What the hell! Cocky? No, confident. He smiled. "Couldn't get free, still on the clock."

"Glad you called."

"Senator Hunter tells me I would be crazy not to ask you out. So . . . you free over the next few days?"

"Well, tomorrow I have a prayer meeting. But Friday for lunch sounds good."

Jack hesitated. *Prayer meeting. Lunch. Who goes to lunch for a date?* "Sure. Can I pick you up?"

"I'm working a promo over at Bell Tower. There's a place called the Blue Point Oyster Bar. I'll meet you there. That okay?"

"I can swing it, not workin' Friday anyway. How's one o'clock?"

"See you then, I really look forward to it." She hung up abruptly.

Jack pondered the short conversation as he made his way back into Naples. Prayer meeting? He'd gone out with some religious girls—there were a million of them in the good old South. He didn't know if he had the will or the patience to work his way around the bases, to go through a prolonged courtship, meet the parents. He was a good-looking guy and didn't have a problem meeting women. He never sought them out; perhaps it was his strong, silent demeanor that drew women to him. His mother used to tell him that he had an honest face.

Lunch, prayer meeting . . . maybe she was playing it safe. So be it. He'd been to the restaurant before, and the seafood was quite good. He'd have a few drinks, get primed, be cordial, say it was nice and be done with it, then he'd call his buddy Perry and see if he wanted to go sharking in the evening. Maybe he would get lucky.

****

"Damn." Jack hadn't left himself enough time to get across town. If you got on the wrong side of the lights in the city of Fort Myers, you could nearly double your travel time. Some of the lights in the state were unbearably long, and if you got caught, you could sit for minutes at a time. There was a constant jockeying for position to get in front of the old people and run the lights, hoping there wasn't a cop sitting at the intersection ready to pull you over.

He sat in traffic stuck in the endless cycle of red lights. He stared at ABC Liquors on the far corner, reminding him to stop later for some Jim Beam and a few Coors Lights for tonight's fishing. He hung his arm out the window. He could feel his skin burning in the hot summer sun. His air conditioning was broken, and the sweat rolled down his back and into his underwear. He put his nose to his underarm, hoping that he was not beginning to smell too bad. Before the light turned, he sent Sarah a quick text telling her that he would be a few minutes late.

The parking lot in front of the Blue Oyster was nearly full, but Jack pulled into one of the few remaining spots. He was fifteen minutes late. Sheepishly, he pushed open the heavy wooden door to the restaurant. The air conditioning blasted him—such was life in South Florida, hot and cold, into air conditioning, into the heat, then back again. He looked around to see where his date was. The room was dark and appealing after being in the hot sun. He scanned the tables—*nothing*. He began to think he'd been stood up, but then he spotted her sitting at the bar, a bottle of Sam Adams in her hand. He sauntered over, trying his best to look casual.

"This seat taken?"

Sarah seemed genuinely startled, sitting lost in thought. She turned to look at him, a wisp of hair falling across her pretty face. She pulled it over her ear.

Damn, she looks good, he thought. She was wearing a tight black skirt, and the way her right leg crossed over her left emphasized the fullness of her hips, the same way her tight zip-up jacket showed off her small but enticing breasts. His eyes were drawn to her hot pink running shoes. His head popped back up—he didn't want to show too much interest. Then it hit him: she smelled really good. It wasn't perfume, it was her. She had her own smell. *Fuck, who has their own smell?*

"I'm glad you made it, traffic can be a bitch around here sometimes." She smiled, and her face seemed to glow. "Let's get you a drink." She waved the bartender over.

"Stella . . . please . . . draft pint," Jack said.

The bartender nodded and moved to the fridge to get a frosted glass.

"Should we get a table?" He was still standing, unsure of Sarah's plans.

"Let's stay here. I like to sit at a bar, the service is quicker. We can be closer and hear each other better."

Closer? I need to get farther away, the smell of you is killing me. Jack sat down, took a deep gulp of his beer, then wiped the froth from his top lip and nodded.

"Let's order some oysters to start. I prefer Malpeque, not the big slimy ones from Florida. They're smaller and slide down easy." Sarah opened one of the menus that the bartender placed in front of them, and handed the other one to him.

"Can I be forward and ask you about yourself, Jackson Walker, or do you prefer Jack? I have heard the odd thing and from what I hear, you are highly rated."

Highly rated? "Is that so? How does one become highly rated?" He crossed his arms.

She smiled impishly. "That's just what I heard. Why would I want to date a man who was not highly rated? It makes perfect sense. Now, about yourself?" Jack felt awkward. He was being interrogated, and her scent was somewhat less potent. *What happened to small talk?* The girl was starting to irritate him, but he figured he'd please her.

"Where to begin? Well, I'm a Southwest Florida boy, born and bred, grew up in the Fort Myers area. I was pretty good at sports. You heard I played pro ball?"

"I know that. It doesn't mean much to me, but do go on."

Jeez. "Oh . . . well, I played well in college, made it to a bowl game, but it didn't really translate into success with the Bengals. I got cut a year ago, and here I am working for the senator. I'll tell you though, I do miss the limelight, the roar of the crowd, and the heat of battle."

"You're educated. That's a good thing, the limelight is superficial. I work for the Republican Party, Jack. You work for a Republican senator. I read your file—everyone has a file. They want to know if you're a lying son of a bitch, or if you have a criminal record. From what I hear, the government knows everything about us. Frankly, I wanted to know as well."

Cannot wait to go fishing.

She put her hand on his knee, sensing his unease. Like a reflex, he wanted to pull back, but somehow couldn't. The hair on top of his head stood on end, and tingles ran down the back of his neck.

"Tell me something else about yourself, something interesting. What you've told me thus far was like something you read off a cue card. That kind of story might work on some girl you might meet at the Lani Kai, but it won't cut it with me. It's boring."

Her hand remained on his knee. He felt paralyzed from the waist down, not wanting to break the contact. *Boring?* He took a minute to gather his thoughts, finishing his beer, and ordered another one.

"Like, what do you want to know? Seems as if you know everything anyway, just like the NSA." He laughed.

Her voice had an edge, like she was losing patience. "Look, if I'm going to go out with you again, I want to know something unique, something strange about you. I don't like normal men, and it's starting to sound like you are pretty normal. Tell me something about you, something you've never told anyone." She wiggled in her seat waiting for his reply.

How badly did he want this girl? He paused for a minute weighing his options. As if knowing what he was thinking, Sarah squeezed his leg encouragingly. *Damn.*

"Okay, I'm hooked on soap operas; never told anyone that." He took a long sip of his beer. "*Y and R*. Used to watch them with my mom." He went silent for a time. She smiled encouragingly, nodding her head. Jack continued, "I'm a bit of a loner, all in or all out. I have my friends, and they are good friends, but not many. The people I hook up with, we're all close." Jack paused and looked into Sarah's face. He was caught by the way her nose turned up cutely at the end. "Never had a long-term girlfriend," he lied. He paused a minute remembering his high school sweetheart; they had dated for three years. He didn't know if he wanted to encourage a relationship with Sarah. "Does my bio say that I'm part Native? My grandfather is Seminole . . . so was my mom."

"No it didn't, and good to know, but still not interesting."

"You have to *show* someone that you are unique, Sarah. I could probably think of a few more things about myself, but that might not be good enough. Hell, what's exciting to me might be boring to you. Beyond what I've said, you're just going to have to find out if I am a 'normal guy.' Take it or leave it. The interrogation is over."

Sarah sat in silence and then smiled, looking him directly in the eyes. "Good answer."

"What about you? I know you're a Republican, and you sure as hell know how to wear a black skirt."

She raised her eyebrows. They both sat in silence for a few minutes looking at the menu.

"Decided what you're gonna have? I'm hungry. The crab cakes sound good, might have a wedge salad with blue on it."

"Sounds good. Two crab cakes with wedges." She repeated the order a little louder, catching the bartender's ear. The server acknowledged with a nod of her head and punched the order into her terminal.

Sarah squished up her cute little nose. "My story. Well, it has some similarities. Florida State, but I didn't play ball . . . well." She smiled coyly. "I was born in Jacksonville."

Jack could not resist. "You mentioned a prayer meeting. Go to church regularly?"

Sarah's eyes turned down for a moment. She pondered her next statement. "It's nothing really, just a group of like-minded people."

"So you don't go to church?" Jack asked.

"No . . . not a church as such. We don't like to talk about things outside the circle. We are nothing like what you must be thinking. If you're worried that I'm a Bible-thumper, don't be." She placed her hand on his thigh in a reconciliatory way.

Jack's heart skipped a beat.

"You're a Scientologist?"

"Not even close." She threw her head back, laughing. "They're a bunch of whackos. I promise we'll talk about it one day if we're still friends, but it's not important now. All this talk about politics and religion isn't the best way to start things off. It's said that many a friendship has been ruined by both."

The bartender delivered the oysters, which looked fresh and were served with diced shallots and horseradish. Sarah dug into the shellfish with gusto, picking up an oyster, raising the edge of the shell to her lips, then tilting her head back to let the delicate meat slide into her mouth. She lightly chewed the oyster before swallowing, then licked her bottom lip.

"Delightful. I have four brothers, so I learned to eat quickly. Dig in, don't be shy. Here, I'll make one up for you."

Sarah dropped a bit of shallot and a pinch of horseradish onto a nice plump oyster and brought it up to Jack's mouth. He reached for it, but she knocked his hand away. She put it to his lips and tipped up the end, allowing the flesh of the mollusk to slide into his mouth. She smiled.

Jack swallowed the oyster and took another sip of his beer. “I don’t date religious girls.” He looked her in the eye.

“Why’s that?” she responded.

“Too much crap; been attracted to my fair share. You get yourself all worked up and then there is the false pretense that you might be willing to see the way of God, Jesus and whatever else is involved . . . parents. You get it?”

Sarah pushed his chin up so that their eyes met again. “You’re afraid I won’t fuck you?”

He nearly choked on his drink.

“I promise you that I will tell you about my prayer group in due time. It’s not important. Let me ease your mind. I’m not a prude and if I feel attracted to you, I might have sex with you. I just might.” She smiled. “Good, here comes our food. The oysters taste nice but they don’t fill a hungry void.”

The bartender placed their lunches in front of them, two large crab cakes with a spicy jalapeno-corn salsa and side salad.

They ate in silence for a few minutes before Jack cleared the air. “It’s not about sex—at least not totally. I’ll be honest, I am a sexual person and I enjoy it, especially with good lookin’ women.”

“Like me?” Sarah smiled devilishly.

“Well, you’re good lookin’, and I have to say, I am fascinated by you.” He envisioned picking her up onto the bar, ripping down her undies right then and there. He shook his head to clear the image from his mind.

“Something wrong?”

“Nah, like I said, it’s not just the sex. It’s the whole religious experience that surrounds that kind of relationship. I’m not gonna take up with the Lord just to get into your pants. I flat out don’t believe in it. I’ve got better things to do on Sunday morning than go to church.”

“Fair enough. I’ll tell you, we don’t meet Sunday mornings, and I would have no expectation of your involvement. Let’s drop the religious thing. Okay?”

Jack felt somewhat relieved, but there was a small niggling feeling in the back of his mind that the prayer group would be an issue if he were to follow through and date Sarah.

“So, have I passed the test?”

Sarah smiled ever so slightly. “So far.”

* * * *

Jack sat at his desk, his feet propped on an open drawer. He shared a large, open office with three others on the senator's staff. The room was drab, with old, curled campaign posters on the walls, worn-out carpet, water-stained ceiling tiles, and the odor of stale cigarette smoke and coffee in the air.

He spent the first part of the morning canvasing for donations, which wasn't his favorite task. He was sure that if the senator's office kept track of his success ratio, he'd be out of a job. Jack didn't take rejection very well, and needed to build himself up for every number he dialed. He was about to punch in the next on his list when he was startled by his cell phone. He didn't recognize the number.

"Jack Walker."

"Hey Jack, it's Sarah, catch ya at a bad time?"

"Hi there. No, you couldn't have called at a better time. Doing cold calls, boring as hell."

"Say, I'm sorry I haven't returned your messages. I've been busy. I'm in the area—got some time?

He hesitated for a moment, looking at the stack of paper sitting on his desk. "Yeah, I can slip out for a bit, as long as I finish this list today."

"Okay, I'll be there in ten, I'll pick you up."

"I'll be out front."

Jack hadn't thought about Sarah since their lunch date a week ago. He figured that he wouldn't hear from her again after she didn't return his calls. Two calls was his maximum; any more than that meant you needed to take the hint. He felt a nervous twinge. Was that a good thing? A week's time had allowed him to cool down. He felt calmer, more in control of his hormones, and wasn't sure that he wanted to take the relationship with Sarah any further.

He mentioned to his supervisor that he had a family issue and was taking an early lunch. Standing in the shade of the building, the heat nearly unbearable, he began to fidget, shifting from foot to foot and looking at his watch. A couple of minutes later, a gold Dodge Caravan came squealing into the parking lot, coming to an abrupt halt in front of him. The passenger door opened, Sarah stretched across the front seat. "Hey, the window's broken, jump in."

Jack slid into the passenger's seat, pulling the door shut behind him. He was hit straight away by her smell. *Damn . . . intoxicating.*

"Glad you could come." She clunked the van into gear and slammed her foot onto the accelerator. "I drive fast, hope you don't mind."

Jack calmly put on his seat belt. He patted the dashboard. "As long as this baby can handle it, I'm okay." The minivan had seen better days, and there was a pronounced wobble as the vehicle accelerated.

Sarah turned towards Jack. "I won't beat around the bush. I'm attracted to you. I gave myself the one-week test. If I still have any feelings after a week, that means it's worth going for it. You only called twice, that's excellent. I feel comfortable when I'm with you. I like the way you look. You seem to meet most of my requirements in a man."

Requirements? He didn't like the sounds of that.

"I'm forward, and life's too short as it is. I think it's important to find out if you're in a bad thing sooner rather than later. On the other hand, if things are good, then you have more time to enjoy them. Make sense?"

"Um, yeah, I guess . . . of course." He was becoming a bit impatient. "No time like the present."

"Okay, there are a few more things you need to know about me before we go on. I'll warn you, they have been deal-breakers in the past."

Christ. "Hit me."

Sarah concentrated on the traffic for a moment, turning right onto Bonita Beach Road. "I have a voracious appetite for sex. I can't get enough of it. I like all aspects of it. I like it romantic, rough, kinky, from behind, you name it."

Jack cleared his throat.

"My partner has to understand. Most men I meet think it sounds great; at first they can keep up, but then they start to waver. All I ask is that you're able to adapt. If you're not feeling up to it, be able to improvise."

Holy crap. Jack sat back in his seat. Sarah was describing every young, red-blooded man's dream, yet he was apprehensive and sat quietly for a time.

"You're hesitating, Jack. That's good. If you were to say exactly what I wanted to hear, I'd have my doubts."

Jack didn't know how to respond, but he felt her pulling him in deeper. If she were to glance at his groin she would know that he was hers. He looked at her quickly; she seemed a bit nervous for the first time. *Had she been turned down before after her proclamation?* She'd mentioned deal-breakers. He needed to maintain some sort of parity in the ensuing negotiation. He could not explain it any other way. This was a negotiation, and he had not experienced anything like it.

"You said there were a couple of things. Well, do tell," Jack said

"The church that I mentioned the other day."

Knew it.

"We worship Satan."

"What!"

Like sticking a needle in a balloon, his erection shriveled.

"Holy fuck . . . You're beatin' me up pretty good here Sarah. I've heard of yin and yang, but this is ridiculous." He wiggled uncomfortably.

She gripped the steering wheel tightly, her hands opening and closing in quick succession.

"Okay, good response," she said. "I assure you that it's not as bad as it seems, and in time you'll see that we aren't bad people. We're better than most religious zealots you see running around."

"Yeah, but fucking Satan? You gonna tie me up and slit my throat like a sacrificial lamb once you bang me?"

"We call him *Set*."

"That's Egyptian, right?" He vaguely remembered the name from his grade school Egyptian history classes.

"Yep, you got it. See, we believe that there is more than one deity. We believe in the Christian God, Allah to some, whatever you want to call him. We also believe in Set, or Satan if you will. Set is the deity of free thought, individualism and creativity. We believe that Set is not evil."

The confidence with which she spoke, and the way her freckled nose crunched up when she paused disarmed Jack . . . somewhat.

"We believe that Set, or Satan, took a bad rap when he defied the Christian God by questioning his judgment. Those who blindly read the Bible have construed this defiance as evil. Set's doctrine is to question and not take blind faith as being good enough—that's all. We don't kill babies or chickens. We are a group of thinkers and individuals. Now, just like Christians and Muslims, there are nut jobs out there who do bad things in the name of Satan. We are against all of that. I can tell that you think I'm too bold."

He canted his head to the side.

"You see, I didn't use to be like this; our doctrines have taught me to be forthright, to ask for what I really want and to act upon it."

Sarah turned off the road into Lovers Key State Park. After paying four dollars for admission, she followed a couple of twisty roads and pulled into a deserted parking lot and stopped the van.

"You're saying that I am to blindly accept all of this?"

"No. To question is one's right; it's one of the tenents of our faith. I don't ask you to join, Jack, but merely to accept me as I am, a good person, hopefully a good companion and lover."

Man, can I pick 'em. Jack pondered the situation. *What do I have to lose? If I don't at least give it a try, I'll wonder about her for who knows how long.* She had a sense of danger that appealed to him, and there was the smell of her. Danger and sex can go hand in hand, but there could be a price to pay if things went wrong, and he had to be willing to pay that price. Like most men, Jack decided to shuffle that thought somewhere deep within his subconscious. He needed to take her—he could always dump her later.

Sarah caught his attention. "Sorry to disturb your thoughts." Jack turned to look at her. "You did say that some things needed to be shown. When you're ready, let me introduce you to some of my friends. They really are terrific people. Some of them are important people within our community. You might be surprised. Tell me, Jackson Walker, do you want to stop? To end this?"

He wanted to say *stop* more than *almost* anything, but he just couldn't. He was just too damn hot for her.

Sarah reached over the console and grabbed his hair aggressively, pinning his head to the back of the seat. Then, like a cat she moved over the console and straddled him. He looked up at the roof of the minivan and said a silent prayer. *If there is a God, protect me . . .* Her aura engulfed him, and her scent tore down his defenses. She bent forward and delicately nibbled his bottom lip. Her breath smelled like honeysuckle, perhaps it was her lipstick. She ran her tongue across the same place she had nibbled. She repeated the pattern, and Jack was helpless. She pressed her body into him and kissed his mouth deeply, passionately. He moved his hand to the back of her head to pull her closer, but she quickly pushed his hands down.

"Don't touch."

She started rhythmically moving her pelvis up and down against his groin. He stiffened and feared what might happen if she didn't stop. Thankfully she abruptly pushed herself away, sliding her knees down to the floor of the minivan. She ran her hands down his chest to his belt buckle, which she deftly undid. The zipper was next. He reflexively lifted his hips off the seat as she tugged his pants to his ankles. She didn't bother pulling off his briefs. Sarah held him, taking a good look.

"More than acceptable," she smiled

She ran her tongue up his length, and he moaned softly as she engulfed him in her mouth. *Damn.* He tried to pull her up on top of him, but she would have no part of it. She pushed his hands away once again. He couldn't put up a fight at that point—he was helplessly lost in blissful ecstasy.

3

THE MCFADDENS

THE GREAT SWAMP HUMMED with wildlife—crickets, frogs, insects, waterfowl, cranes together created a chorus. The night was still and very warm, and the air smelled sweet and musky, except for the occasional waft of swamp sulfur. Mosquitoes and no-see-ums were thick, searching for exposed flesh. A full moon provided ample light for those creatures that needed it, be they man or beast.

Three men stood on a low, flat aluminum skiff which moved slowly down the middle of a wide marshy river, leaving a clear trail in the brown-gold algae that covered the water. One of the men stood on a platform raised above the outboard motor. With a long pole, he pushed the craft forward. The figure in the middle of the boat held a flashlight, which he aimed at the grassy bank of the river. The third held a high-powered rifle cradled in his arms.

Jimmy McFadden grinned as he poled the skiff along. "Like shootin' fish in a barrel, ain't it. Eric?"

His older brother shushed him. "Just keep the damn boat straight, you dumb bastard."

Isaac shook his head. He'd been listening to this back and forth banter for most of his forty-five years. Eric had raised Jimmy and Isaac after the death of their parents nearly thirty-five years ago. It was said to have been a freak accident, but Eric knew the details of their suspicious demise. They drowned inside their car in one of the old drainage ditches close to home. Eric was the only sibling old enough to remember; he had been fifteen at the time. His most lingering memory was standing in the funeral home, greeting the various people who knew his parents and came to give their respects—sugar cane farmers, local businesspeople, and colored folk who lived close to their property. His mother was kind to the Negroes. The faces, though, were blurry—except for one. In the procession of mourners and well-wishers, only the old woman stood out. *The old woman,* that was her name, at least as far as Eric McFadden was concerned. Eric thought she was creepy. He didn't like the way she smiled. It was forced, her perfectly straight, brown, stained teeth displayed behind tightly stretched thin lips. She seemed to look right through him, and her breath smelled of stale wine.

"Your parents were fine members of this community, boy. They will be missed." She placed a hand on his thin shoulder, pulling him in closer to her face and the corrupt smell that emanated from her mouth. "Do you intend to carry on the family business, boy?" Eric didn't answer; he was too numb. She gave him an envelope, pressing it between his clasped hands. Later that night, he sat alone in the McFadden home's large and ornate parlor, his parents' caskets displayed at the end of the room, surrounded by garish-looking flower arrangements. He pulled the envelope out of his breast pocket and opened it. It was full of crisp hundred-dollar bills.

Eric looked back on that moment as a turning point in his life—the day he put his parents in the ground and sold his soul. He often wondered if his father had done the same in his youth. He remembered his daddy talking about the old woman, how she had supported their family for as long as he could remember. He was quick to say, "Never cross her, lad, or you'll have the devil to pay." Eric was never sure if this comment was to be taken seriously or figuratively.

Eric had always worked with his father. He hadn't spent a day in school: as far as the Lee County School District knew, Eric McFadden didn't exist. His mother taught him to read, write, add, subtract and multiply. Young Eric tagged along with Jed McFadden wherever he went, never questioning his judgment. Morality was not an issue: he didn't know any better, he simply did as his father requested. When asked to cut the lawn, he did it. Later, when asked to dispose of a dead body with a bullet hole in the forehead, he did it. This was just how things were. His daddy showed him how the great swamp could swallow up a soul without leaving a trace.

The McFaddens and their ancestors were cleaners. They disposed of things great and small, including scrap metal, old cars and trucks, road kill for the county, and dead bodies. If the pay was good, they would kill. As far as Jed could recollect, the business had existed prior to the Civil War.

Upon his parents' deaths, Eric simply continued. His father's clientele came to him because there was no one else to go to. They came to him with dirty jobs and he took care of them, no questions asked. It was a natural continuation. The McFadden's best customer was the old woman, who loved her poison.

As Eric's younger siblings grew older, the roles within the McFadden family shifted. Eric taught the family business to his two younger brothers, which, simply put, was fixing other people's mistakes. Isaac, the middle brother, used the money he inherited from their parents to put himself through school. Eric figured that at least one McFadden should get an education, and would whip Isaac if he was lax with his studies. His high school marks were exceptional, the highest in Lee County during his graduating year. He was accepted at many exceptional colleges and chose Cornell University in upstate New York, an Ivy League college. He graduated with an MBA after completing his undergraduate degree.

Isaac inherited his mother's taste for clothing and the finer things in life. His style was impeccable, and he was always perfectly dressed for the occasion. For instance, when gator hunting, Isaac would outfit himself in pressed safari khakis and a large brim hat. During business hours, he was seldom seen without a casual suit and tie, Ivy League all the way. Tall with dirty blond hair, his face, like his mother's, was sharp featured, with a long, hawk-like nose—handsome if you could get past the seriousness of his demeanor.

Isaac came home to run the family business, His brothers acquiesced to his exceptional ability to manage their affairs, but only as long as he left them alone to pursue their own idiosyncrasies. McFadden Holdings, Inc. was truly a unique undertaking. They did things that other people did not want to do, or did not know how to do, and were paid very well to do it thanks to Isaac's business acumen.

Cleaners needed to be much more careful these days. It had been easy to dispose of things when his father was around, but the modern world put such questionable dealings under a microscope. Issac understood the value of appearances, and made sure that the brothers were diversified and ran front businesses. Isaac formed a small but successful accounting firm. Jimmy was a taxidermist extraordinaire. Eric ran fishing tours out of Pine Island.

****

Isaac turned back to Jimmy. It was his birthday and the two older brothers were taking him gator hunting, one of his favorite activities. Isaac didn't care much for it, but he was a good shot and it made his brother happy. Jimmy would bring the carcasses back to the homestead, then clean and freeze the meat for sale. He would preserve various body parts and sell them to souvenir shops.

Isaac looked back at his brother. Jimmy was not stupid; *simple* was a better word. As far as his brothers knew, he hadn't suffered birth defects, which might account for his behavior and dysfunctional personality. Isaac liked to call him marginally simple with psychopathic tendencies. Jimmy understood good and bad, he just didn't see that one was any better than the other. He did things with no feeling other than a joyful enthusiasm. He would offer you the shirt off his back, or be the first person to help an old lady across the street. Conversely, he did not see the wrong in necrophilia, torture for his own enjoyment, and murder in general. Isaac saw his brother as a useful and loyal tool to be used with discretion.

As a young boy, Jimmy didn't have any use for school. He was a round peg in a square hole, and Eric worried that he might do something bad to other kids. Jimmy liked to kill, dissect, and preserve the bodies of animals of all sizes and types. Eric could well imagine Jimmy bringing home a little friend to show off his veritable house of horrors in the back shop—or worse, sticking some kid in the belly with his pocket knife over something trivial. Eric was wary of the boy when he had a knife in his hand. Thus, Jimmy stayed at home.

Jimmy knew the great swamp and its deeper secrets. Much of this knowledge came from his older brothers, and the rest came from long days exploring, as young kids do. As Eric had learned from his father, Jimmy found that virtually anything could be disposed of in the vast watershed of the Everglades: cars, trucks, planes, garbage, and most importantly, people. Wild pigs, gators and bull sharks will dispose of a body in no time, as long as the bigger bones are broken up, especially the skull and teeth. The slow-moving current of the river of grass swallowed the finer details. Jimmy was expert at making things disappear permanently, and he enjoyed doing it. He found the deepest holes while fishing for catfish, the ones that held the largest gators. No one looked in such places.

Their homestead was located on a large creek that ran into the Estero River. Jimmy liked to pour a bucket of blood and small animal parts off the end of the dock several times a day. The chum attracted a number of large and vicious bull sharks, including one in particular— Jezebel. Although smaller sharks would migrate in and out of the Gulf of Mexico, this shark had lost one of its eyes and stayed pretty close to the dock. Jezebel was nearly ten feet long, and was fat and lazy. She could finish off a normal-sized human, minus the head and teeth, with little difficulty.

Jimmy was methodical, seldom leaving things to chance. He would first dismember a body, then distribute the various parts between the sharks, gators and wild pigs he kept penned behind the barn. The pigs ground down the bones, leaving no trace. The only problem was they took their time.

Jimmy was not ugly in the conventional sense, though he was awkward, and cursed with a permanent look of disgust. He bore a perpetually screwed-up pucker, as if he'd eaten something bitter.

Eric was the perfect balance between his brothers. He didn't have the intellect or the good looks of Isaac, nor did he have the psychotic disposition of his baby brother. He was the worker, the de facto parent, the glue that made things work. He was a decent-looking man, though his face looked weatherworn from the hot Florida sun. He cared little about his outward appearance, but he did clean up nicely if he was with his girlfriend Beth, who lived in St. James City on Pine Island. When he wasn't working for McFadden, Inc., his time was spent on the water operating one of the better fishing charters, specializing in tarpon.

Eric was happy to leave the business end of things to Isaac, and the morbid aspects to Jimmy. Eric was adept at extractions and, when called for, assassination. Within hours of receiving a call, he could have a body removed and, if at all possible, the evidence cleaned up. He drove a restored 1970s GMC van, well-equipped with the latest forensic technology, carpet cleaners and body removal paraphernalia. If he couldn't fix the problem, he would make sure the place burned down.

Eric was very good at killing people. His favorite weapon was a thin blade, perfect for a quick stab to the temple while his other arm held the victim's neck and throat. The temple provided a convenient soft spot for the blade to enter, and it wasn't terribly messy, as the wound could be staunched with the retrieval of the blade. His father had preferred the garrotte, a piece of piano wire with two handles on either end. It was messy, though; the head sometimes fell off, and blood was a real concern. The knife, poison or chloroform over the nose were much simpler. Once the extraction was made, Eric turned the body over to Jimmy, never to be seen again.

* * * *

Eric directed the light onto a pair of eyes, which shone like two beacons just above the waterline. Isaac didn't waste a moment. He raised the rifle and exhaled as he squeezed the trigger. The animal thrashed just after the bullet split the eyes, taking off the top of the head and the brain with it.

"Nice fuckin' shot, Isaac. That's a big one—big female, by the look of the belly when she rolled." Jimmy did a little dance on the back platform. "Let's get 'er in the boat." Jimmy poled the craft over to the shore quickly; they didn't want the gator to slip down into the water. Eric picked up a large gaff and snagged the reptile under the jaw. At this point it was a matter of tying up the beast and hauling her onto the bow of the low, broad boat. If the animal was too big, it would need to be dragged back home.

The McFadden boys pulled the boat up to the dock. It was still dark, and the light at the end of the large wooden structure was engulfed in a mass of bugs. Jimmy jumped up on the wood planking and pulled the boat forward onto the lift. Once the boat was out of the water, he and his brothers dragged the huge gator onto the dock. The blood that dripped down into the water between the cracks would soon attract predators, so Jimmy wasted no time untying the beast and rolling it onto its back. He unsheathed a large fillet knife from his belt and inserted it into its throat and then sliced the large reptile deep into its belly down to its anus. He pulled the insides out, cutting them free from the inner cavity of the body, then pushed them over the side of the dock. Within a couple of minutes, the water began swirling—probably Jezebel, but it would not be long before the gators and catfish arrived. By the time he dragged the rest of the gator to shore, there was a full-on feeding frenzy below the dock. He took extra care not to slide on the slippery wood; it would not be the best time to fall into the water. Eric helped Jimmy hang the carcass up on the front of the boathouse veranda, which jutted out over the river.

"Happy birthday, you sick bastard. Let's get her hung up high. There'll be gators up on the grass in no time."

Jimmy grinned, but it came off more as a look of doubt, the way his face puckered up. "Ain't nothin' to do 'bout bein' sick, Eric, this is what I do."

"If these were dead people, you'd still have 'em gutted, and hung up. To me that's bein' a sick bastard."

"Yeah, but you'da brung em' to me. Who's sicker . . . asshole?"

Eric shook his head, stifling a smile on his leathery face.

Jimmy pulled along one of the many meat hooks hanging on a long metal track. They tied a rope around the gator's head, then slung it around the bar to pull it up to the hook. It took twenty minutes to get the large reptile hung up to bleed. It was the same process that Jimmy used to dispose of human bodies, which have to bleed the same as a gator, though he used a bucket to catch the human blood—no traces could be left.

Eric shook his head again, deep in thought. Jimmy liked to get to know the human corpses, especially the females. He would talk to them for a while. Most of the time they were dead when he got them, but the odd time, they would still have a flicker of life left in them. In those cases, he would slowly bleed them by making small cuts in their toes. He liked to see the terror in his victims' eyes. It empowered him. He would have his way with them sexually, whether male or female, dead or alive. It didn't matter much. He had no remorse.

A number of years back, Jimmy had been quite taken by a young woman and had preserved the body. Eric and Isaac drew the line. It wasn't so much the dementedness of it, but rather the risk of being caught. In the end, Jimmy saw the reasoning behind the decision and disposed of the body.

4

FISHING

JACK PADDLED THE KAYAK into a warm wind that blew steadily off the Gulf of Mexico. It was one of life's simple pleasures, as far as he was concerned; it gave him a sense of freedom with a bit of daring. The water was slightly choppy, and a large full moon hung almost orange in the July night sky. Shark fishermen called it a hammer moon. The odds of hooking a great hammerhead shark were higher, because the shark was better able to see its favorite prey in the moonlight—the stingray.

Jack removed the plastic-coated wire leader from between his teeth as he reached what he guessed to be about three hundred yards. He looked back toward the shore where his friend Perry waited with the rod. He could see him waving a flashlight, a small speck of light compared to the multitude of lights in the high-rise condos that loomed behind him. Jack took the leader, weight, and the bait, half a cow nose ray, and carefully dumped it into the water.

He felt so peaceful, he didn't hurry back to shore. He leaned back in the kayak seat and opened a can of Coors. It was a difficult feeling to explain. Friends would ask him, "Aren't you afraid out there? Dropping a bloody bait, aren't you going to get attacked?" It didn't work that way, at least so far. Once a shark had circled him, but that hadn't bothered him. He was fatalistic out here. If he was going to go that way, then so be it. He had the big-game hunter mentality. Before heading out, he didn't like the idea of dragging a bloody bait into shark-infested waters, but once on the water he seemed to forget his fear, and the thrill-engaged adrenalin took over. It wasn't as easy to catch a shark as everyone thought. They weren't the mindless, meat-eating beasts that most people believed them to be. They were actually quite skittish, and would only bite if conditions were right. A big, bloody piece of fish could be dropped out into the ocean and it might sit there for a day without as much as a nibble. Crabs would do a better job some nights. He'd dropped bait hundreds of times, it wasn't a big deal and he was still alive. He feared the waves and the storms that circled southwest Florida in the summer more than he did the fish.

He finished his beer in one long gulp and ventured back to shore. As the bow touched, Perry helped him pull the kayak onto the sand. "Took your time, bro."

"The summer wind off the Gulf is just gorgeous, and the sound of the waves lapping up against the side of the boat was too nice to pass up."

"True enough, true enough. We got three baits soaking, let's chill for a bit."

He sat down in his beach chair and cracked open another Coors. Perry slumped into his chair. The two had bonded and formed a strong friendship through their deep love of fishing.

"Things okay over at the restaurant?"

"Same old. Pretty dead in the summer, but we're keeping our heads above water. The boss has some pretty good specials going, and a lot of the locals like our shit. You?"

"Job's going okay, don't love it. I met this girl, works at the same place, a different office though."

"C'mon, so?"

"Well, she's different, but I think in a good way. She's pretty cool."

"Pretty cool? Bro, you must be serious. You usually say yeah, she's a good fuck, or she's stuck up, or it ain't workin'. What the hell does *pretty cool* mean?"

"Um, we've only had a couple of dates, but I'm pretty sure I'd like to pursue it a bit more."

"Two dates? Pursue? C'mon . . . "

Click, click, click.

"Something's nibblin' on the twelve ought."

ZZZZZZZ . . . Line started ripping off the huge Penn reel, a sound like no other. Then it stopped. Both men were on their feet staring at the rod. Perry reeled back a few feet. "Let 'em chew a bit. Jackson, I know you better. You are the slumdog football hero. Tell me more." Both men fell back into their chairs.

"Well, we went for lunch the other day. I tell ya, I was so hot for this chick, Sarah. Anyway, halfway through lunch I thought I was gonna have to go whack off in the restroom. Then she mentions religion. Bam, there goes the hard-on. Thought she was a religious nut—we've both dated them, waste of time. But man, was I wrong. Well, it was all nicey-nicey and then she says she has to leave and get back to her job.

"Next week, she calls me up at work. I thought she'd forgotten about me. Comes and drags me out. Says she needs to talk to me. So I clear it with the supervisor and we go for a drive. We talk for a bit, and she says she's a Satanist."

"What the fuck, bro!" Perry stood up looking down at Jack.

"I have to say I was taken back. But then she explained that what she did wasn't evil, that her religion was merely a point of view. Anyway, I'll keep you briefed. I'm not terribly concerned."

Perry looked at him, placing his hands on his hips. "Point of view, what the fuck is that supposed to mean? Is it voodoo or something? You're weirding me out now, bro. I wouldn't touch that shit with *your* dick, I don't care how hot the girl might be."

Perry looked down at Jack, his face pulled tight. He didn't do that very often unless it had to do with fishing. "Don't fuck around with that shit, bro. I don't want to lose my fishin' buddy over some devil woman. I mean that in two ways. Those fuckers can warp your brain and shit. I've heard about it. Before you know it, you're doing shit that you didn't want to do. Second, you work for a state senator. They get wind of that shit and you're toast. You won't get a job on a shrimp boat after that. My advice is to dump her right away. The pussy don't own you yet. You go in there and they own ya."

Jack sat for a few minutes pondering Perry's words, taking a long swig of his beer. "I've thought about all that. I promise to let you know what's up. I'm just checking things out. You know how it is—sooner or later the blow jobs stop. As soon as things start to get weird, if they do at all, I promise I'm outta there."

"Blow jobs? I'm not following."

"Have you ever gotten a blow job from a chick after dating her for more than a year?"

"Good point."

"So anyway, we drive for a bit and end up at Lovers Key. We park, and before you know it we're going at it hard."

"No, c'mon, in the minivan?"

"Yep, right in the front seat."

ZZZZZZZ . . .

"That's a solid run. Get your belt on."

Jack strapped on a fighting belt and Perry handed him the screaming rod. He took it and started running backward towards a stand of mangrove. Once he had a head of steam up, he threw over the drag lever. *Wham*, the hook took hold and the fish was on, and none too happy. The line zinged off the reel at an alarming rate.

"Big one, Perry. Not a black tip. Either a hammer or a tiger—taking . . . too . . . much . . . line. Maybe a big bull?" He sat down in the sand and dug his heels in and began rocking forward and back, gaining a bit of line each time he moved forward. The fish calmed a bit and he added a little more drag. It began to take more line, but not as much as the first run. "Not a hammer, but she's solid."

Perry would not relent. "So you're in the fucking minivan and she bangs you? Afternoon delight, I am so jealous, bro. How ya doin'? Can you gain some line?"

"She's turning, I think." Jack stood up and quickly ran toward the surf, reeling as he ran. Then he started walking backward toward the trees. "Memorable head, Perry, no sex. Fucking memorable head." He started to gain some line. "She's going right, need to keep it off that buoy out there." Jack ran to the left and was rewarded with some slack. He added more drag and began reeling as hard as he could. "I'm sure that I want to bang her, but it's scary what she can do with head, you know? I just want to see her again so that I can get some more. Crazy."

"C'mon, it's really that great?"

"Believe me Perry, it just fucking is."

"You're givin' me wood, bro."

"Well then, stay away."

It took Jack another half hour to get the fish to the beach.

"Here she comes, Mr. 'Memorable Head.' Nice bull!" Perry ran into the surf and grabbed the leader. "Got it, grab the tail."

Jack put the rod in the holder and calmly moved to the back of the thrashing bull shark. He waited until it calmed a bit and the tail stopped flapping back and forth. He quickly grabbed its tail and with one big heave, ran it up onto the beach as far as he could, which was only a few feet.

"Beauty, Perry. It must be eight-plus feet, and she's fat."

The shark started to flip again; both men stepped back, respecting the strength of the animal. Finally, Perry stood over the top of the fish, his feet on the pectoral fins, and pulled its jaws open. Jack used pliers to pull the hook out of its mouth. The shark was tagged, measured, dragged back into the Gulf, and released with no harm done.

The two friends did a high-five and went straight to the beer cooler, their adrenalin still kicking in at high gear. It was a rush that neither of the two friends would ever tire of.

"You give me your word. You're outta there the second things don't add up, right?"

"Sure thing. Now let's get another on the sand. Sorry I brought the whole thing up."

"No, man, that's what friends are for."

****

Jack hesitantly agreed to pick up Sarah at one of her prayer meetings. He arrived at the low block building located five miles inland on Immokalee Road just as the sun began to set. There were twenty or so cars in the gravel parking lot—an odd assortment of vehicles ranging from a beat-up Hyundai to a black Bentley. It was a surprisingly cool night for late July, and the wind was strong. Jack stared at the dashboard, contemplating Perry's words from the night before. Deep down, he knew that his friend was right. *Why am I pursuing this girl?* The physical attraction was strong and he liked being with her—a lot. *Love?* It could be, but there were things that needed to be sorted out, namely her association with the Brotherhood of Set. He pushed his forehead against the steering wheel. "Okay Jackie boy, promise yourself, if things get weird, you're out." He felt marginally better having said the words aloud. He stepped out of the car and slammed the door, hurrying to the front entrance of the building, not wanting to mess up his hair. There were no signs on the building and very few windows. Sarah had told him to come straight in.

He opened the door, trying to make as little noise as possible, and was immediately in the midst of at least forty people who were standing around, drinking tea and eating bite-sized sandwiches. The hum of conversation stopped as he entered the large, low-ceilinged room. The congregation turned to look at him and he could feel his face heating up. The details of the room captured his attention. It was like a legion hall, but without the banners and memorabilia. It was sterile and very bright. Fluorescent lights in the ceiling seemed to burn into his brain while he was being scrutinized by the perfectly quiet people staring directly at him. It was unnerving.

Sarah excused herself from a conversation with an older couple and moved toward Jack. She grabbed both of his hands and turned to the rest of the assembly.

"Everyone, this is my friend Jackson Walker." She turned Jack, presenting him to the congregation. "I promised that we wouldn't scare him away just yet. Please welcome him."

To a person, they placed their cups and food down and clapped gently, nodding in his direction, almost as if it were scripted. Within moments, cups were picked up and the hum of conversation returned. Jack let out a long sigh of relief.

"That wasn't so bad, now was it? I am so glad that you came. Come, I want you to meet some people."

"Whoa. I didn't agree to this." His internal alarm sounded.

"Really now, they're just ordinary people like myself, with similar beliefs. They won't bite, nor will you go to Hell for talking to them."

"I agreed to pick you up. I told you that this . . . this was to stay out of our relationship."

"It will, I just wanted you to meet some of my friends. I promise to do the same with yours . . . come on, now."

Reluctantly, Jack allowed himself to be pulled over to the older couple Sarah had been speaking with. He could hear Perry's words clearly in his head: *"I wouldn't touch that with your dick."*

"Carly Henderson, Buck Henderson, let me introduce you to my friend Jack."

Both looked to be in their early seventies and were very well-groomed. Carly had that permanent Florida tan with white-blonde hair so common to older ladies who lived in Naples. She was in a casual but impeccable dress. Buck was a large man, nearly the same height as Jack. He offered his hand and Jack could feel the strength in the handshake. "It's a pleasure, Jack. I'm originally from Cincinnati. Too bad what happened with the Bengals. Personally, I think they made a mistake letting you go. They don't know their asses from a hole in the ground—bad organization."

Jack was used to this kind of *quasi-plumping up,* as he called it. People want to get close to you as a celebrity, so they try to commiserate and get your guard down so they can talk your ear off about stuff that really doesn't interest you anymore. He'd been offered well-paying gigs to show up at functions so that people could say they hung out with him. He'd done it a few times, but felt somehow prostituted. He felt sorry for the ex-athletes who had no choice, the ones who had families and had blown all the cash.

He slipped into his scripted mode. "No, sir, I respect them totally. It's a business, and I wasn't performing. I had a good run at it, and I am not sorry that it is over. Not everyone is cut out for professional sport. What's important is that I've met this lovely girl." He gestured to Sarah. "She asked me to meet some of you folks."

Sarah smiled for a brief moment and then stared at him, her brows scrunched down, her head tilted to the side.

"Son, I can see right through your armor," Buck said, catching Jack off guard. "I don't give a rat's ass who you were. I'm a minority owner of the Atlanta Braves. I speak on a regular basis with higher-profile athletes than you ever were. I was padding your ass, Jack. What I'm interested in is who you are. Are you good enough for our Sarah?"

Jack was at a loss for words.

"I wouldn't have chosen him if I didn't think he was worthy," Sarah said, clasping his hands harder.

Buck grinned. "This place drives me nuts. I feel like I'm in an incubator. Why don't the four of us go out for a drink? We won't be missed."

Jack looked at Sarah, raising his shoulders in question. *Do Satanists drink?*

"We'd love to. Where are we going?"

"We'll meet you at Handsome Henry's, on Third."

"I know the place, it's . . . a bit old and karaoke?" Jack said, his face turned up in question.

"Well, we're old, and we like karaoke." He offered a hand to Jack.

"Okay, fair enough. Meet you there."

* * * *

Jack parked his rent-a-wreck car behind a black Ferrari and smiled as he got out of the jalopy. At one point not that long ago, he had envisioned a Ferrari, but now he laughed at the irony of the whole thing. Sarah poked him. "What you thinking?"

"Not a whole lot. Just thought one day I would have one of those." He gestured to the sports car.

"I'm glad you don't. I wouldn't have had the chance to meet you. If you owned that, you'd be looking for a supermodel."

Jack pulled her close and put his hand on the back of her head, looking her in the face. "You're hotter than any supermodel. To me they all look like spindly-legged colts. You make something inside me go off, Sarah. From the moment I set eyes on you, I couldn't get my mind off you.

"That's a crazy thing for me to say. I've not been in a relationship since high school. I've been fucked up these past few years. I think fate has more to do with things than anything else. You could step across the street tomorrow and be struck dead by a car. Bullshit. I've tried to live in the present these past few years. I met you for whatever reason, and I'm happy."

He leaned down, pulling her mouth toward his and kissed her strongly. Once again, her smell engulfed him. Her mouth tasted like cherries. She pulled him in deeper with her hand.

Jack put his arm around Sarah's shoulders and led her across the street toward the restaurant. Henry's was hopping. Most of the diners had finished eating and were listening to a singer cover the golden oldies from the '60s and '70s. He was singing "Sweet Caroline" as they walked in.

The place was focused around a large patio, with several palms covered in rope lights. The restaurant itself was an indoor-outdoor affair, covered by a roof but open to the elements, as was the bar.

Carly and Buck were sitting at the bar and gestured for Jack and Sarah to join them.

Once everyone had a drink in hand, paid for by Buck, they moved to comfy chairs beside the singer.

"This guy is great, we come to listen to him all the time. His name's Reggie, originally from Jersey."

Carly smiled, her eyebrows raised. "Yes, this is what it has come down to, listening to washed-up old singers once a week. Buck likes it, though, and if that makes him happy . . . " She shrugged her shoulders. "Take some advice from an old woman. As marriage goes on, your perspective changes. I let him sit here and have a few drinks, then he leaves me alone when we get home. He's a horny old bugger, you know, but he can't get it up after a few rye and Cokes."

Jack nearly choked on his Stella.

Sarah winked at him. "I won't let that happen in any of my relationships. Any man of mine is going to have to keep up his stamina. Health drinks, exercise, whatever it takes."

"I like your attitude, honey. Don't get me wrong, we're still romantically inclined; it just changes once you're pushing seventy. Would you guess that I am seventy-six and Buck here is turning eighty in December? I think we're doing pretty well for a couple of old-timers."

Sarah raised her glass of wine. "Here's to sex after eighty."

Glasses were clinked and the conversation went on, topics ranging from Republican politics to the state of the US collegiate sports system and scholarships. Jack found himself liking the old couple. They were interesting and witty. He found it funny how Carly would interject, mostly with her wry sarcasm directed at Buck. The fondness between the two was obvious, and Buck enjoyed the challenges she presented. It was a long-practiced banter, and Jack hoped that he would be lucky enough to find such a soul mate.

After a couple of hours passed—quite pleasantly, as far as Jack was concerned—Carly stood.

"Okay Uncle Buck, time to move that big body of yours out the door. Let's leave these two a little time to themselves." Buck rose slowly, favoring what appeared to be a sore knee.

"See, Jack, I didn't tell you that I played in the Canadian Football League after I graduated from Rutgers. I didn't make much money, but I did get this bum leg. Count yourself lucky you got out when you did. You seem to have your head on your shoulders. And look after our little girl here. You'll have to answer to me if anything happens to her."

Jack shook the large man's hand. Buck's smile was warm and wide, but somehow Jack knew that the man made the comment with intent.

"Here, take my business card. You need anything, don't be shy to give me a call. Let's get moving, girl." He gently took his wife's arm and escorted her out after she gave both Sarah and Jack a kiss on the cheek.

Jack and Sarah finished their drinks. Jack swirled the remainder of his beer around the bottom of the glass. "You know, they seemed pretty normal. I'm glad you tricked me into meeting them."

"Did you expect them not to be normal? What do you mean by that, Jackson Walker?"

Jack hesitated, wanting to get the words right. "I mean, I have this preconceived notion of what a Satanist is like. You know, come to think of it, they didn't mention religion once."

"Why should that surprise you? They're normal people. Well, they are very rich normal people. I told you, we're not fanatics. Would a Presbyterian speak any differently? I doubt they would, but they probably wouldn't have a drink. Look, I don't want to put any pressure on you. I just want you to be comfortable with the fact that I am what I am. I'm not a monster."

Sarah stared at the table for a moment, and when she raised her eyes, there was a twinkle in them. "Say, let's get out of here. Buck already paid for our drinks. Should we walk down to the Naples Pier? It's turned out to be a gorgeous night now that the wind's died down."

"Yeah, it's been a while since I was down there. My dad used to take me there when I was a kid. He'd drop me off with my fishing rod and some money for bait and I'd be set for the day."

Jack took Sarah's hand in his as they made the ten-minute walk towards the Gulf.

"It's another world in this town, isn't it?" Sarah said. "I feel like a beggar walking past all of these wonderful homes with their perfectly manicured hedges and properties."

"Yep, it is. There's big money in Naples. I think it has one of the highest incomes per capita in the States—a lot of old money. Too bad I didn't make it in football, mighta been able to afford something. Cape Coral just might have to do." He chuckled.

They reached the pier and walked up the old wooden steps. The structure ran roughly four hundred yards out into the sea. There was a structure a third of the way out where bait and refreshments could be purchased during the day. Now the pier was deserted except for a couple of old hard-core fishermen down at the end. They walked out to see if anything was being caught. After a brief conversation with one of the men, they turned to walk back. Sarah stopped halfway and stepped to the side, leaning her arms on the wooden railing.

"You never know what you're going to get out there," Jack said, joining her. "I've seen tarpon, large sharks, barracuda, lots of stuff."

"It's like you're in your own little world out here," Sarah said softly.

Jack wrapped his arms around her from behind, leaning into her. "It can get pretty busy in the day, but yeah, you're stuck out here, like in the middle of the Gulf." Her smell was pure intoxication, and the warm salt air added to the allure.

"Now, Jackie. I want you now."

"What?" he said reflexively. "People could come along any time."

"So? Do I look like I'm concerned about people?" She hiked

her dress up around her waist, and pulled her thong panties to the side. "Take me from behind right now." She pushed her perfect round bottom up against his now very hard erection.

Jack looked left and then right. It looked clear for the moment, though there were people milling around the entrance to the pier. He quickly unbuckled his belt and top button and slipped his pants and briefs to the ground around his ankles. "Right here? You can get in trouble for this kind of thing." Sarah reached behind and grasped his erection and deftly guided it into her.

"Fuck me hard, Mr. Football Star."

He looked around one last time. "Damn it." He didn't need any more encouragement. He grabbed her hips and began thrusting, holding nothing back. He was too hot for the moment to do any differently. What he hadn't anticipated was that she was a screamer. He'd experienced a few of them in the past. He resisted the urge to put his hand over her mouth; somehow he knew she wouldn't let him. Sarah had no concern for the noise she was making. Jack was sure the fishermen could hear, as well as anyone coming onto the pier. She took one of his hands and placed it on her breast.

"I like my nipples to be squeezed hard."

"Jesus," he obliged, making her squirm under him, bucking harder into his groin. She let out a very loud, primal moan. He wasn't sure if Sarah had climaxed, though he figured she must have. He lost final control and released himself into her. She kept pushing onto him for a few moments. Jack could see some people wandering onto the pier. He hoped they had not been lured onto the dock by their little show. He released himself from her warmth and quickly pulled up his pants. He blushed as he couldn't lose his erection and turned toward the railing.

She turned around and shifted her clothes, the hem of her dress dropping to its normal length. She smiled, putting a naughty finger to her lip.

"Yes, Jackson Walker, you will do for now. Are you embarrassed?" She gave him a quick peck on the cheek as two couples walked past them; it was clear they had seen or heard what just happened by the awkward looks on their faces.

She grabbed his hand and started walking toward the pier's exit. "They just wish they had the guts to do what we just did."

5

SATANIC RITES

"WE'LL BE LATE IF we catch another light. The priestess doesn't tolerate lateness."

"I wasn't the one who decided to go back for round two, Sarah. Besides, I'm still very uneasy about the whole situation. Frankly, I wouldn't mind being a bit late, or maybe missing it altogether. I agreed to meet some of your friends, and I've been to a few of your tea parties. I get that you're not bad people, but I'm very skeptical about the devil-worshiping thing. I promised a good friend of mine when we first met that I would stay clear of any hocus-pocus."

"Hocus-pocus?" Sarah scowled. "Who's your friend?"

"You know, the guy I told you about, my fishing buddy Perry."

"We've been together for nearly two months. Do you think I would lead you into something that might harm you?"

"I'm not worried about being harmed, Sarah. I'm thinking about my job and the associations. No matter what you say to me, whatever you want to call it, Devil worship is not normal. I don't want to lose you, but I can't afford to lose my job either."

"I want you to see the whole picture. I don't want there to be any skeletons in the closet or secrets between us," Sarah said. "I don't want there to be a reason for our relationship to develop any problems. I'm not asking you to take part. I just want you to see the things you might be the most bothered about. I won't ask you to come again. Keep an open mind." She squeezed his leg.

Jack could not shake off his unease.

"Would you mind stepping on the gas?" Sarah checked her watch again.

Jack frowned. "I'll get us there. It's not too far, I think, from the directions you gave me. Pretty close to Goodland. I know the area well, used to fish there a lot."

Jack pulled onto a dark gravel road, which passed into a thick forest. The large trees draped over the road, moss hanging nearly to the ground. A white hand was painted on a tree trunk indicating the turn, according to their instructions. "What's with the hand?"

"It represents the left-hand path. It's a phrase used by the followers of Set to describe their view of religion and its place in the world. Our congregation is called The Church of the Left-Hand Path."

"Okay, you're weirding me out again, and this road is getting pretty rough."

"No need to worry, it's just a point of view—just keep driving." She smiled at him, scrunching up her nose. "Satanists believe that there is an inner sanctuary, or understanding, suppressed by more conventional beliefs. Mainstream religions use the power that is brought forth for the greater good of God, sometimes to the detriment of their followers. Look at some of those Southern evangelists who scammed all of that money from their devotees and built a theme park. *'Thy will be done.'* This phrase is known as the right-hand path; it stresses the importance of pure devotion to God, whether it is the Christian God, Muslim, or whatever religion: *'you will do My will.'* On the other hand, *'my will be done'* is the directive of the left-hand path, that of Set. It stresses the importance of the individual and his or her personal enlightenment. Many who follow the left-hand path do not refer to a specific deity, but rather to a greater entity whose name does not particularly matter. He has been known as Lucifer, Set, Satan, and many other names throughout the history of the world. It's the individual who is important, not the god. We are free to think what we want. Some, tragically, take this philosophy to extremes."

"Heavy stuff," Jack said. "Something irks me, though. Why do you have to belong to this group to believe that the individual is important? If the point is to have your own opinion, why do you have to belong to a group of people?"

Sarah hesitated for a moment. "Good question. I ask you, why do people go to college? I'd say, besides getting a good job, enlightenment. There is comfort in the fact that you can discuss various issues or philosophies with others. Group discussion pushes you to delve deeper into issues than you would on your own. Sometimes a concept needs to be brought to your attention, something you might never have thought about—at least that's how it was for me. I guess ultimately there was one being who started all this and we believe him to be a higher, greater entity." She smiled. "The Church has given me the opportunity to see that the left-hand path makes more sense to me in our modern world. I don't know . . . I find that enlightening."

A red glow emanated from the road ahead. As they came closer, Jack saw several vehicles parked along the side of the road. He parked at the end of the long row of cars. As he got out, he could hear the hum of people talking. Together, they walked toward the glow, which he guessed might come from a fire.

He was correct. Flames from a large bonfire lit the night, casting shadows upon the moss-covered trees that surrounded a large clearing. Dozens of people sat cross-legged around the pit that contained the flames. He recognized several of them from the discussion nights. He nodded to those who looked up as they approached. Jack stepped over the ring of white powder encircling the group. One woman sat alone within a smaller circle, closer to the fire. The heat didn't seem to bother her. She wore a very sheer, dark grey dress which emphasized her generous figure. She held herself confidently as she gazed at those who joined. She nodded to Sarah and then to Jack as they took a seat.

Sarah whispered, "I'm sure she was waiting for us. This ritual is supposed to clear your mind, opening it up to Set."

Jack squirmed where he sat, clearly distressed with Sarah's last comment. He remembered going out on a fishing charter a few years back. The weather had been wicked and he'd spent the entire trip vomiting. He'd promised himself that he would never go deep-sea fishing again, and hadn't. As he settled in next to the fire he promised himself to never go to one of these horror shows again. He was pissed that Sarah would think that he would be remotely interested in it. *This crap is like something out of a movie.* He shivered as he put his mouth to her ear. She shook him off, gesturing toward the priestess. *I should get up and walk the fuck out of here.*

The woman raised her hands, breathing deeply; her movements were smooth and practiced. Jack could see that within her circle, etched in powder, was a pentagram, each point of the star nearly touching the edge of the circle. A thick, heavy-looking candle sat on each point. He had seen enough demonic horror flicks to recognize the symbol. The woman, he surmised, was the priestess. She lit another candle, this one a bit smaller, and raised it over her head.

"Azazel," she said in a loud, even, slow vibrato.

The hair on the back of Jack's neck stood on end. He looked at the others around the fire and realized that he was the only one not caught in rapture. He needed to leave, but somehow couldn't; his legs were glued to the ground. The priestess brought the candle down, close to her groin. *"Belial."* After a few moments of meditation, she raised the candle to her chest, and then to her right shoulder, chanting, *"Asmodeus."*

Jack moved to whisper something to Sarah but she cut him off before he could say anything. He tried again. "Sarah—"

The priestess stopped, her eyes turned to Jack, riveting him to where he sat. There was a momentary silence. Jack looked up to see the congregation watching him. He lowered his eyes, his face reddened.

The candle drifted to her left shoulder. *"Asteroth."* She clasped her hands to her chest while still holding the candle and chanted, *"Baphomet."*

Jack tried to rise, but he couldn't. It was like he'd lost the connection between his brain and his legs. He made a low growling noise as he tried to stand, but couldn't.

The woman paused for a couple of minutes, deep in meditation. He looked around the circle and could see that he was the only one with his eyes still open, including Sarah. The congregation seemed to be in a trance-like state. He was more determined to resist whatever was going on.

His attention was captured by a movement from the priestess. She stood and faced what he guessed was west and the Gulf. *"Leviathan."* She turned to the south. *"Samael."* Then to the east. *"Lucifer."* Then finally to the north. *"Lilith."* She addressed the congregation, her eyes still closed. "Let us pray." The group as a whole was evidently familiar with the words and resonated as one. "Around me flame the pentagons, the star of force and fire. Within my breast the Eternal One, the infinite immortal star." She then raised her hands. "Let us meditate. Let all of your thoughts be of yourself and your singular existence on this earth. Open your mind. Embrace the left-hand path."

Jack sat mesmerized, but somewhat relieved. *Singular existence, okay, this is more along the lines of what Sarah talked about.* He was not so much fixated on the priestess as on the members of the church. He had been to a few of their tea meetings, all of which seemed fairly sedate and harmless. There had been no mention of Lucifer or . . . Amadeus or whoever. It had all been very intellectual and for the most part, enjoyable. He was uncomfortable watching the members of the congregation apparently lost in religious fervor. It reminded him of the Sunday morning prophets he saw on television when he was a kid. As much as Sarah espoused the merits of her religious points of view, it still stank of overlording. And someone was getting some cash out of all this. He smiled: *All the same, just a different angle.* He breathed a deep sigh. He could handle all the nonsense. *All make-believe. A little hocus-pocus, get some cash off the rich folk like Carly and Buck, and everyone goes home happy.* He would placate Sarah, but would be careful not to be implicated by the association. He could relax and enjoy his relationship and the great sex. It was a big relief.

He gazed at the congregation sitting around the fire, their hands and arms waving slowly out in front of them. "Isn't she wonderful?" Sarah said, her face aglow with religious enthusiasm. "The priestess will want to speak with you. Don't worry, there will be no pressure, she only wants to meet you. I've talked to her about you, and she'll understand your hesitation. It is not our way to try and convert people; our way is but another path to self-enlightenment. I showed you this only so that you could see who I am, what makes me tick."

"Sarah, relax, I totally understand. I am my own person. I can handle the situation. I can see everything for what it's worth. I no longer feel threatened, though I don't agree with the premise."

Sarah shrugged.

"Let's go meet the woman, I look forward to it," Jack said, trying to show some bravado, his shoulders pulled back, and his step purposeful.

Sarah frowned. "That's a sudden big shift in attitude. You're making me nervous, Jack."

"Why the devil should I be making you nervous. See? I said *devil*. Don't worry, lead on." He chuckled.

Sarah guided him by the hand toward the priestess, who was bringing herself out of her trance-like state. A number of her disciples milled about, waiting to have a word with her. She saw Sarah guiding Jack in her direction and motioned to those who stood waiting.

"My esteemed members, I will be with you shortly. Please let me have a word with our young Sarah. She has brought a new friend."

Sarah guided Jack forward. "Priestess, this is my friend Jackson Walker."

The priestess smiled. "We have heard a great deal about you, Jackson."

Jack nodded. He was having a hard time keeping his eyes off the woman. The sheer material of her gown did little to hide her body underneath. She held her hands out to him and he returned the gesture, reaching out and accepting both of her hands. She guided him to the ground where they both sat cross-legged, their hands still connected. Her hands were warm and soft. He didn't want to let them go, and he knew that she would not let them go. He wanted to recoil, but he couldn't find the connection between his brain and hands to carry out the impulse. Sarah sat down beside them. He raised his eyes to meet the priestess', while fighting the urge to lower them. He had the will to move, yet he was frozen in place. It felt warm and safe, but all his alarms were sounding.

"Jack." Her voice was like honey, her eyes like black lodestones pulling him into her being. Despite himself, he wanted to curl up in her lap and go to sleep forever. He forced out the words.

"Sarah has told me a lot about you." He no longer felt the urge to pull his hands away, yet he felt that he couldn't even if he tried.

"I seek to sustain Sarah's happiness, Jack. I wanted you to meet us so that we could eliminate any misconceptions you might have about Sarah and her connection to our congregation. I am sure that she has told you we are not bad people, but saying is one thing, showing is another."

Who the hell holds voodoo sessions out in the woods praying to the devil? This thought felt far away, but he could hear its whisper.

"There are a lot of false notions about our faith. Many of these are raised by others who have twisted the concepts we espouse. The same thing occurs with those who follow the right-hand path. Great evil can be found within Christianity and Islam, just as it can be found in Satanism."

Jack nodded, his hands still ensconced within hers.

"Evil is the desire to bend another's mind or will to attain goals that benefit others, goals that are not to the benefit of the individual. Deceit, avarice, are a requirement of blind faith. There are those who need to follow, who do not have the intellect or the will to choose a path that is right for them. It is not a sin to be a follower, as long as one does not follow a corrupt path knowingly. The world is mostly full of followers."

Bend the will of another? Isn't that happening to me?

She squeezed his hands gently. He wished she would keep on doing so. He could see her nipples pushing out through the sheer gown.

"Our way is the way of the scholar, the way of the philosopher. We are intellectuals, Jack, not bloodthirsty cultists. What has drawn you to Sarah? She is a pretty girl, of that there is no doubt. Is it her being, her oneness with herself, that which shows her inner confidence? All of these strengths were there before she met us. We were simply here to show her how to draw upon those strengths."

Sarah put her hand on Jack's shoulder and squeezed it gently.

"The ritual you have just witnessed is merely a clearing of

the mind, a calling of a divine being who supports the individual spirit that lies within most of us. Call it devil worship if you will. The devil is only seen as evil by those of the right-hand path. Ha-Satan was an important member of the court of Yahweh, or as most know him, God. His main task was to test the faith of men. Punishment was not brought down by Satan, but rather by Yahweh's angels. We put our faith in Satan, or *Set*, as we call him. He is the demigod of the individual. We believe him a good deity."

The priestess released Jack's hands. He recoiled, falling back on his elbows. He was cold. He wanted to grab the woman's hands again, but somehow found the will not to. He shivered, feeling as if he'd just walked away from a hot fire on a cool night. His throat was dry and he croaked. "What the hell?" He looked to Sarah who was still caught in rapture. His eyes returned to the priestess. "I think it's time we went home."

The priestess frowned. "Is there something wrong, Jackson?"

He wasn't sure what to say. He crossed his arms. "I get what you're saying. It makes sense superficially, but I don't buy into it, just the same as I don't buy into Christianity. I think you people know all the angles, you talk all nicey-nicey, but this is all just a bit over the top for my liking. I'm feeling . . . wrong. It's time to leave."

Jack slowly got up, his knees aching from sitting cross-legged for so long. He looked to Sarah, and saw that the spell on her was broken. She had an uneasy look on her face. "I'm glad you met the priestess." She turned toward her.

The woman nodded. "It is of your own free will to return to us." She folded her hands in front of her. *"Xeper,"* she said in parting as she walked away from them to talk to others in the congregation.

Sarah did the same. *"Xeper."*

As Jack walked back to the car with Sarah, he had to ask, "What the fuck is *Xeper*?"

"It means to become, to come into being, finding oneness within you."

* * * *

Jack turned the car around and slowly drove back down the old gravel road. He wished he had a can of beer—no, a shot of Jim Beam, maybe two.

Sarah looked at Jack with an anxious expression. "So?"

He didn't say anything for a few minutes, keeping his eyes on the road. "So. That was interesting. Is that where you take all your boyfriends?"

Sarah frowned. "What do you mean, Jack? No, I've never taken anyone to meet the priestess. I thought it important because I'm starting to feel something for you. To me, this was the next step. We can back off anytime you wish." She crossed her arms.

"Hey, I get what you're saying. I am glad I saw it, and I'm equally glad that we've left. It's just . . . What the fuck did that woman do to me? It wasn't right. I feel like I've been bent over and abused. Say what you want about Christians, but I don't think you would see that happen at The Church by the Sea on Ft. Myers Beach. That just wasn't right."

"She has a forceful personality, Jack. She does that to everyone."

"Well then, she's spooky. I'd call it witchery."

"No such thing as witches. That's the kind of thing people say that makes us look bad. She is deeply rooted in her beliefs and she has a way of capturing your attention and holding it. She is a remarkable woman. She should be a politician."

"Yeah, why not? We have a nut bar in the White House, why not chuck in a witch; that will really fuck things up."

"Come on, Jack, you're taking things a bit too far."

"Yeah, guess I've been listening to the senator too much. Anyway, I've had enough hocus-pocus for one evening—in fact, for the time being. I appreciate the show, but that's enough for me. I don't mind going to the occasional old folk meeting. That's harmless. Okay? Don't expect me to do that again. If you do, this is over."

Jack could see that she was crestfallen, but he had to take a stand. He didn't believe in what he'd just seen and experienced, but he didn't want to be tarred and feathered with it as well. "I still love you, but I've not bitten on the devil worship."

"What did you say?"

"Figure of speech, darlin'."

She smiled and sank into her seat for the ride home.

6

BUSINESS

ISAAC SNAPPED THE LEDGER book shut and looked up at the man handing him the check. "Pleasure doing business with you, Mr. Jacobs. We'll see you again this time next year?"

"I can't deny that you do a good job, Isaac, and I thank you kindly. I appreciate the work that you do . . . on my taxes."

Isaac shook the chubby, balding man's hand. "That's our goal, Mr. Jacobs, that's our goal. Now you say hello to Mrs. Jacobs for me and that pretty daughter of yours. What was her name?"

"Virginia, and you keep your eyes off her. She's a mite too young for you."

"Suppose so, suppose so. Good day, sir."

Peter Jacobs smiled and left Isaac's office, closing the door behind him.

Isaac straightened the papers from Jacob's file and stuck them in a manila folder. His office was just off Fifth Avenue in Naples. The property and the one adjacent to it were owned by the McFaddens and had been purchased by his great-grandfather in the 1920s. It was a solid investment, as now the properties were worth several millions of dollars. Isaac's clientele consisted of many of the older, well-moneyed families—Naples' upper crust. It was a good network of people to be associated with, especially with the diversification within McFadden Holdings, Inc. The rich were prone to having their problems the same as the common folk.

A year earlier, Peter Jacob's daughter was raped by a couple of young men from North Fort Myers. The boys had been let off due to insufficient evidence. Isaac and Eric orchestrated a couple of tragic occurrences for the men in question. Both were alive, but would have to deal with deformities for the rest of their lives. Jacob had just settled his rather large but justifiable accounting bill for services rendered.

There was a knock on the door. Before Isaac could respond, the door opened and his brother Eric entered, his face tanned and leathery, darker than normal.

"Saw Jacobs leaving the building. Did we get paid?"

"Yes, and promptly."

"Great. I need some cash. One of my Mercs bit the dust yesterday. I didn't know the impeller was shot and I fried it. Tarpon are running. Got a couple of charters set up this week and I have a line on a new motor—cash deal."

"I'll have ten grand transferred to your account after lunch. Good enough?"

"Great. More than enough, but I'm due to bring the girlfriend out somewhere special, maybe get away for a few days. It's been five years. Can you believe it?"

Isaac smiled in response. He was fond of Eric, and the two would jump off a cliff for each other. Isaac controlled the purse strings; it was an agreed-upon arrangement. Neither Eric nor Jimmy had a clue how much money they had, or what McFadden Holdings, Inc. was worth. They did not care, as long as Isaac kept them flush. Isaac knew the company's finances down to the last dollar. The boys had enough money that they would have a hard time spending it in a lifetime. Neither Eric nor Jimmy had expensive tastes and were easily placated with a small monthly stipend. It was rare for Eric to ask for additional funds; he made a decent living off his fishing charters. Isaac wasn't bothered by

Eric's request. It was the least he could do for his older brother, who never asked questions.

"Anything new on the books, little brother? I'd like to plan the next week or so. I'm pretty busy with charters."

"Nothing concrete, but I did get a call from the old woman. She was asking questions about the Indians, if we had seen them doing anything strange. She asked if I knew anything about some flunked-out football player named Jackson Walker. You know anything about him?"

"Nope. The name rings a bell, though."

"Well, maybe you can ask some questions. I'd like you to keep an eye on him if you can find him."

"Will do, little brother. Jackson Walker, right?"

"That's correct."

Eric wrote the name in his pocket book.

7

CLEWISTON

JACK HAD CALLED HIS buddy to go for a drink before Perry began the dinner shift. They met at the Boat House Restaurant on the back bay. It was a quasi-tourist/local hangout. The food was pretty decent and it was happy hour all day long on the weekend.

Perry crossed his arms, resting them on his slight paunch. "How's things with Sarah?"

Jack took a swig of his beer, frowning ever so slightly. "Really good. We get along and the sex is still great. You know how things can tail off after a while. I think it's the danger thing. I don't have any desire to get involved with a nice girl. The fact that I'm playing with fire makes it more intriguing. It's like watching one of those taboo porno sites, only it's me that's in it."

"Unforgettable head, was that what you called it?" Perry reached for his beer.

"We've graduated from that. I tell you, she wants it all the time. She warned me, though, and I agreed."

"Agreed what?"

"Anytime she wants it."

"Wants it? Anytime? You're kidding me?"

"Nope. For real, man. I thought she was just putting me on. Sarah is a for-real, certified nympho. I tell you, my dick's getting sore—rubbed it raw the other day."

"Poor bastard." Perry laughed, slapping his thigh. "Gotta ask. So what happens when your dick is bleeding and the call comes?"

"Sex toys."

Perry broke into hysterics.

"No, really, sex toys. She likes me to tie her up and as she says, 'push the envelope.'"

"It's the demon shit. This is how they hook you. I've been reading about it since we went fishing. No normal chick likes that shit. They only do it because they know you like it. Normal women would never suggest that. So does she like it from behind?"

"What do you mean *behind*? Doggie style?"

"No. I mean be-*hind*."

Jack's face flushed.

"Okay, you answered me. Normal girls don't like that either, which proves my point: she is a demon bitch. Dump her now."

"I wouldn't go that far. I think it's just the way she is. What I wanted to talk to you about was the ritual crap and the meetings. I think I'm falling for her, but I don't want anything to do with the Satanist bullshit anymore. I'm going to give it one last chance and see exactly where she thinks the relationship is headed. I'm going to give her an ultimatum. If she's willing to back off, or even better, leave the cult, I'm willing to take things to the next level. If she's not willing, then I'm done . . . I've been to four of their meetings. They pretend it's just *intellectual* discussion and harmless. But I'm feeling pressured. Some of the leaders are really old and kind of creepy . . . I'm done with it."

"Now you're talking. Has any of this crap gotten back to your work?"

"I don't think so. The senator is pretty straight with me. If there was a problem, he'd let me know. He's been tied up the past few weeks with some gambling bill and I haven't seen much of him."

They both sat for a moment looking out at Estero Bay as a large fishing charter unloaded its catch.

"I think he's getting it on with his secretary and it's going to blow up in his face."

"Christ, you sure?"

"Pretty much. It's the way they are around each other, and I've seen the little winks and touches, pretty obvious. I think they know that I know, too, which is making me damned uncomfortable. My biggest worry is that it's going to bring him down. Guys in his position get slammed for this shit all the time. I need the job, Perry. When I think of all the money I blew . . . I could have squirreled it out for a few extra years. I was just in such a bad place."

"You're complicated, my man, and you know I loved to watch you play. My best advice is mum's the word on the senator bonking the secretary. As far as Sarah goes, I'd be straight with her. Tell her you aren't going to any more of the death cult meetings. See how it goes. You'll know that she's for real if she can accept your point of view and still keep things going between you. As far as your dick, I would think about using some KY."

Jack hesitated for a moment and smiled. "You pretty much said what I was thinking, but I needed to bounce it off someone."

"That's what I'm here for, bro. But if I were in your shoes, it'd be different. I would dump her now, no bullshit. A few years ago I wouldn't have had to tell you this stuff. You were the shit; now you're soft."

"I did promise to go to one more of her meetings tonight."

Perry grimaced.

"I know I keep saying the same fucking thing, but this is the last time you're going to hear it, and this time Sarah knows it. She says there's someone important coming and she wants me to meet this person. That it would mean the world to her. So I said I would. We had it out the other night—no more Satan bullshit. It's been a real long time since I've had real affection from a female. I've had sex, but nothing that feels like anything resembling love."

"Love?"

"I mean cuddling up on the couch to watch a movie, cooking together . . . never done that shit before. I lived football from since I was fifteen. I just might be able to be happy with this girl."

"Okay, I buy all that shit, but one more meeting? No fucking way. You just jinxed yourself. That's like going on your last recon mission in Nam, your last tour of duty. You know how many of those guys bought it right at the end? *Love?* This is like a bad fucking movie and you're missing the fucking plot."

"Calm down, man, it's all been pretty harmless so far, and I can't go back on my word. I'll call you tomorrow and tell you how it goes. Time for one more?"

"I do, and it's on you: counseling fees. You deserve to pay for being so fucking stupid."

****

Sarah locked her fingers into Jack's as they walked toward the meeting hall. Jack found it strange that they never met in the same place twice. Tonight it was in an old theater on Sanibel Island. It was a cozy spot with wood siding on the outside. The inside was casual, with a low stage at the back. Chairs and tables were dispersed as usual. The members of the congregation were spread around the room having their little conversations. This was Jack's fifth meeting and he was becoming friendly with a number of people who attended. He shook Buck's hand as he moved past him.

"Good to see you, Jack. So we haven't scared you off yet?"

"Not yet, sir."

"Forget *sir*, it's *Buck*. Now you keep that little girl of yours in good company and maybe we'll talk a bit later."

Jack nodded and moved on to the back of the room where Sarah was waiting for him. It had been a long day and the beer he'd had earlier made him quite hungry. The mini sandwiches were good, as usual, and he managed to eat more than his fair share.

"There she is." Sarah pointed to an old woman.

Jack estimated the woman was roughly seventy-five, and pretty well preserved. She wore a few pieces of jewelry that he was sure must be worth tens of thousands of dollars each. Her face was wrinkled, yet there was a youthful look in her eyes.

"She is wonderful, isn't she?"

"She's well preserved, I'll give you that, but *wonderful* is not the adjective I would use to describe her. She looks a bit creepy to me."

Sarah frowned deeply, her lips pulled tightly together. "She's over a hundred, you know."

"Okay, I might give you *remarkable."*

"She is the matriarch of our brotherhood. Her name is Henrietta LePley. I don't know why, but she has asked to meet you. She likes to meet all who are involved."

"I'm not fucking *involved*, Sarah, and I tell you, she is creeping me out."

"She's a beautiful woman, Jack, and you will not meet anyone who is as captivating. She'll have you feeling at ease within moments."

"At ease? Great. I might just ease myself out of this place. So let me see, you have a priestess and now this old woman. How come I never see the priestess at these meetings?"

"I'm not really sure. I think she likes to remain mysterious."

"And now this old lady, how come I've never seen her before?"

"Again, hard to say; she seems to come around when there is a special occasion or when she has an agenda."

"She wants to speak to me? No way, I told you I was done with this shit."

"Come on. She won't bite."

"I'm not worried about bites, Sarah. I can survive a bite. Remember, I've been through pain therapy management."

She gave him a vulnerable look.

"Oh, all right, I guess she is the reason I came one last time, so let's get this over with."

Sarah pushed him toward the old woman. Jack could feel the hairs on the back of his neck tingling. As they neared, Henrietta turned toward him. He almost stopped in his tracks as he was hit full force by the greenest eyes he'd ever seen, and they were looking right through him. His mouth went dry.

"Miss Henrietta, this is Jackson. I told you about him some time ago. You asked to meet him." Sarah curtsied.

The woman's eyes were like magnets. He turned his head away slightly, but was no match for her stare. Henrietta reached forward and gently lifted his chin, engaging his eyes directly. The irony of the situation struck him; he was the big football player, yet he was powerless to hold the old woman's gaze. She lifted his chin as if he were a hundred-pound weakling.

"Jackson, it is a distinct pleasure to meet you. I have heard so much about you from various members of our congregation."

Her breath smelled of old wine, but her voice was even and calm. She spoke with a distinct Old South Floridian accent. Her voice was calm, taking her time pronouncing her vowels, the dialect people had if they'd lived in the state their entire lives.

She did not look or sound like she was over one hundred years old, yet there was something unexplainable happening. It was like she was totally in control and Jack could do nothing to even things up.

"Nice to meet you, Miss Henrietta."

"I hear that you played ball up north?" she said putting her hand on his knee.

He resisted the urge to recoil. "Up north, well, if you call Gainesville up north, then yes, I guess so. I really didn't play much in Cincinnati."

"When I was much younger, I would take in the odd Dolphin game, Miami Hurricanes as well, but that was some time ago. Sport is a means to an end though, isn't it? You're still young, mid-twenties; what if we were able to pull a few strings? I could get you a walk-on with the Saints. We have strong connections over in New Orleans. What if I could guarantee that, Jackson?"

His heart started to beat so hard he was sure the woman could hear it.

"You really don't think your job with Senator Hunter is going to amount to much, do you? We could get you back on track with your career. It's not *what* you know, son, it's *who* you know, isn't it?"

Jack shrugged.

"We know about the drugs and the effects they had. It wouldn't take much to set you up in a rehab center. We could guarantee that you are given a clean bill of health."

Jack interjected. "Pardon me, ma'am, but drugs are not an issue anymore. I've been to rehab and I've passed GO."

She smiled. "Let's say the worst-case scenario is a back-up job. You could be pulling in two, maybe three million a year. That would guarantee our little Sarah a good life." She cocked her head to the side for a moment in thought. "Let's be honest;

it's not about you, it's about Sarah. She is our prime concern. However, you might grow in our esteem should you step up to the plate and take care of her in the way she deserves to be taken care of."

Christ, we've only just begun dating! Jack had to collect his thoughts. He paused for a few moments, his eyes dropping from Henrietta's. "I don't have what it takes to play pro ball, ma'am. I was cut, fair and square."

"Nonsense." She lifted his chin again. "We both know that isn't the truth; you were an abuser of drugs. You were cut because you became a liability. I have talked to those who know. You are a uniquely talented passer. You can read a defense with the best. Deep down inside, you know this is the truth. Is it not?"

Jack hesitated. "Ma'am, I would like to think what you're saying is the truth. I'd love to believe what you're saying. I loved the game. But there are so many other talented players out there. Why would an NFL team pick me up, especially with my past? Okay, I'll say it: I messed up, I abused drugs, and I wouldn't give my own ass a contract. This is a crazy conversation, and how do you know all of this about me?"

Henrietta lifted Jack's chin again, her breath smelling somewhat better . . . cherries? "I am telling you, I can do this for you."

Jack looked into her eyes. He wanted badly to believe what she was saying. Her green eyes drilled into his head. "What would it take?" he said in a low voice. His will was slipping.

"There's a good boy. You need only promise that you will look after our Sarah. I am not going to push our ways on you. That is not our objective. We hope that in your own time you will see the truth. This is all we can ask. We do not seek your enlightenment, Jackson, we can only hope that you better yourself and find your own way. I think that you would benefit from some self-indulgence, which is our hope for the congregation as a whole."

Jack's eyes dropped to her hands, which were amazingly smooth for a woman her age. "What about my current job with Senator Hunter?"

She looked at him. "The senator need not know about our little gambit, and it will take some time to put things in motion. His office won't find out about things until they are well underway."

"Okay, so what's the cost?"

Henrietta smiled, her perfectly straight but brown-tinged teeth glaring at him. "There is no cost, Jack, other than your devotion to Sarah." She turned toward Sarah, who was beaming with admiration for the woman.

"That's it?"

She nodded, a smile forming on her thin lips. "We may call on you from time to time to do us favors."

"Favors?"

"Don't worry, they will not be anything too dramatic or burdensome—nothing devilish. One hand has to wash the other. If we could revive your career, Jackson, wouldn't the odd favor in return be worth it?"

Jack stood, looking down at the old woman. "I am not convinced that I want to be tied up with a Satanist church." He paused to consider. "But all you're going to do is make some calls and maybe get me a tryout, and the rest is up to me?"

"Of course."

Jack felt a large hand on his left shoulder. He turned to see Buck, his welcoming smile looking him level in the face. He had been so intent in his conversation with Henrietta, he had not noticed the large man walk up behind him.

"She speaks the truth, boy. I have the connections and I can promise you a walk-on."

Jack took a moment to contemplate his options. He weighed Perry's comments about the risks of his 'last tour of duty.' But then he imagined himself, once again the center of attention, flush with cash, living the high life. He sat down in one of the fold-up chairs that filled the room. Sarah sat quietly next to him.

"Okay, much as it feels wrong, I'll go for it. But I am not a Satanist. I am doing this for Sarah." He looked Henrietta straight in the eye. He didn't believe in the devil—Satan, or Set, whatever they wanted to call him—yet he couldn't help but feel he was selling himself, well, to the devil. He shook his head. *No such thing,* he told himself.

"Is there a contract or anything that I have to sign? Do I owe you any percentages if I get a contract?"

"Absolutely not. I am a wealthy woman, Jackson. Having a piece of your soul is payment enough." Henrietta laughed. "Of course I am just kidding. We Satanists are allowed humor."

Jack felt the tingling of goose bumps forming on his arms and scalp.

"I will ask you for one favor, though. I have a large sum of money that has to be delivered to one of our benefactors, and a letter for his wife; she's such a dear friend. I never did learn how to drive. He and his wife live up on Lake Okeechobee on an old plantation. Alfred Marsh is his name."

He looked to Sarah. "You'll come with me, right?"

"I can't, Jack, you know that I have a big day tomorrow. You wouldn't get back until quite late, and I need the evening to prepare for a conference. It's only an hour and a half drive."

Out of the corner of his eye, Jack swore he saw the old woman make a slight nod toward Sarah.

"For your trouble, young man, please take this as a measure of my gratitude." She handed him five crisp one hundred dollar bills.

"That's not necessary."

"Take it Jackson, I insist."

Jack reached out to take the money and the envelope, and he could not help but feel dirty. He looked to Sarah. Her face seemed to beam in acceptance. He stuck the envelope into his pants pocket.

"Buck, will you keep the young man company?" Henrietta smiled.

Buck put his hand on Jack's shoulder. "Well, I don't have any plans. When you're over seventy, your night life involves watching TV and going to church meetings." He turned to his wife, who stood silently, smiling. "Unless you had some sex planned for the evening, sweetheart?"

She blushed.

"Jack, get it while you can; once you're my age, it becomes a semi-annual event." Buck hugged his blushing bride. "We can take my Caddie?"

"I don't mind driving, unless you have an aversion to riding in poverty. But I'm okay to go on my own."

"It'll bring me back to my youth, son. My wife will give Sarah a ride home." Buck nodded to Henrietta.

"Then it's settled," Henrietta said. "You're a good lad, Jackson. So mote it be." She lifted his chin again and stared into his eyes. "Does the walker choose the path, or the path the walker? Good night son." She turned and moved toward another group of people.

Jack stood for a moment staring off into space. Buck clipped his shoulder. "She is priceless, isn't she? Don't let all this bullshit bother you. Let's get that envelope delivered and get back,. Maybe we can have a nightcap if it's not too late."

"Sounds good. Let me say goodnight to Sarah. Ah, hey—what the hell does *so mote it be* mean?"

Buck looked caught off guard for a moment. "Pretty much the same as *amen.*"

* * * *

Jack nodded to the large man and led Sarah from the meeting hall. Outside he began stomping around in agitation, his fists clenched. Sarah put her hands on his shoulders. He pushed her off, backing up a couple of steps.

"What the fuck? What the fuck just happened?"

"Calm down, Jack. I know you don't want to be invol—"

He cut her off with a wave of his hand. "I went for a drink with Perry earlier and he warned me not to have anything more to do with your people. He compared it to a soldier's last tour of duty."

"What do you mean, *last tour of duty*? Are you planning to dump me?"

"No Sarah, I'm not. I do, however, want to get things straight. I don't like the Satanist bullshit. I don't feel comfortable with it. If you want me to be committed, I have to draw a line. That woman creeps me out. I don't know why I couldn't say no. I don't believe in all this *yada- yada* horseshit about finding one's path and all that crap. My better judgment has been compromised. You shoulda stepped in and intervened. I'm pissed. You just sat there staring at that woman like she was God!"

Sarah stood for a moment, her hand resting on the hood of Jack's car. "I told you in the beginning. I don't have a problem with your autonomy. I just want you to understand. I can ask no more. Wouldn't you like another try at football?"

He contemplated her words. "Why do you people all say *'I can ask no more?'* And why not get some other schlep to deliver the money?"

She shrugged. "I hadn't noticed that we said that. Maybe I've just become accustomed to them saying it and hadn't realized." Her eyes turned to the ground.

"No more meetings. This is the last one. Frankly, I think that the lot of you are whacked out on Prozac. I will *not* go to another one of these gatherings. No more. That whole thing was like a scene out of *Rosemary's Baby*."

After a few moments, Sarah quietly said, "Agreed." She looked up again.

"Serious?"

"Absolutely." She put her arms around his waist, looked up into his face, and stepping up on her toes placed a gentle kiss on his lips. Her breath smelled divine.

Jack sighed, not pulling away this time. "So you can't come?"

"Nah, got a full day tomorrow. Come back when you're finished and I might be able to wake myself for a little snuggle." She looked up and squished her nose with her forefinger.

"Okay . . . for you."

"It's not for me, Jack, it's for Henrietta. Hell, five hundred bucks, you can take me out to dinner this week."

He looked her in the eye. She held his gaze. "Would you consider dropping the Satanist bullshit?"

She frowned. "I don't know that I can promise that, but I will at least give it some consideration."

Jack walked back to his car, his lips still warm from Sarah's parting kiss. He opened the door and took out the envelope full of cash and stared at it. He muttered out loud to himself. "Last tour of duty, you stupid fuck." He stood waiting for Buck to emerge from the old theater.

Buck came rambling out of the hall a couple of minutes later, his big frame hesitating, his eyes searching until he caught sight of Jack.

Buck sauntered through the parking lot surveying Jack's car as he neared. "Sure you don't want to drive the Caddie?"

"Runs like a charm, Buck."

"Okay, your choice, let's get going." Both men got into the car. Jack stuck the envelope under his seat as he sat down. He wasn't sure if Buck intentionally turned his eyes away from the action, but he saw a serious look on Buck's face for the briefest of moments. He engaged the ignition and jolted the old Ford into gear.

****

The ride across the causeway from Sanibel to Ft. Myers was one of Jack's favorite stretches of road. In the daytime you could see for miles in either direction. He followed it onto Summerlin and made his way towards Interstate 75. Traffic was pretty light at this time of night and he was able to get off at Palm Beach Boulevard. Buck was quiet for the first part of the drive, his big thumbs typing away on his smartphone.

"Amazing things, these devices. I can get twice as much done in a day as I could 20 years ago. You younguns, don't know any different, you're spoiled." He laughed. "Hey, remember that game six years ago against Clemson? You're in a bowl game if you win that one. Why'd you run four times on that last goal line stand? I lost a lot of money on that game. You'd been passing beautifully all day."

Jack tensed. He wasn't in the mood for this type of discussion. He gripped the wheel a little harder with both hands. Not wanting to be rude, he answered, "It was the coach's call and it was my second year. I wanted to go opposite of what they thought was coming. I wanted to go play action on the first two downs. He disagreed and called two straight running plays. On third down, where we should have passed, he lost his nerve and called another run. We got stopped on the goal line. We went for it on fourth down. They came at us hard and I did my best to hang onto the ball. The rest is history. Believe me, I was pissed, but play comes through the headphones and you don't run it, bad news, man."

"I get it, just a bit frustrating as a fan."

"That's sports, you live and die by your good plays and your bad plays. I know all about that."

The county highway was like most inland Florida roads: dark, straight, and boring. As it veered away from the Caloosahatchee River the scenery turned to oranges and sugar cane. They stopped at a 7-Eleven in Labelle for a coffee before making the last part of the drive to Lake Okeechobee.

As he pulled back onto the highway, he was tempted to call

Perry. If Buck hadn't been in the car, he would've. He wasn't sure why; perhaps he wanted moral support, or maybe he was questioning his wisdom in accepting the envelope and heading out here with Buck. Buck seemed trustworthy enough, but Jack was no longer in his comfort zone. He knew what Perry would say, so he put his phone back into his pocket. He didn't need to hear that he was stupid. Why did he feel compelled to complete this little job? He'd accepted the money in payment for a service, and he wouldn't go back on an agreement. But it wasn't like he needed the five hundred desperately.

He thought about Henrietta's green eyes. He hadn't been able to say no; it had been impossible. So what was stopping him from simply returning it to the old woman? Was he caught up in the possibility of playing football again? Henrietta had dangled that carrot in front of his nose. *Was it Sarah? Or was it Buck's presence?* A little bit of all of it, probably.

He was lost in thought as the orange trees flew by his side window. He was falling in love with Sarah and hoped for a future with her, but this seemed dangerous and stupid. He was starting to enjoy his work with Senator Hunter, and he could tell the man was taking a shine to him. His Aunt Rebecca, who had set him up with the job, told him that he needed to get in on the ground floor. Once he did, his competitive nature would take over. Do a good job and things would evolve. He didn't want to get on the bad side of his aunt, the matriarch on his father's side of the family. No one crossed Rebecca; she would disown him if she found out he was doing this.

Jack hadn't told anyone but Perry about the devil worship. If his boss found out about it, he'd be fired. Jack resolved that he would finish this one favor and be done with the whole thing. He wouldn't accept the football tryout, even if that came through. He would go back to Sarah tonight and tell her that it was over unless she was willing to dump the Satanists. He knew she wouldn't, but he needed to draw the line. It was time to step up and be the man in this relationship.

Jack looked over at Buck. He'd been quiet for some time; his head was rolled over against the side window, his mouth hanging wide open. "Good company," Jack muttered under his breath.

Jack's eyes were starting to pinch. He was jolted awake by the

Welcome to Clewiston sign; *Sweetest Town in America* referred to its roots in the sugar cane industry. He pulled to the side of the road for a moment to punch the street address into his phone. He was glad to see that he wasn't too far away; the property was no more than five to ten minutes northwest of town. His stomach began to churn as he neared his destination. It was similar to the feeling he would get before a football game—nervous energy, he called it, a lack of confidence in his own abilities coupled with a jolt of adrenalin. He started to feel queasy and jumpy, so he twisted in his seat, trying to get comfortable. The reality of the situation struck his funny bone and he laughed to himself. He was driving to some old estate in the middle of Hell's Half-Acre, Florida, delivering an envelope to someone who worshiped the devil. There was every reason to feel uneasy, and he did.

"Okay, you crazy bastard, drop off the envelope and get the heck out of here," he murmured. The deep resonance of his voice helped him settle down a bit, and it also startled Buck out of his nap.

"Where we at, boy?" He sat up, rubbing his eyes.

"Clewiston."

"Okay, I see where we are, just a little farther—take that upcoming right."

Within ten minutes they were idling in front of the driveway they sought; an old crooked sign with *Marsh* printed on it confirmed the correct address. He turned into the dirt laneway, which was in poor condition, full of potholes and tree debris. It led through a large field of uncut grass, roughly three hundred yards square. He figured he must be nearing Lake Okeechobee, as he had been following its shore to his right for the past five minutes. As he guided his car forward he could see a large stand of moss-covered trees ahead, their majestic old branches hanging low, nearly touching the ground. Behind the old trees loomed a rundown multi-story plantation house. Lights were on in several rooms, mostly on the main floor.

An old Mercedes sedan sat out in front. He pulled up behind it and turned off the ignition. Reaching under the front seat he pulled out the envelope that had been given to him, stuck it in his pants pocket, got out of the car and stretched his arms. The night was warm and clear, and the bright moon and stars made it easy for him to see. He could smell the mustiness of the lake and hear the omnipresent crickets and frogs.

Buck eased from the car. “That ride’s gonna give me a bad back, son. Now let’s see how the Marshes are doing.” He looked at his watch. “Ten thirty, not bad timing.”

“Why me, Buck? Why not someone who knows these people?”

Buck stopped and faced him. “That’s her way, son. She’s a hard-assed businesswoman. She’s testing you. She’s offering you a chance, but she wants something on you. She’s got something on all of us.”

Jack looked up at the stars, then back at the large man. “Maybe I don’t want shit on me. Here, you take the envelope. This is stupid.”

Buck put his hand on his shoulder. “Let’s just get this over with and get back to civilization in time for a drink.”

Jack stood, looking away from the man for a few moments, weighing his options. It was like standing at the edge of a cliff before jumping into the water below. You knew it would be okay, but you still had that niggling feeling that it might hurt a bit, or be really cold.

Buck smiled and turned towards the house. “I’ll go with you, but let’s take the stairs slowly. My knees are bad, especially after being squished up in that thing you call a car. Besides, I haven’t seen the Marshes in some time.”

Jack hesitated for a moment, but then followed Buck.

The two of them walked up to the front porch. As they neared the house Jack could see that the place was in a bad state of repair. Shutters hung sideways off many of the windows, and it looked as if a paint brush had not touched the edifice in dozens of years. Most of the wood was grey and untreated.

The stairs that led to a large wraparound veranda groaned with Buck’s weight, and when Jack added his, he thought the steps would buckle. As they approached the front door, he noticed that it was cracked open four or five inches. Light flooded out from between the door and its frame. Buck grabbed a large brass doorknocker and dropped it down three times on the door; the sound of metal on wood echoed within the house. He waited for a few minutes, but no one came to the door. He banged the knocker again, this time harder.

"Gotta be home; maybe they're out back." Buck pulled the screen door open and stepped into a large foyer. "Hello?" His voice resonated through the quiet house.

Jack reluctantly followed him in. The old place reminded him of the church his mother had taken him to when he was a young boy. It smelled of polished wood and stale air. His better judgment told him to leave, but he had been told that the envelope was to be hand-delivered, and he was already here. A grand circling staircase with an ornate wooden banister led upstairs from the center of the room. To the side were two large openings. The headers were intricately carved with leaves and intertwining vines. Both rooms were dark. Jack knocked on the wall one more time. "Mr. Marsh?" He moved to place the envelope on a side table, but Buck shook his head.

"There's a lot of money in that envelope. I'd feel better if I saw it in the old guy's hand." He stepped aside, his weight creaking on the old hardwood flooring.

Jack stuck his head into the room on the right. The windows were open and the sound of crickets and frogs could be heard through several screened windows, through which streamed beams of moonlight. The room was large and ran to the back of the house. The walls were covered with portraits of people, most from a long time back, judging from the clothing. What caught his eye was a large photo of Seminole Indians sitting along the bank of a lake or river, with dozens of fish laid out on the grass in front of them. There was another of a male Seminole adorned in full tribal regalia. In the middle of the room was an old snooker table. There were numerous burn marks around the wood coping, and the cloth on the table was old and faded.

He turned and went back to the other room. Buck followed him in. The windows were similarly open and afforded enough light to see a large dining table in disarray. There were three place settings with half-finished steak dinners and a nearly full bottle of red wine. Forks and knives were scattered randomly. It looked as if the diners had left in a hurry. A napkin lay on the floor. A swinging door led from the room to the right; it was covered with years of dirty handprints where it had been pushed open. When Jack turned on the light switch, he could see more signs of distress. An overturned chair on the far side of the room, and a broken wine glass beside it.

Buck walked around the table. “Looks like someone crashed the party.”

“Look Buck, let’s just leave the damn envelope in here and get going. What the hell do you think happened in here?”

Buck cleared his throat. “Let’s go see if they’re out back. Then we’ll call the police if we can’t find them.”

Calling the police was the first sane idea he’d heard since they arrived.

Buck put his hand on Jack’s shoulder and ushered him through the doorway into the kitchen.

Jack shrugged the man’s hand away and gave him a stern look. “Don’t do that again,” he said as he folded the envelope and slid it into his pocket.

Buck backed off, raising both hands in the air in apology. He looked to the side instead of eye-to-eye with Jack.

Jack moved to the door, gingerly pushing it open to get a peek into the expansive country kitchen. The room was dark, but there was just enough light to see the oven clock. He tried to flip a couple of wall switches, but none worked. He moved slowly toward the other side of the room, one foot after the other. He could smell the strong scent of garlic, onions, and cooked meat. His foot crunched on broken glass—very fine glass. He bent down and saw the remains of several light bulbs that had been taken out of a light which hung over the large central cooking island.

“Time to get the fuck out of here,” he whispered to himself. He heard the crunch of glass next to him. He looked up to see Buck smiling down at him, holding a gun. There was another figure by the kitchen door. Before he had a chance to react, he felt a heavy thump on the back of his head. His forehead hit the countertop just above his left eye, and then there was darkness.

8

ESCAPE

IT WAS A BAD dream—surely it had to be. The winding road, sugar cane, thick like a jungle on each side, pushing in, brushing against him. His head hurt; the smell of garlic. Jack rolled onto his side, but there was no pillow. He reached to the side to find it. Instead, his hands encountered something wet and slippery, and the hard floor. He put his hand to his mouth and jolted upright. *Christ*! He wasn't dreaming—there was no mistaking the smell and taste of blood, but it was cold. He felt the all-too-familiar sensation of his head and ears ringing, and had an acrid taste in his mouth. It was slowly coming back to him.

He'd been hit hard many times in his football career, but this time he hadn't been wearing a helmet, and he took a few moments to gather himself. He must have caught the corner of the counter; a crust of blood was beginning to form just above his eye. He touched his head gently—there would be a good welt. Damn, it hurt. There was blood on his hand, lots of blood. He was lying in a pool of it. There simply was too much blood to have come from his small head wound. He felt around; the floor was covered with it. There was a knife beside his left hand, he pushed it away. Grabbing the edge of the sink, he pulled himself to his feet and nearly toppled over. He fumbled around the counter looking for a tap, and in the process he knocked over a stack of dishes and cooking utensils. He did his best not to let any drop to the floor, but there was really no sense in trying to be quiet anymore. He put the dishes in the sink, turned on the water, and did a quick clean-up of his hands, wiping them on his pants to dry them.

He tried to calm himself. A cold sweat formed on his brow, and his heart was pounding. His eyes darted to the ground to his right. He could see that something—or more likely, someone—had been dragged through the back door of the kitchen. It was an old screen door that looked like it led to an outdoor porch. *What the hell had happened here?* He pulled open the door; the handle was covered in sticky, half-dried blood. His eyes were drawn to the middle of an expansive backyard. In the distance he could see moonlight reflecting off Lake Okeechobee; however, he could also see several large candles lit in what appeared to be a large circle halfway to the water's edge. He moved down the steps quickly and ran toward the light, stopping for a minute as pain wracked his head. He was dizzy and nearly dropped to his knees. He looked around for signs of danger but didn't see anyone. *Where the hell did Buck go? Is he still here?* He remembered the gun in Buck's hand. He remembered the other man.

As he neared the candles, he could see that there were two lumps in the middle of a large circle. People—dead people, by the looks of it. They lay side by side, and as he got closer he could see that their throats were cut nearly two-thirds through their necks. They were placed upon a chalk dust pentagram, their eyes blankly staring up at the starry sky. Jack fell to his knees and retched up whatever remained in his stomach. The description of the Marshes fit: mid-seventies, both with grey hair, well-dressed. He looked up at the moon; if he'd been a dog, he would have howled. Everything was sinking in. *They set me up.* The deception had been so simple, now that he could look back at it. *"Fuck!"* he yelled.

Jack's head jerked toward the house as he heard the sound of two car doors slamming shut. He ran toward the corner of the plantation house. "Shit!" He pursed his lips as he realized that he had left the knife in the kitchen. His fingerprints would be all over the place. "Fucking perfect . . . bloody fucking perfect." He moved around the corner of the house and looked into the window of the game room. He heard knocking on the door through the screened window, then he saw someone step into the front foyer. "Christ, it's a fuckin' cop," he whispered under his breath. He saw the beam of a flashlight coming his way as a second police officer cautiously moved toward him, most likely heading for the back door of the house. Jack had no choice and ducked down under the foundation of the house. He prayed that there were no snakes or spiders as he slid a dozen feet under the old building. It seemed an eternity for the officer to pass where he was hiding. The flashlight probed back and forth and occasionally under the house, but thankfully nowhere near where he lay.

Jack waited for the man to pass into the backyard. He knew that there wouldn't be much time once the bodies were discovered. Inching his way from under the house, he thought about turning himself in, but the whole mess looked incriminating. Without dusting himself off, he tiptoed to the front of the house. He heard a female voice shouting from the backyard. There was no time to be cautious at this point—he broke for his car, which fortunately was not blocked, the cops having parked their dark, unmarked car beside the Mercedes.

Jack fumbled for his keys and prayed that his car would start. It usually took a few tries when the engine was cold. With numb hands, he pulled up the handle for the door, his fingers feeling like useless sausages. The door opened with a creak and he slipped in. He pulled the door partly shut to avoid making noise, then pulled the envelope full of cash out of his pocket and quickly stuck it under his seat. He turned the key in the ignition and the engine groaned. He turned the ignition again, stomping on the gas pedal. The four banger engine chugged to life, as did the headlights. He jammed the car into reverse and slammed the gas pedal down, firing backwards down the driveway, bouncing through potholes until he reached the grass field, which made up most of the property. He swung the front end around and then jammed the gear shift into drive, nearly dropping the transmission out of the bottom of the car.

Jack turned his head and saw the lights of the police car come to life. He stomped his foot to the floor and the Ford Taurus groaned and whined before lurching toward the side road. It took him less than a minute to reach it. The police car was in pursuit, its lights bouncing up and down as the vehicle pounded through the potholed lane. Jack took the corner onto the road to the left a little too quickly and banged into the signpost on the driveway, making a gouging noise along the side of his car. "Damn," he muttered as he pushed the accelerator flat to the floor. The old Ford whined once again before the gears found some traction, the front wheel drive bucking up and down as the car gained forward momentum.

The county highway was just ahead. He could see the headlights behind him in the rear view mirror turning onto the road. He caught a movement out of the corner of his left eye; perhaps it was that split second that saved him as an old Chevy pickup shot toward him from a concealed spot in the brush at the side of the road. Jack jammed on the brakes and the pickup shot in front of him, the back corner of the truck clipping the front right corner of the Taurus, causing his assailant's vehicle to spin backwards. He floored the gas pedal, reaching the highway within a minute. Jack didn't spare a glance to see if any other cars were coming until he reached the highway.

Then he quickly looked over his shoulder. The pickup, luckily, had slowed down the police car for a few precious moments. Jack's heart was beating hard and it took a little skip as he thought through his options. He passed through Clewiston, doing more than one hundred. He was not worried about speeding—oddly enough, he found it quite liberating. Taking a deep breath, he looked back and saw the headlights of the two vehicles. He didn't know the involvement of the pickup in this mess. *Buck?* He figured his car should be able to outpace it, but he knew that the police car could catch his old beater and sure enough, it was making ground on him.

The cold hard reality hit him like a brick as he navigated the dark road. He'd been duped, played like a bad hand. *The fuckers were all in on it. Fucking bastards.* "THAT FUCKING BITCH!" The sex had been more than exceptional . . . he shook his head. "Too good to be true . . . Buck, *fucking Buck.* I'm so damned stupid." He banged his hands on the steering wheel.

Jack turned the car through a long, gradual turn. Coming up on his right was a strip mall; ahead, the road curved to the left. He pulled the gear shift into low gear and the car sounded like it was going to explode as the engine revved, pushing the tachometer into the red. The car slowed, however, without the brake lights coming on. He swung the car to the right, barely stopping it from rolling over as it hit the new asphalt in the mall's parking lot. He pulled the car in behind the buildings and slammed on the brakes, then got out of the car and ran to the edge of the wall and peeked around the corner. His head was killing him and a wave of nausea rolled through him. He watched as the police car roared through the turn and continued down the highway. He waited for a few moments, anticipating the arrival of the pickup. A minute or so later he heard the growl of the truck's engine, and watched it slowly moving its way through the small town. He could see two men in the vehicle, their heads moving from side to side as the vehicle passed. Jack ducked back behind the wall, holding his breath as if it would matter. The truck stopped, and Jack resisted the urge to run. After a minute, and to his utter relief, the truck accelerated and moved on down the road. As it cleared the last of the commercial area, the engine revved and the vehicle sped off down the highway.

Jack leaned against the brick wall, the howl of a dog in the distance giving him a shiver. He moved back to his car and slumped into the driver's seat and turned on the ignition. He pulled onto the highway and turned back toward the lake house. He decided to double back toward old US Route 27. He didn't want to take any chances and figured he could hook up with County Road 70 a ways north at Lake Placid. It would take him at least an hour to circumvent County Road 80, but as long as he had the gas, it should keep him clear of his assailants and the police. He had to assume the police would be looking for his car.

Jack had a rotten feeling in the pit of his stomach and he was furious. The old matriarch Henrietta was cunning. But then, he couldn't forget the feeling of helplessness when she asked the favor. He didn't believe in the paranormal, but there was no other logical way of explaining what had happened, other than him having been bewitched. *Did Sarah do the same to me?*

"Fucking witch! Goddamned no-good whore." He was silent for a few minutes. "I'm gonna kill that fucking bitch."

Jack followed the back roads until he hit the outskirts of North Port. In his fury, he had a hard time keeping to the speed limit. The streets were quiet and he made good time, regardless. He headed south on I-75 to Punta Gorda. It would have been faster to continue via the interstate, but he feared that the authorities would be looking for him along that route. At every bend in the road he expected to see a road block, or flashing lights. He drove on until he reached Highway 41, which ran south along the coast. Sarah's apartment wasn't more than three blocks from the highway.

****

It was just after one in the morning when he pulled into the driveway of Sarah's apartment complex. The building was a 1970s three-story condo, with stone and stucco facing on either end. Jack looked down at himself. He was covered with dried blood; he prayed that no one would see him. Shaking his head, he cursed at himself. "No choice now, you dumb bastard. She's still here, she's dead." He walked deliberately to the lobby door and entered the code on a keypad. A green light went on and he stepped into the lobby, depressing the handle as the door buzzed. The entrance was dark and musty, and the orange and black carpet was stained and threadbare. He decided to use the stairs to get to the third floor; he thought running up the stairs might burn off a little nervous energy. The stairwell was dark and smelled of mold, and his feet echoed as he took the steps two at a time. At the third floor, he opened the door to the stairwell and walked briskly to Sarah's apartment, which was almost directly across the dimly lit corridor. Sarah had given him a key three weeks earlier; it seemed like a natural steppingstone in their relationship.

He unlocked the door and pushed it inward. He stood back from the entrance for a moment in case there was someone waiting for him inside, then he walked in and flicked on the kitchen light. The room was empty. Cupboard doors stood open and the contents were cleaned out. His heart thumped heavily in his chest. The living room was empty, as were the bedroom and bathroom. Sarah was gone.

He'd been methodically played. Panic rose in his throat and his heart skipped a beat, his chest tightening to the point that a heart attack seemed possible. He let the sensations subside; to fight them would only make them worse.

As he stood in the bedroom surveying its emptiness and feeling sorry for himself, he heard a squeak on the floor in the living room. He put his back to the wall as he heard another step in his direction; someone had walked into the apartment. They were not Sarah's feet. *Too heavy*. The movement stopped no more than six or seven feet from the bedroom doorway. He cursed under his breath, realizing he hadn't locked the apartment door when he came inside. His hands felt strangely numb, as did his feet. He clenched his fists several times and decided that he needed to be proactive. There was the possibility that the intruder might be a concerned neighbor, but if he was being hunted, he needed an element of surprise. He stepped into the doorway, not wanting to be stuck in the confined space of the bedroom. In front of him was a fit-looking man, possibly in his forties, with tanned, leathery skin and dark eyes small and close together. In his right hand he held a long, lethal fillet knife. The man grinned and stepped toward him. Jack crouched low, his hands spread to either side like a defensive back. The man stopped, surveying his quarry. Jack moved into the room to avoid being cornered in the doorway. He moved to the right, trying to circle the stalker, not taking his eyes off him.

The man stepped in the other direction to keep Jack from getting closer to the exit and flexed his hands, the corded muscles in his forearms bulging. It was his attacker who broke the silence.

"Your little run is over."

His voice was native Floridian and the confidence with which he spoke sent a chill down Jack's spine. The killer grinned, revealing perfect and very white teeth. "You were lucky to evade us at the lake. You won't be so lucky this time." As he finished his last word, he lunged forward, the knife swinging in a wide arc. Jack dodged to the left, barely missing the path of the blade as it whipped past his face. He pulled away into empty space, barely keeping his balance.

"You're slow," Jack snarled. "I've dodged defensive tackles much better than you. Come on fucker, I've had enough bullshit tonight." Jack tried to goad the leather-faced man forward, but he would have none of it.

Leatherface lunged again, this time striking a glancing blow on Jack's thigh. The knife was razor sharp; Jack couldn't feel any pain, but saw the strip of red appear through the cut in his jeans. Jack made a move to the right, edging closer to the door, and the man lunged again. This time he overextended himself just a little; Jack saw the opening and slammed his elbow down onto his shoulder. Groaning in pain, the man dropped the knife. Jack brought his knee up into his assailant's jaw; he heard and felt the crack of the man's jawbone breaking. Jack bolted for the door, not bothering to press the attack. The assassin jumped back to his feet, staggering for a moment, the knife once again in his hand.

Jack ran through the apartment door heading straight for the stairwell. He opened the door and glanced back; the man was only a dozen paces behind. He pulled the door shut behind him and instead of running down the steps, ducked to the side of the door. It seemed an eternity before the door was slammed open and his assailant ran toward the steps, hesitating as he caught sight of Jack beside the door. Jack charged forward and wrapped his arms around the man's waist, driving his shoulder into his belly, the force of the attack carrying both men into open space above the stairs. They hung in the air for a few seconds, their momentum carrying both bodies towards the bottom of the stairwell. Jack remained on top of the man as they crashed into the wall at the turn in the stairs with tremendous force. The wind was knocked out of Jack's lungs and he lay stunned on top of the man for a few deathly quiet heartbeats, before rolling off him. The fishing knife was stuck in the side of Jack's hip. Jack rolled sideways to feel for a pulse on his enemy's wrist and found none.

He sat on a step and put his hand on the handle of the knife. It would be impossible to walk with the blade sticking out of his leg. Taking off his light jacket, he bundled it up to press it down on the wound to staunch any flow of blood. "One, two, three," he panted, and pulled the blade out. There was little pain, but he knew he had to get treatment on the puncture or it would fester.

Blood from the wound made a small pool on the cement floor and Jack pondered whether to clean it up, but having watched television shows like *CSI,* he knew there was no way he could cover up what had happened in any meaningful way. He reached over and searched his dead assailant. All he found was a set of keys in his pants pocket. Jack guessed he drove that old blue Chevy pickup.

Using the wall as a brace, he pulled himself up to his feet and walked down the rest of the steps and into the foyer, then straight out the door to the parking lot. Next to his car was the old pickup. *Too easy*, Jack thought, but then again, his assailant hadn't planned on losing the confrontation. He unlocked the driver's side door; the cab was full of papers scattered on the seat, empty coffee cups, and other debris. The truck smelled of cigars and the ash tray was full. He bundled up the papers and stuck them under his arm. Reaching under the seat he found an old leather wallet, which he shoved into his jeans pocket.

Jack leaned up against the old pickup for a moment. It wasn't prudent to be here any longer than necessary. He needed to get lost and could think of only one place: *The Everglades.*

In the recent past, he'd turned his back on his native ancestry—his mother was Seminole. Since his well-publicized drug problems, he had avoided his native relatives, his mother's family, out of humiliation. But there was no other place to turn. He made the decision to head to his grandfather's house, which was located on an Indian reserve off Highway 41, halfway to Miami. But first he had to get rid of his car; there was no sense making it easier for his pursuers.

Jack parked the old Ford two blocks away on a side street, locked it, and then made his way back to Sarah's apartment complex, making sure that the place was devoid of any activity. Within five minutes he was driving the old Chevy pickup south toward Naples.

* * * *

"You went where? Clewiston?" Perry was furious. "Dead people, and you're being chased by the cops? I told you! Fucking Satanists. Where's that bitch?" He didn't even wait for Jack to answer. "You know they can trace an iPhone; it's all part of that find-my-phone thing on the latest download. The police have got ways of doing this kind of shit. Probably can see where you are now, maybe tap into this call. You're gonna get me in trouble."

"This is getting fucked up fast, Per. I went back to Sarah's place. It's cleaned out."

"No shit."

"Nothing, nothing there at all. Then I get jumped by some guy with a knife. We scrap it out for a minute or so then he ends up chasing me into the stairwell. I jump him and we fall down the stairs. The force of the fall, with me on top, breaks the fucker's neck. Dead as a doorknob."

After a long pause, Perry said, "You okay?"

"Got stabbed in the leg. I don't think it's too big a deal."

"You're fucking lucky, bro. This is seriously out of hand. You gotta chuck that phone of yours into a drainage ditch, feed it to the gators."

"Call my Aunt Rebecca in Atlanta, here's the number. Let her know what's happened. I'm a fugitive now. If I turn myself in, it's not looking good, so I'm gonna have to figure a few things out first. I think this whole thing is linked to Senator Hunter in some way—I don't know why, but I do. I'm going to see my family. Can you call Aunt Rebecca for me?"

Silence. Then: "Yeah, I'll do it. Ditch the phone." Click.

Jack contemplated turning north and heading out of Florida, but that would be expected, and he couldn't run for long on the five hundred dollars Henrietta had given him. His credit cards were useless. He continued south and waited until Highway 41 made the turn to the east before he chucked his phone out the window into a drainage ditch full of water that ran along the side of the road. He lamented the loss of his connection to the outside world, but knew that it was the safer choice.

As he stopped at a red light, a police cruiser pulled up beside him. He saw the officer punching something into his onboard computer. He did his best to remain calm. There wasn't too much traffic at that time of night and he was sure he was being given the once-over. The cruiser moved ahead when the light turned green. Jack took a deep breath and followed, not too closely, making sure he held the speed limit. The officer turned right at the next light and Jack sighed in relief.

Within forty minutes he passed into Big Cypress Reserve. His Gramps and many of his cousins lived in a small town just off the highway. They ran airboat tours into the Everglades. He hadn't been there for some time, but not much had changed. He went north along Route 29, which used to be not much more than a dirt path, at best. Now it was paved and provided a link to I-75. He came in the back way down a dirt road to a small encampment of chickee huts—small squat buildings with reed roofs. A short distance past the huts stood a more modern bungalow. He pulled up close to his grandfather's home and slid out of the truck. The wound in his leg was starting to ache. As he moved toward the house, half stumbling, three men wielding high-powered rifles emerged from the shadows. He raised his hands above his head and didn't move. The dome light was on in the truck and he hoped it was bright enough that the men could see his face. One lowered his rifle and moved toward Jack, obviously recognizing him.

"Jackson, you son of a bitch. What the hell are you up to at three in the morning, man? Lucky we didn't shoot you. We saw the headlights and we came to wake up Gramps."

Jack stepped towards the man. "Josh, glad as hell to see you." He embraced his cousin with a bear hug. Josh was slightly taller but with a similar athletic build as Jack. His face was lean and tanned, with eyes that showed a keen intelligence. His hair was cropped, unlike the two other men who wore their black hair tied back off their faces in ponytails. Jack and Josh had been close in their youth. Jack thought it was a shame that Josh hadn't taken the opportunity to better himself. His grades had been excellent.

"Last time I saw you was on TV, getting carried off on a stretcher. You don't look much better now. You look like a bag of shit. What's with all the blood?"

Jack grimaced. "Asshole, I shoulda been a lineman like you in high school—be the hitter, not the one getting hit. At least I made it and played university ball. You shoulda gone."

"Florida State is the only college, cousin. You got Seminole blood in you and you played for the fuckin' Gators?" Josh stiff-armed him in the shoulder, knocking him back a yard, then Jack fell to one knee, obviously in pain. "You alright Jack?"

"Not exactly . . . I've been stabbed." Jack looked at the other two men. He recognized the one on the left, a childhood friend of Josh's. "Hey Nate, or should I call you Nathan now?"

Nate smiled, his brow furrowing slightly. He had always been quiet, and was still on the chubby side. "Nate's fine. Good to see you Jack, it's been years. We must have been fifteen?" Nate came over and clasped hands with him helping him to his feet.

Josh motioned to the third man. "This is Bobby. He doesn't speak too much, but he can shoot the eye out of a gator at a hundred yards." Bobby nodded. "Like I said, he don't talk much."

Josh put his arm around his cousin's shoulder and pulled him towards his grandfather's house. "K, Jack. Wassup? You're lucky we were up smokin' a joint and havin' a few beers. You mighta got a rude welcome. Don't you call before you show up here? You know better. It's shoot first and ask questions later after sunset. Use your phone, brotha."

Jack shrugged. "Tossed it in a ditch."

Josh shook his head. "I'm not stupid. You're in trouble. You ain't homesick for this bug-infested shithole. Gotta be bad, we haven't heard shit from you in five years. Gramps has been pissed about it. He won't say shit against you, though."

"Would Gramps be pissed off if we woke him up?"

"Does a bear shit in the woods?"

Josh rubbed his hand across his face. "Gramps always liked you. Don't know why, you being a half-breed and all. He's probably just sick of seeing our sorry asses all the time. He's the head cheese around here now. You in trouble, you gotta speak to Gramps. What kinda shit you in?"

"Big trouble, cousin. I mean real big."

Josh smiled. "No trouble too big. I'm glad as hell you came home, had some sense. We look after our own, even if you are a half-breed. Boring as shit around here, driving white folk around in an oversized Jeep on stilts to see a few fuckin' gators, losing my fuckin' mind. Another fat-assed white guy asks me how dangerous they are, I'm gonna toss him over the side and say, 'Real dangerous, bite your arm off in seconds.'" Josh chuckled.

Bobby laughed. "Bite your fuckin' arm off."

Josh shook his head. "Real quiet, then he just says shit."

Bobby just stood and grinned.

Josh directed Jack toward the old man's residence, but when he put a hand on his cousin's arm Jack retorted, "I haven't been away so long that I don't know which house my grandfather lives in. Where's Grandma?"

"She's still shacked up with some guy in Hollywood, haven't seen her in years."

* * * *

Gramps's house sat in the middle of a line of huts that backed onto the swamp. It amazed Jack that his people still lived in these primitive dwellings. It seemed that as the Seminole people got older, they moved closer to their roots. Many of them owned fairly expensive homes in bigger cities, paid for with gambling money or other Seminole business interests. Gramps, as far as Jack knew, was worth at least a few million. Yet he lived in this little house off Highway 41 in the middle of a swamp. He swatted away a mosquito that landed on his cheek.

As they approached Gramps's place, the door swung open and out walked a tall, older, native man. His face was wrinkled and brown from the Florida sun and his hair was brush cut and grey. He didn't look as if he had been sleeping; he was dressed in jeans and a well-tailored shirt, his eyes intently watching the group as they approached.

Jack moved towards him and bowed his head. "Gramps."

The old man stared at Jack, his eyes narrowing. He crossed his arms, not lowering his eyes. He took a pipe out of his jacket pocket, followed by a pouch of tobacco. He placed a small pinch of the weed into the bowl and pushed it down with his thumb. Josh held out his Zippo lighter, flicking it, and the flame was sucked up into the old man's pipe as he inhaled deeply. The aroma brought back memories; Jack had forgotten the pipe. He and Josh had spent many hours sitting around a campfire years ago, their grandfather telling stories, blowing smoke rings that would rise up towards the stars.

"You only come when you need help?" He looked at Jack, his eyes like tiny daggers. "You forget about your heritage, but it is the rock upon which you fall. We should let you stand on your own . . . "

He let Jack squirm for a few moments.

" . . . But the spirits tell me differently. Come in, let's talk." He turned to Josh and the other two. "Josh, you are family, you can come in. Nate, you and Bobby can watch the door."

Gramps frowned and led his two grandsons into his hut. The interior of the dwelling was a surprise. His grandfather seemed to have moved up a notch in the modern, technological world. The house was furnished with expensive leather couches, a formal dining set, up-to-date kitchen appliances, and modern art interspersed with three giant flat screen TVs on the walls. Two laptops sat open on a coffee table in front of one of the couches.

Gramps moved toward Jack and embraced him. "You have your mother's eyes. I miss her." He motioned for the boys to sit and walked over to the fridge and pulled out three Coors Lights. He returned and handed them to Jack and Josh. "I suspect that you might need this."

Jack nodded, cracking open the beer and downing the whole thing in one long swig.

"In the old days, we would do an augury to find out if things were wrong. Today I still make an augury, but I have the help of the late night news. I woke up three hours ago and I knew that you would be here. The spirits woke me. When I slept I saw great evil. I saw you trapped within its web. I saw you here. As I waited for you to come, I turned on the television and saw this."

The two young men turned their attention to the largest TV in the middle. Jack saw the old estate house near Clewiston cordoned off with yellow tape, and a dozen police cars sitting in the driveway. A news reporter gave details of a grisly murder, apparently tied in with a Satanic cult.

"The prime suspect is Jackson Walker of Fort Myers. A former NFL player, Walker works for Senator Hunter in his Naples office. Hunter has not been available for comment. Walker is believed to be armed and dangerous."

Jack wondered why the press suspected him. He'd been set up big time. Why had the police shown up? *Buck!*

Gramps turned down the sound. A picture of Jack in his Bengals uniform flashed on the screen.

"Satanic cult? What the heck, Jack. What have you done? What is your involvement? All of this is no coincidence. There are no coincidences in life."

Jack walked over to the fridge and helped himself to another beer. “Okay. I’m here now, I may as well tell you the story. It’s one fucked-up mess, and I can blame no one else for my actions and involvement.”

Josh and Gramps sat in silence as Jack finished his tale. Gramps sat for a few minutes longer without speaking. “You talk as if these Satanists are not bad people. Herein lies your misconception. They are real. They are dangerous, and they are using you. Satan is real and he is manipulative. The cult that you speak of has been in existence here in South Florida since before the first Seminole war. The name has changed. What they call The Brotherhood of Set was formed forty years ago. Before that they were called the Congregation of Set, before that, The Brotherhood of Satan. We have been watching them and they have been watching us. Let there be no mistake, they know your heritage.”

He sat for a moment in silence.

“You see, there are only a few who know of their real intentions, and I am one of them. I know Henrietta LePley. She is old Florida blood and she is a witch.”

Jack raised his eyes in question.

“Yes, there are witches, and this one is powerful. That old house in Clewiston, it’s on the reserve. The Marshes were good people.”

Jack’s jaw dropped. “Fuckin’ hell. Witches with brooms?”

“No, nothing like that. There are those who follow the good path, and there are those who follow the bad. There are channels that flow between good and bad, grey areas. I believe that good people don’t stray from the path that is more socially acceptable. Henrietta and her coven chose the path less travelled. If you have the dark conscience to go that route there will be rewards, but there will always be a price. Henrietta has sold her soul to Satan. She draws upon the devil’s powers of deceit. You are a victim. I don’t think you are a major piece, but rather a fly in her web. You are caught, and it will be hard to get you unstuck. It will be difficult to disprove something that has existed in secret for close to two hundred years. We will have to clear your name through normal means. It would be senseless to try and prove that witches exist. Most people look at these cults as crackpots. I believe your employer must be the real target for some reason.

You are collateral damage because of your Seminole blood."

After a pause, Gramps continued. "What has Senator Hunter been doing for the past while?"

Jack thought for a moment. "He has been working on a clean water bill, you know, revitalizing the Everglades. I don't know much more than that."

Gramps nodded. "We are in agreement with the government and in negotiations to help them with their bill. It is good for the Everglades, but bad for the businesses that operate within the watershed. The bill which you speak of affects Henrietta and her investors. Growing sugar cane and feeding cattle require that much of the valuable Everglades water be diverted into drainage ditches, and Lake Okeechobee threatens to overflow every summer.

"The Everglades are dying. Every summer, the water is let out of the great lake and into the rivers, instead of being allowed to flow slowly through the great swamp into Florida Bay and some of the other main tributaries. The fisheries and wildlife are being destroyed. Henrietta's people have been against the bill, as it would kill their business interests. Moreover, they feel that we cheated them when the gambling authority was first given to us." He took a long drink from his beer. "Is there anything else?"

Jack thought for a moment. "Well . . . I think the senator is screwing his secretary."

"Oh ho!" Gramps slapped his leg. "How long has she worked for him?"

"I don't know exactly, but it hasn't been for long, maybe a year and a bit."

"Hmmm, makes sense. The same ploy they used with you. Female sexuality mixed with a little voodoo. It works most of the time. It is said that the priestesses within our tribes had the power to ensnare young men's hearts. They did not use it for evil, but rather to ensure that our kind survived and procreated. Young men in their prime don't want to settle down. They want to fight, hunt, and cause trouble. Unfortunately grandson, you are a horny bastard and are paying a high price for your sexiness."

Josh laughed. "Sexiness?"

"Yes, sexiness. Your cousin Jack is a good-looking Seminole man; he is desirable to women, and this trait is what probably attracted the Satanists to him. He was an easy target."

Gramps stood and paced the room for a few minutes, his hands clasped behind his back. He moved and stood over Josh and Jack and looked down at them, placing a hand on each man's shoulder.

He looked Jack in the eye. "Now tell me son, and look me in the eye as well. Are you involved in any wrongdoing?"

Jack pondered the man's words for a moment. "No, on the surface . . . no. I don't know why I was drawn into that house. I suppose I unlawfully entered. Then I touched a lot of things, including the blood in the kitchen. I'm not sure, but I think I killed that bastard in Sarah's apartment building. Not good."

Gramps nodded. "You're in deep." He put his hands on both boys' shoulders once again. "You were spellbound; you could not break the incantation. You were unaware of it and not strong enough to do anything about it, and it made you stupid for a time. Unfortunately, white man's society does not account for the occult within its governance. It will be difficult to prove your innocence. We need to get you low. Josh, you need to take your cousin on a long hunting trip. You need to get lost. Follow the old trapping route that we used to take when you were a teen. If I need to contact you, I will do so at your next checkpoint. Leave something at each one so we can tell where you have been. Leave a pack of matches with a note in it on the window sill. If we can keep you safe long enough, we might be able to figure this mess out. If they catch you now, there will be no chance, much less a plea bargain."

Jack interrupted. "I told Perry to contact my aunt in Atlanta. She's wealthy and she likes me. I know you don't like my dad or his family, why would you? But she could help. She's always treated me well."

Gramps looked at him. "You need as much help as you can get. I once met Rebecca. She is a powerful woman." He grabbed the sleeve of Jack's shirt. "Look at this. You are a mess. We will need to get you some clothes. Josh, lend him something of yours." Josh nodded and left the hut. "We also need to get that leg cleaned up before we send you into the wild. Is it sore?"

"It's starting to hurt."

Gramps gestured for him to take his pants off. He left and

came back with a bag.

"You know that I'm the village medicine man." He laughed as he cleaned the wound with some peroxide and then iodine. "I can put a Steri-strip on this for now, but you will need to keep it clean." He handed Jack a Ziploc bag with some cotton balls and peroxide. "Here's some antibiotics. Take two a day until the bottle is empty."

Josh returned with a duffle bag filled with clothing for Jack.

"You're going to need help, boy. Now you get going. Take Nathan and Bobby with you. Take an airboat to camp, then use kayaks. You're going to have the police down on you from what I can see on TV. They won't enter the reserve unless they have a damn good reason, and then only with permission of the council."

Jack looked to his grandfather in admiration.

Gramps finished his beer. "We're family here. I know you have been away, but you are blood. There are no coincidences. You were meant to do what you've done and be where you are. We will look after each other." He looked into both of their eyes. "We do not leave anyone behind. We do not surrender; we do not get captured. Are we clear? Family is bigger than the individual. If we had not been negotiating the Clean Water Bill, you would not be mixed up in this mess. We have withstood the US military in three wars; we will prevail."

Jack blanched. Though he was part Seminole, he never truly felt like he was native. The look in Gramps's eye drew out something from within him, something primal, something he had never felt before. He smiled. "I am sorry to have brought y'all into this mess."

"Nonsense. I will say this one last time: there are no coincidences, we were meant to help you."

Josh stood. "We have been in this mess together for a long time. We are one. I will die for you, Jack. Will you die for me?"

Jack did not hesitate. He grasped his cousin's arm. "We are one."

The three men embraced, rocking back and forth.

Gramps looked up to the boys. "There's a storm brewing. I can feel it in my bones. It'll hit land in less than two days. Get into the swamp, lay low. Storms are an omen of change, bringers of death and rebirth. It will also help give you cover. You can't stay here any longer. They will seek you out. I have no doubt that they will be here at daybreak. Be gone. May the strength of our forefathers guide you and keep you strong."

The old man chanted a few words in the Miccosukee tongue. Jack had not heard the language in years. Though he could only make out a few words, the sound of his grandfather's voice brought him comfort. The old man pushed them to their knees, his hands upon their heads. "I have placed a ward upon you. Do not fear the devil's magic for the time being."

Jack stood. For the first time in several years, he felt like he had made the correct decision. Jack reflected on the past four years. His fall had been gradual, a piece here, a piece there, and then a snowball of events. In hindsight, he could have brought an end to the cycle, yet it never works that way; it's never that easy. He'd believed he was taking the correct steps by getting a job with Senator Hunter, but it had been that very job that had created the final pen stroke in his fall from grace. When you reach bottom, you have to grab onto something or you die. He had his family.

9

JANIE

THE SUN BAKED JANIE'S bare chest. She loved the warmth and the tightness of her skin after getting her daily dose of vitamin D. She had been warned by her dermatologist to be careful. She'd recently had a couple of suspicious spots removed. It's not that she didn't care, she just figured she would probably die from lung cancer before melanoma. Her sun worship was an addiction, but what the hell, she had worse vices. Janie had smoked a pack of Marlboro Lights a day, sometimes more, since she was sixteen. What else? She needed a few drinks to start the day, and she loved young men. She had no time for forty- and fifty-somethings with their beer bellies and screwed-up attitudes. She liked the feel of a hard body.

She spied her empty pack of cigs. The thought of smoking and how bad it was for her triggered the addiction response. She opened a new pack and lit up. She drew in the heavy smoke and rolled over. *One more won't make it any worse.* Janie worked for Peter Robertson, a criminal lawyer in Bonita Springs. Peter had called her first thing that morning—a big client was coming in, a relative of the man accused of the double homicide in Clewiston, and she needed to be on the ball. She was a little short on cash so she said she'd be there with bells on. Peter relied upon her for his dirty work. Janie had lived in Southwest Florida for nearly thirty years, graduated from law school in Connecticut in the early '80s, but had failed to pass the bar exam. She moved to Florida, drawn by the lure of sun and fun. In her twenties, Janie had been a knockout—smart, attractive, the quintessential blonde beach babe. She'd bounced around for a number of years as a bartender, moving from one hot spot to the next, until she hit the wall that most sun seekers reach—no longer young, no net worth, and suffering the toll of booze, late nights and sun. Janie was still attractive, but she looked all of her forty-five years. Her skin was wrinkled and she had a smoker's voice. Her laughs became coughs, her voice gravelly and no longer sexy.

Janie pulled herself up off the lounge chair and walked into her house. She instinctively reached for the bottle of Stoli that she kept in the freezer. She paused. No, she needed the money, and Peter got upset if she drank during a job. She rolled into the shower, stripping off her string bikini bottoms. *Not bad for an old broad*, she thought, looking at herself in the mirror. She had a few sags here and there, but plastic surgery worked wonders.

Peter had mentioned that the case was high-profile and she should be on her game when she came in. Janie had built up a reputation as a diligent investigator; she wasn't necessarily fast, but she would turn over every rock in her path to get what she needed. She knew the beaches, barrier islands, and the stretch between Naples, Fort Myers and Port Charlotte better than most. She had been a party girl, knew what bars to drop into for a quick drink where people would talk, and had an endless stream of friends built up over twenty years of being a socialite.

The client was a woman, so she would need to wear something conservative, nothing too sexy, though she knew Peter liked that look. She decided on a dark blue pantsuit, low black heels, and a simple white top. She dragged a brush through her shoulder length hair, pulled it up into a swish as she called it, and stuck in a clip to hold it in place. A soft muted burgundy lipstick. Perfect.

It was hot. It was always hot in Lehigh Acres. Being five miles inland during the summer was hell. She turned on her car to let the air conditioning do its thing and had another quick smoke while she waited. Janie drove one of her boss's old BMWs. It was pushing 180,000 miles, but still ran like a charm.

She pulled into the parking lot with a few minutes to spare and lit another cigarette. The drive took the better part of half an hour. When she finished she popped a piece of gum in her mouth, thinking it would mute the smell of cigarette smoke.

Robertson and Robertson was located in one of the myriad taupe stuccoed office buildings that filled up commercial strips throughout southern Florida. She walked through the entrance and saw Peter talking to Myrtle, his secretary of at least twenty-five years. Peter was a nice-looking man for sixty-five, always well-dressed and groomed. His hair still showed a hint of black, and his eyes sparkled with a quick intelligence.

"Janie darlin', glad you're on time. Our potential client should be here soon. Come to my office and I'll give you a briefing." He wrinkled up his nose. "I do wish you wouldn't smoke right before a meeting. It cheapens our image." Peter spoke with a well-cultivated Southern drawl, which Janie thought was a bit put on at times.

Peter Robertson's office was large, and like the front office, finished in dark hardwood veneer. Two walls were covered with bookshelves stuffed with an assortment of books, many looking as if they had not been pulled in the last half century. The rest of the wall space was filled with diplomas, pictures, and two large windows. There were several low back green leather chairs spread out in front of a stately mahogany desk.

"Janie. Our client is moneyed, as I have stated, and I suspect a good prospect for the firm. Things have been a bit tight of late." He smiled calmly. "You look perfect, by the way."

Janie nodded. Peter could be a dirty old man; she was aware of his eyes running up and down her length. The innuendo was more of a game than anything. Janie respected Jack's wife Isabel too much to act on the many passes he'd made over the years.

Peter gestured for Janie to sit down in one of the chairs. He didn't waste any time beginning his briefing. "What do you know about Jackson Walker?"

"Christ. Well, isn't he that Satanic fuck who murdered a bunch of people out in the swamp? Been all over the news."

"Okay, you know who we're talking about. Mrs. Dempsey is Jackson's aunt; I think she is from Atlanta. She believes the boy has been set up. Now I stress to you that we are under the veil of secrecy and I was asked to sign a confidentiality agreement before she would meet with me. The boy is in hiding. You know damn well that there are dozens of cops on the case by now. The papers and television are on it. The whole goddamn thing is a clusterfuck. But as you know, these cases come along once in a while. It's not just what we might make from Mrs. Dempsey, but rather . . . the exposure. We need to get my face on television. This could be a decent payday, Janie.

"Once she walks through this door, there's a slight chance you might pick up a tail at some point. The police will find out who Walker's relatives are, and if they cross-reference that she bought a ticket to Fort Myers yesterday, they will be on her."

Janie nodded, her interest growing. "So we're going to have to prove this guy Walker is innocent. Been here before, Pete; what if he's not? I have to mess around with some sick fuck. I read what he did to that poor old couple. I don't know. Can I smoke?"

Peter shook his head. "Sorry, Janie. Let's just have a listen to Mrs. Dempsey. The guy was a local sports hero of a sort. He's got alibis. You want out?"

"Like hell I want out. I need the money."

"Just listen and try to look smart."

"That should be easy."

Peter's phone rang. He picked it up and listened for a moment. "Please bring her in."

A minute later Myrtle knocked on the door. "Mr. Robertson," she said as she opened the door, "Mrs. Dempsey is here." A well-dressed middle-aged woman stepped into the room. Peter stood and walked over to her, extending his hand. "Mrs. Dempsey, pleased to make your acquaintance. Peter Robertson, my clients call me Pete." He motioned towards Janie. "This is Janie Callahan. She is one of my top investigators."

Janie stood up, easily six inches taller than the woman, and politely shook her outstretched hand. It was delicate, yet strong. "I'm pleased to meet you, Mrs. Dempsey."

Janie watched Rebecca Dempsey as she elegantly sat down in the chair across from Peter's desk. She calmly crossed one leg over the other and placed a small dossier on her lap. Her hair was long and fashionably made up into a coil on the back of her head. Her face was stern, her eyes unrelenting.

"Mr. Robertson," she said in a slow, Georgia drawl. "You have been recommended to me by some close friends, whom you represented to their satisfaction. Trent and Patsy Hughes."

Peter paused for a moment to think. "Yes, Mrs. Dempsey. The Hughes have been good clients. I represented Trent successfully ten years ago."

The woman smiled, aware of the association. "You can call me Rebecca. Your family has practiced law in the state of Florida for generations, Mr. Robertson. You have a good reputation."

Peter smiled and nodded, accepting the compliment. "My great-granddaddy started this firm in 1910, Rebecca. We have been representing the unjustly accused in Fort Myers for more than a hundred years. How can we assist you?"

Rebecca chose her words slowly. "I am sure that you have been following the papers. We have had an incident. My brother's son Jack, Jackson Walker, has found himself in a predicament."

"We have been following the events with keen interest but are not privy to the details, only what can be gleaned from the papers and television."

Rebecca acknowledged Peter's words with a slight nod. "Yes, it is sad, but it is also an unjust story. Now, as you probably know, I live in Georgia. I don't see my family here very often. But I do know that Jack is a good boy, very clever, always very respectful. My sister-in-law was the salt of the earth, and she raised the boy until her untimely death. He has good values."

"Rebecca, pardon my skepticism, but we hear this sort of thing all the time. If the courts believed what they were told by parents, spouses, and relatives, the jails would be empty."

Rebecca nodded, accepting Pete's point. "Jack's friend claims the boy has been set up, or rather, is a victim of poor associations and circumstance. You have been doing this for a long time, Peter. And yes, I am sure that you have heard the same story from most of your clients. The boy might be guilty, but I owe it to my dead sister-in-law to try and help him." Rebecca paused. "Peter, my brother John was an alcoholic and an abuser, and beat Jackson's mother to death three years ago in a fit of rage. It is a sore point in our family history. I have a soft spot for the boy and am willing to pay you to investigate, whether or not we might have a defense. If we could, we would retain you to handle our case. If we are successful, we will continue to use your services with a civil action against those who have wronged Jackson. There are slanderous words being tossed around. He is an aide to Senator Hunter, and I am sure that the senator's office is trying to distance itself from the inferences being made about Jack. Being associated with a cult is not good for re-election."

"If Jack is on the run, Rebecca, he is only going to find a bad end. He needs to turn himself in. We need to speak to him. He needs to stop before he does himself more harm."

"He has indicated that he won't turn himself in until he has found a way to clear himself."

Peter pondered Rebecca's words. "The odds seem long, but this is what I propose. I would have you pay my firm a retainer of $20,000. We will need a week or so to investigate the circumstances surrounding your nephew's, uh, situation. If at that time we feel there is sufficient evidence to pursue the defense, we will enter into a more formal business agreement. I think you will find our connections and diligence outstanding. Janie knows the streets better than anyone I've ever met."

Rebecca gestured with her head and arms indicating accord. "I was told that you were not afraid to charge."

Peter didn't blink. "You get what you pay for, my granddaddy always said. We will keep a strict accounting of the time spent. Janie is the best, and not a time waster, if that is fine by you, of course? She may be putting herself at risk and there needs to be appropriate compensation."

Rebecca turned to Janie and nodded. "The onus is on you, Peter, to show me that we have a case. Let us consider that we have a temporary agreement." She stood and Peter went around the desk to shake her hand. She offered her hand to Janie and then sat down again.

"Jack's mother was Seminole. They have him stuck out in the Everglades somewhere. We will arrange for you to talk with him. It might be tricky, as you may well have figured."

Peter stood and began to pace. "I assure you that we are discreet."

"Someone from the family will contact you shortly," Rebecca said.

Peter pondered things for a minute. "I have an under-the-radar cell phone. I will give another to Janie." He turned his attention to Janie. "I would suggest you get another one as well, one with a pay-as-you-go plan. Sooner or later we will be watched."

Rebecca nodded.

"Janie, see what you can find very quickly, and then lose yourself for a day. We've done this drill before. I mean invisible."

Janie nodded. Somewhere she'd missed the part where she was to decide if she wanted the case or not. It no longer seemed an option. Perhaps there would be a big payday; she needed a face lift, her chin was beginning to sag. Once this case was over, she would fly out to California and go to one of those places that pamper you for a week.

Janie shook Mrs. Dempsey's hand again, her voice suddenly gravelly. "Good day, Mrs. Dempsey. Pardon me, but I need to get lost." She winked at Peter.

* * * *

Janie left the office building and walked to the designated smoking area, quickly lighting a cigarette. *How in the hell am I going to dig up any decent dirt so fast?* She decided that she would visit the obvious spots before she went underground. She slowly glanced around the parking lot and picked out a blue Ford that looked like it might be a cop car. She tossed her half-finished cig on the ground, squashing it with the toe of her shoe. She decided to head to Walker's place of work. She knew where Senator Hunter's office was as she drove past it every day on her way into work. It was close. The Ford didn't follow.

After a five-minute drive from Peter's office she saw the strip mall in which the senator's office was located. She pulled into the parking lot, making a mental note of the green Malibu that had stopped at the side of the road in front of the building.

Stepping into the front office, a blast of cold air made her shiver. She was greeted by a pleasant young brunette receptionist.

"Hello there." The girl's large bright eyes met Janie's. "It's hot out there today, isn't it? What can I do for you?"

The receptionist was overly eager, perfect. Janie didn't have a lot of time to waste. "Hello, darlin', hot as hell assuredly. I'm supposed to meet someone here. His name is, uh, Jackson Walker, said he'd meet me just before noon. I'm a reporter for the *Gainesville Sun*, we're doing a story on post-concussion syndrome among college athletes. We want to see how they're doing after graduation. It's a sad story for the most part. Is Jackson in?"

The receptionist blanched. "Jack . . . Jack is . . . not in today."

"Strange, we set this up weeks ago and I confirmed it on Tuesday."

"Umm . . . hold on a minute." She buzzed someone on the intercom. "Graham, could you please come out here?"

"I hear Mr. Walker has a girlfriend who was supposed to meet with us. What was her name?"

"Oh . . . Sarah, Sarah Courtney."

"Is she from Fort Myers?"

"Yes, but, didn't you hear—"

At that moment a man stepped out of an office and interrupted the receptionist. "I am sorry, ma'am, can I assist you?"

"Yes, I was saying to the young lady here that I had an appointment with Jackson Walker. I'm here from the *Gainesville Sun*, doing a sports story?"

"Ma'am, Jack doesn't work here anymore. He was let go earlier this morning. He is no longer associated with Mr. Hunter's office. I'm sorry, but we are closing for the day. If you have any other inquiries, please make an appointment with Mr. Hunter's press secretary."

The girl behind the desk looked flustered.

"Okay sir, thank you. I will do just that."

Janie stepped out of the office, the heat of the day blasting her like a hot sauna after being in the very cold building. She stood and lit up a smoke. The green Malibu was sitting out on the street and she could see two men in the front seat. At this point, it really didn't matter if she had a tail. The police would most likely be watching the senator's office. She was still anonymous at this point.

She took out her little red notebook and started making notes. Senator Hunter was in damage control, disassociating his office from Walker. The police would have had Sarah Courtney's name 10 hours ago. They would be steps ahead at this point, but she still had to do the follow-up. She would have to bribe someone for the forensic reports, and that would be tough. Her ace in the hole was the aunt and her link to Jackson, and she needed to talk to him. *One thing at a time, Janie.*

She tapped Sarah's name into the Yellow Pages app on her smartphone and found the address. It took Janie forty minutes to arrive at Sarah's apartment. She parked out front in the visitor's lot. She lit a cigarette as she crossed the parking lot. The front lobby hadn't seen a facelift in twenty years and the place stank of moldy, dirty carpet. She went over to the intercom and pressed the button beside *S Courtney*. There was no answer. She looked around the ceiling for any signs of surveillance, though she doubted this place would have any. Once she was comfortable that there weren't any hidden cameras, she rummaged around in her large purse and pulled out her lockpicks. It only took her seconds to access the inner lobby and cross to the elevator.

Sarah's apartment was nearly straight across from the elevator. She moved casually to the door and knocked lightly. Nothing. She fiddled with the door lock for a moment and smiled as she heard the telltale click of the lock disengaging. She opened the door and slipped in quickly. The apartment was empty, which could mean a couple of things. She needed to talk to Walker.

Her cell phone rang, the display indicating that it was Peter.

"Just a heads-up. The police just called looking for information. They know that we have been retained by Walker's family. It's time for you to disappear."

"Walker's girlfriend's apartment has been vacated."

"That corroborates."

"Let me know as soon as the family contacts you. I can't do too much else without interviewing Walker."

"Will do. Talk soon."

Janie's friend owned a small condo on the south part of Fort Myers Beach at the Estero Beach and Tennis Club. She had the code to get into the place. She decided to ditch her car and take a cab. She would have Pete pick it up tomorrow. As she headed towards Edison Mall, a dark-colored Malibu pulled out of the condo parking lot and fell in behind her.

She drove purposefully slow, reaching over to the glove box, keeping one eye on the road.

The car followed as she pulled into the mall. It must have picked up her license plate at the apartment; Sarah's building would be watched, as she was the suspect's girlfriend. She parked at the back of the parking lot under a large tree, then stepped out of her car and locked it. The Malibu parked three rows over. She lit up a cigarette and walked casually towards the mall entrance. Janie noticed that the driver remained in the car, and no one followed her in, or entered the mall entrance. *Good, a lazy cop. He'll be watching my car for a while.* She smiled.

Within minutes, she slipped out the far end of the mall and hailed a cab.

"Where we going, lady?" said the taxi driver.

"Fort Myers Beach. Drop me off at the South Florida Grill, down the bottom part of the beach, Santini Plaza."

"Might be evacuating the beach with that big storm coming, lady. Sayin' it could turn into a hurricane."

Janie smirked. "I'll take that into consideration. Please hurry!" The driver frowned as he looked at her in the rear view mirror. "Okay, lady." He punched the meter and made a U-turn in the opposite direction.

Janie let out a long breath. Her thoughts turned to the approaching weather. Summer storms were a daily occurrence in South Florida. She didn't think the storm that had materialized over the Keys would amount to much—they seldom did. She'd be off the beach by tomorrow afternoon, and the weather was due the next night.

After a half hour's drive, mostly sitting at frustrating traffic lights, the cab crossed the tall bridge at the north part of Fort Myers Beach. The top section of the beach was, for the most part, filled with honky-tonks, beachwear stores, tattoo parlors, mid-priced restaurants, bars, and large multi-level condo developments. Janie didn't mind the cheap touristy end of the beach; she fit in perfectly. The lyrics for the Rolling Stones song *Honky Tonk Women* popped into her head. She smiled. "Story of my life."

"What's that?" said the driver.

"Drive the car. Just talking to myself."

****

The scenery changed as the cab made the six-mile trek to the south section of the beach. It was less commercial, with higher-end residences and condo developments.

Janie paid the cab driver from the thick envelope Peter had given her earlier in the day, adding a good tip. "Thanks, ma'am."

She stepped into the dark interior of the restaurant and found a seat at the large granite-topped bar. One of her favorite bartenders, Tory, had a large chardonnay ready for her within moments of sitting down. "Cut me off after a couple, got a big day tomorrow."

"You're the boss, Janie. How's things, haven't seen you in a while?

"Same old. You?"

Tory shrugged.

"Blue cheese salad and some of those appetizer ribs, please, dear. And I've not been here tonight, right?"

"Like I said, you're the boss."

****

Janie was woken by her cell phone. It took her a few moments to register where she was and what was making the noise. She looked around the condo; the sun was just rising over Estero Bay, nearly blinding her as she looked out the window. She turned her head to look out over the Gulf. She'd slept on her friend's couch as she did not want to mess up the bed. With some reluctance, she picked up her phone and pressed the green talk button.

"Janie?" She could tell from Peter's tone that something was up. "I'm going to give you an address. You are to meet a native man, his name is Bob, I think his last name was . . . Okay, here it is: Bracken. Write this down and get a cab there by noon. Now, turn off this phone and don't use it again. Git it?"

"Yeah, yeah. Gotcha." She hung up and wrote down the address.

Janie forced herself to her feet and stretched, then put the phone down on the table. "Goddamn it," she said out loud. "I'm getting too old for this shit."

It didn't take her long to shower and dress. She figured something low-key: jeans and a designer T-shirt. She looked in the mirror and fussed with her hair. "Not bad, Janie." She checked her purse to make sure she had her Glock 19 semi-automatic. She'd never used it, but in her line of work, a woman needed protection. She had flashed it a few times, which proved to be a sufficient deterrent.

She called a cab and took the elevator down to the lobby. She found an inconspicuous place to wait outside and lit up a cigarette. A green and yellow cab rolled up to the front of the building before she had time to finish it.

The drive didn't take too long. The address was that of a fruit shipping company close to downtown Bonita Springs. Janie paid the driver and went inside. A young Latina sorting out some bills on a large counter turned to look at her. "Can I help you?" she said with a Spanish accent.

"I was to meet Bob Bracken here at noon. My name is Janie, Janie Callahan."

"Just a minute, I'll ring him." She picked up the phone and punched in a short number. After a moment she said, "Okay, I'll send her back." She turned to Janie. "Go through that door to the back of the warehouse. He's just finishing up a load."

"Okie-dokie, thanks."

The warehouse was large and smelled of fermenting oranges, and the fruit flies were thick. She followed the girl's directions and went to the back, where she found a man closing the back door of a medium-sized cargo truck. He turned towards her. He was short with a clean-shaven face, she guessed nearly fifty. He had a pleasant smile, which instantly put her at some ease. "You must be Janie?" he said with a South Florida drawl. "Hi, I'm Bob." He extended his hand to her as she nodded. "I'm Jack's cousin. I'm going take you to see him. Jump in."

He gave her a hand up into the cab of the truck, which had worn, fake leather seats and smelled of body odor and cigars.

Bob opened the back door to the warehouse and then jumped up into the driver's seat. The old diesel truck roared to life as he turned the key. They pulled out of the warehouse and into the fenced yard behind. He took a minute to close the sliding gate that protected the parking area.

Bob didn't say a word for five minutes or so, intent on navigating the busy traffic. Once they eased out of the commercial district he broke his silence. "You a lawyer or somethin'?"

Janie paused for a moment. "Paralegal, actually. I work for a lawyer. I'm a researcher, I do all the bullshit work so my boss can charge the big bucks."

Bob grinned and made the turn off of Highway 41 and headed inland on Corkscrew Road. "Jack's in trouble I guess?"

"It would appear so." Janie looked at the ashtray brimming over with cigar butts and ashes. "Mind if I smoke?"

"Nope, as long as you got one for me."

Janie was relieved and passed one to him, then held the lighter for him before lighting her own. Finding a fellow smoker these days was like finding a soul mate. Never any questions asked and no prejudice.

"We can fly under the radar in a fruit truck. I'm gonna take you into the swamp a bit where you will meet some more of our boys. They'll take you to him. Then I'm off for another load. Hopefully we can get you back to civilization in one piece once you've done your thing."

"One piece? Okay. How long a ride?"

"Not that long, actually, forty-five minutes, an hour maybe. Not sure exactly where your drop-off is. There's an old bridge a ways from here. Know it when I see it. You know . . . Jack's not a bad kid. Couldn't see him doing it, that's why we're all behind him."

"Who's 'we?'"

"His family, his people." Bob drove in silence for a few minutes, finishing his smoke. "He's half-blood. He don't know the history, makes him a perfect target."

"Target?"

Bob sat for a minute collecting his thoughts. "Got another smoke?"

Janie offered him the open end of the pack and lit another for herself.

"We're sure he's been framed. You see, this all goes back a hell of a long way, least a hundred years."

Janie tipped her growing ash into the nearly full tray on the dashboard. "Like cowboys and Indians?"

Bob smiled. "Closer than you might think. We like the term *native,* but don't worry, I won't hold it against you."

"So sorry."

"There are some old families that have lived here in Florida probably one hundred and fifty years. Some say they were outcasts, criminals, who knows, but they were not wanted where they came from and they were not wanted when they arrived. If you get a chance to talk to Gramps—he's Jack's grandfather—he might tell you more. It's not like all of the old white families are bad, just a few. See, that's the root of it. We were once a very much more spiritual people. The old timers like Gramps can tell you. Our ancestors could see them for what they were. In English they're called *devil's spawn*. Some might call them bad witches. They're powerful, not just in an occult sense. They're behind a lot of shit that goes on down here. We don't like them and they know it. It's not like an all-out feud or anything. Shit just pops up every now and then; always seems to happen when they have an agenda. That's what makes us nervous."

Bob tossed the butt of his cigarette out the window.

"So you're saying that Jack Walker has been framed in order to deflect attention away from something else?"

"Don't really know. It could be that they're just trying to piss us off. I wouldn't doubt it. They never did like the fact that we have the gambling rights here. Anyway, it's all conjecture on my part. We just want you to prove that he isn't guilty."

Janie sat in silence. She could see the possible motive behind framing Jack; however, the evidence against him was pretty damning. If he was framed, the perpetrators had done a good job.

"You mentioned bad witches. Are there good ones? Is there such a thing, or are you just trying to get a rise out of an old broad?"

"Ha. Yep, they exist. *Witch* is what they call them in movies. We call them *spirit talkers*. There are good ones and there are bad ones. Gramps is a good one—the last of a kind."

"So what about this Satanic cult, do you believe that stuff?"

Bob paused. "I do and I don't. I'm not sure that I believe in the devil stuff, but I do think there's a bunch of old families down here that have a political agenda. What I find strange is that they're at odds with the Republicans. I could see if there was a Democratic agenda at hand. These folks are deeply Republican. I think they like to control things down here. They're clearly not getting their way with that Clean Water Bill. I look at Senator Hunter as a rebel. Rebels are not taken kindly to down here in the South. He'll find himself dead. These people are not to be messed with."

Time passed quickly as she pondered the information given her by Jack's cousin. It was all a little farfetched, and certainly hard to prove. Before she knew it, Bob was pulling off the road just before a small bridge that ran over a river.

"They'll be down below in an airboat. I dare not stop. Nice to meet you, Janie Callahan, I think you'll do a good job. I can sense it, even if you are a hot old broad." He smiled.

She accepted his handshake and climbed down out of the truck. Before she could blink, Bob's truck was moving and back on the road heading east, leaving her in a cloud of dust. She felt uneasy. What if her next contacts were not here? It would be one hell of a long walk back to Bonita.

* * * *

She cursed her shoes as she cautiously made her way around the abutment. She half-slid, half-hopped down the gravel hill to get under the bridge. She was relieved to see an airboat up on the bank.

Two young men standing next to it, one with long black hair, turned her way as she unceremoniously slid down the rest of the way on her backside to end up in front of them. The closest young man quickly moved to give her a hand, which she gladly accepted. He was tall and athletic and wore a long-sleeved hoodie and khaki shorts. His face was handsome—a kind face with a wide smile, which set her at ease instantly.

"You must be Miss Callahan?" said the other young man. He was shorter and a bit on the chubby side; he too disarmed her with a kind smile. "I'm Nathan, this is my cousin Josh. Hop in, we should get going right away."

"Janie Callahan—Janie is just fine. Do you mind if I smoke?"

"Knock yourself out. Better do it now, because once we're moving you won't be able to."

Janie lit up, drawing a curling wisp of smoke from her mouth up to her nose. She looked at the boat dubiously as she was helped in. It was a long flat aluminum shell with seats and a huge, caged-in propeller and motor on the back. Its bottom was littered with fishing equipment and dried blood, probably from fish—at least, she hoped it was from fish. It was rusty and dented. A rifle sat on one of the bench seats, and Josh picked it up as the three settled in. Nathan fired up the motor, which shuddered and spat out dark black smoke before it settled down to a somewhat steady roar.

The craft lurched forwards, slowly picking up speed, until they were moving faster than Janie figured they should be going. She faced forward and let her hair fly directly backwards almost into Josh's face. Nathan veered sharply to the right and headed directly into the long grass. Janie was relieved to learn that there was water under it. Josh yelled in her ear, "Don't worry, he knows where he's going, done it a thousand times. No one will see us through the grass!"

Janie nodded. She wanted some time to contemplate the information she'd received from Bob, but the wind, the tall grass, and the noise from the motor made it nearly impossible to think. She crouched forward and bided her time. They rode almost an hour before Nathan slowed the craft. He veered into a canal that seemed to stretch for miles. He then turned the boat sharply to the left, and within seconds they were in a small lake. On the far shore Janie could see a small collection of huts with grass reed roofs. They sped across the small body of water and approached an island where Nathan expertly beached the craft. Janie was helped out by Josh.

"I'm supposed to tell you that you should keep it to an hour, if possible. We'll need to get you back before dark. There's a big storm moving in."

Janie nodded. Her attention was diverted to a young man walking towards her. He was a little over six feet tall. She recognized his face immediately from the case file and TV news. Before he had a chance to speak, Janie extended her hand towards him.

"So, you must be the infamous Jackson Walker?" Unexpectedly, he blushed, his eyes looking down towards the ground. This was not the face of a killer. "Sounds like you've had a hell of a couple of days. Let's get away from these bugs." Her hair was a total disaster, she was coated with a layer of sweat, and she needed a smoke. She didn't bother to ask permission.

"Yes, it has been quite the fiasco. My aunt says that Peter is a good lawyer?" He guided Janie towards one of the small huts.

"Damn good, but we need to give him something to go on. So let's not waste any time."

Janie squashed her cigarette with the toe of her shoe before they entered the dwelling.

The inside of the hut was very basic and smelled of mold. Perhaps it would have been better to stay outside with the bugs.

"Have a seat, Miss Callahan." He offered her a chair at a small table. He noticed her looking around. "They are called chickee huts. My mother's people used to live in them and they're still scattered throughout the Everglades. Now they use them as fishing huts, way points. Pretty basic, I'm sorry."

"Janie, please. I guess it's a good place to hide."

"Okay, Janie it is." Jack's voice was deep and calm. Janie was drawn to his big, sensitive blue eyes. "I guess so. I think the fact that we're on the reserve is more important. The authorities won't come out here."

"Where should we start?" She opened up her notepad and clicked on the end of her pen. She looked him in the eye. "Your file states that you have had substance abuse problems?"

"Jesus Janie, nothing like poking at a sore spot. I'm sure my aunt didn't bring you out here to dig up the past." He slumped in his seat, his cheeks a bit flushed.

"Character background, Jack. Sorry, if we go to court, the district attorney is going to rip a hole in your history to draw a connection between past indiscretions and present. Satanic killer, drug abuser, they will beat the hell out of you for this."

Jack took a few sips from his beer. "I've had my problems, but no more than most professional athletes."

Janie put down her pen. "Look, Jack, if we're going to get anywhere, you're going to have to lay off the bullshit. I buy the steroid story, that's old news on the sporting front, but the cocaine and marijuana charges, sorry, that's not common, won't help us . . . nope. Your last charge was over a year ago, four ounces of marijuana. When's the last time you smoked up?"

"Months ago."

"Come on Jack, you expect me to believe that? If I'm going to help you, I have to believe that what you're telling me is the truth. I can see in those big blue eyes that you're lying, a jury will see right through you."

Jack looked up at Janie. "Nate and I lit one up last night."

"I want you to cut that stuff out right now. We don't want any traces of it in your blood. You will eventually have to turn yourself in. You don't want to get caught."

"Like hell I'm turning myself in!"

"Okay, just please me and let me use the position as a premise."

"Fine, but I ain't doing it."

"Any other drugs?"

"A bit of Ecstasy, Sarah liked that shit. She had me put some coke on her private parts. I suppose I may have ingested some of it."

Janie tapped her pen on the table, resisting the urge to joust with the comment. "So what's your story, Walker?"

"I'm probably going to sound like every criminal you have ever spoken to, but . . . I'm not guilty. I didn't do what they say I did. Unless you believe this basic apriorism, we're wasting our time here."

"I am not paid to believe you, Jack. It's my job to disprove the premise that you're guilty, sometimes an inch at a time. Let's put it this way: I want to believe you. You seem like a believable young man. Prove to me that what you say is true. Now let's start at the beginning. No bullshit."

Jack started at the old lake house where the bodies were found and gave his accounting of the events. Janie took notes, prodding him here and there for more detail. When he finished she sat for a moment in thought.

"Okay, it sounds like a reasonable story. It still doesn't prove anything. Your prints are all over the place. You evaded the police."

"Maybe I should have turned myself in right there, but the situation was just too bizarre, that's why I bolted. I was scared. Who wouldn't be?" He paused for a moment. "The part that doesn't make sense to me is how they knew to come to the house? How did they know to come right at the time I was there? It was pretty late at night and there wasn't another house close to that place. Someone called this thing in. Wouldn't the cops have a log on that sort of thing?"

Janie tapped her pen on the desk. "Now there's something. I'll make an inquiry once I am able to. From what I can see, that might be the only tangible point to be taken from the set of events. However, the Marshes might have called 911, which is totally plausible. This should be easy to check."

"The police car got messed up with the blue pickup truck, like, banging into each other, and the cops passed the truck. Both were looking for me. I just don't see how they would have known that anything was wrong at the Marsh house. I think someone tipped them off. Maybe Buck called them in. Why go through such an elaborate set-up and not have the cops come?"

"Okay, I just might buy that. Anything else you can think of that might be important?"

"Well, actually, lots. I think I might have killed a man later on in the night."

Janie dropped her pen on the table, her eyes meeting Jack's. "Do go on." She pulled out her pack of Marlboros and lit one up. "Got an ashtray in this place?"

Jack went into the kitchen and brought her the old tin can he had been using to drink out of. Somehow he felt bad downgrading the can's purpose; it had been the only useful item available to him over the past day and a half. "This'll have to do. Would you like a beer?"

She declined after a bit of hesitation. "Thanks, but I need to keep a clear head. Maybe when we're finished. The can will do nicely."

"Where to start . . . I went directly to my girlfriend's apartment—you see, I think she is involved in all this."

"Who is your girlfriend?"

"Well, we met four or five months back at work. Her name's Sarah Courtney. That part's all normal, but she was a . . . devil worshiper, belonged to this cult. The way she explained things, it wasn't all that bad, more of a philosophical point of view than a religion. I started going with her to weekly meetings. I didn't support their point of view, but I did appreciate the intellectual discussions that took place. I didn't know if anything was going to come of our relationship, but I was willing to go along with it to keep seeing Sarah. I'll admit it, she had me whipped pretty good."

"Too much information, Jack, but do go on."

"No, I think it's important. She was almost too good, if there is such a thing. It was like she was professional or something, perhaps she was getting paid really well to fuck me. At least that's what it seems like in hindsight. Either that or she had a spell on me, maybe both?"

"I don't believe in spells, nor do juries."

"We were at a meeting the night all of this started. There's this old lady who runs the church; her name is Henrietta. She asked me to deliver an envelope to the lake house. She started making promises about getting me a tryout with the Saints, pretty unrealistic now that I think about it."

"Do you have the envelope?"

"Dammit, no, I left it in my car. I parked it a couple blocks away from Sarah's place. I could shoot myself for that."

"What's your license plate? Do you have your keys, and what's the make?"

Jack reached into his pocket. "Yeah, here they are, it's a faded red Ford Taurus."

"I'm going to call it in and have the car broken into. That envelope could be your savior."

"It's under the floor mat."

Janie had discounted much of the information Bob told her, but there were more than a few coincidences, the occult stuff set aside.

"So, you take this envelope up to Clewiston and go into the house." She paused. "Why did you go into the house?"

"Well, I forgot to mention, I went there with one of the church members, an older guy named Buck. We knocked several times and no one answered. He said he knew the people and didn't think it would be a bad thing to go in. I didn't want to leave a wad of money sitting on the front step, and the door was slightly open. I thought I would just leave it in the front foyer. Once I get in there, I started seeing that things were not right, and one thing led to another. It was a set-up. I think it was planned from day one."

"Okay, I buy that. I don't know if a judge will. We need more."

Jack frowned. "Buck seemed like such a nice old guy, but then the fucker pulled a gun on me. I told you what happened after that point."

"Do you know where Buck lives?"

"Well, no, you see, I don't know where any of those weirdoes live. It was all hush-hush."

"Okay."

"So then I go to Sarah's apartment. Oh, I did make a call to my friend Perry, and then tossed my cell phone. I'm not sure if that's important."

"It could be. Anything that corroborates your story can help. I'll have to talk to your friend, what's his number? Go on."

"I get to her place and go in. I have a key. The place is empty, she's gone. My alarm bell starts to go off and before I know it, there is someone in her apartment with me—a man. He tries to take my head off with a fishing knife. Anyway, we get into a struggle and I manage to break free and head for the door and the stairs down. I stop in the top of the stairwell. Okay, the guy comes out and flies through the door, making for the stairs. He glances at me as he lunges for the top step, so I tackle him and he lands awkwardly at the bottom of the flight and cracks his head real hard on the cement wall. His neck is broken. So things are a real mess at this point. I ditch my car and drive to my grandfather's in his old truck. The rest is history."

"Anything else?"

"Oh, when I swapped vehicles, I found his wallet in the front seat." He handed it to her. "His name was Eric McFadden, lived on Pine Island."

"I'm going to take this."

"Absolutely."

Janie sat for a moment without speaking. "Jackson, that's quite the story. Can you think of any little details you might have missed? Everything is important. How did you meet Sarah?"

"I work for Senator Hunter. Sarah works for the Republican Party. We were in touch with their office all the time. Met her one day and she asked me out. Like I say, the rest is history."

"She asked you out?"

"Yeah, like I said, she was real forward."

"The police will leave no stone unturned. I really think you should turn yourself in."

"No, too many balls in the air, Janie. This thing is bigger than it seems. Since I've been here, I've learned a bit about my family history. The people that I dealt with have some sort of feud with my mother's people that's at least a hundred years old. There are no coincidences, I am finding out. I still don't understand the reason for it all, but I'm not going to turn myself in until I have a better idea of what I'm up against. It's kinda too late now anyway, I may as well ride it out until something gives."

"You will be linked with the killing of that man at your girlfriend's apartment. I would give it a few days. If the police haven't caught you by then, they will come after you hard. I know this is a damned big swamp, but they will bring in the means to track you down. You're a killer of three people in their eyes. The media is already hyping this thing up. Someone tried to hit you in that apartment building. It wouldn't take a rocket scientist to figure out where you are—roughly. If I were you, I would keep on the move. I'll give you a cell number to use if you decide you want to come in, or if you can think of anything else."

Janie realized something. "Why would that guy try to kill you?"

Jack sat for a moment in thought. "I've been trying to figure that out. The guy did say that I was lucky to have escaped *them* at the lake house. I figure that whoever is doing all this wanted me caught red-handed at the scene. This whole thing is premeditated. The one positive thing is that I'm just the little guy in all of this, as best I can figure."

Janie stood and gathered up her things. "I'm going to get out of here now. You're not a safe person to be around. If we can make anything out of this mess, I'll contact you through your aunt. You know how to get me. Be safe, Jackson Walker, and remember: you will be caught. Come in before that happens. I can see you doing time if you offer a plea."

"See, that's what I figured. I know I'm not guilty. I appreciate your efforts, and I hope you can help me out, but I'm not going to leave my fate in someone else's hands. The one advantage

I have is that the US government is careful when dealing with Native Americans. I qualify; they will have to dig up something big before they step foot on the reserve. My mother's people have their own police, I'm sure you know this. There would have to be concrete evidence given to them before they would allow me to be handed over. Janie, if the Reserve Police wanted me incarcerated, they would have bundled me up twenty-four hours ago. I'm sure that Gramps has talked to them. I have a window of a few days to help my cause. Hopefully between us we can figure something out." Jack stood and shook Janie's hand. "Have a safe ride back. Nate and Josh will look after you."

"Stay low, Jack."

10

THE POLICE

"MY GOODNESS, IS IT hot, and these little bugs are eating me alive," Lani Green said as she scratched the back of her neck. She turned her head to observe the tall young man walking beside her. Rick Ramirez smiled, his broad white teeth lighting up his distinctly Cuban face. Rick had grown up in Miami and didn't seem bothered by summer weather in Florida. It was a different story for Lani, a Wisconsin native. She'd transferred from Kenosha to Tallahassee twenty years earlier, but still couldn't get used to the summer heat. Most Northerners dream of living in a southern climate—great in the winter—but fail to take summer into consideration. The heat was acceptable near the coast where there was always a nice breeze, but as soon as you went a couple of miles inland it was sweltering. Sweat dripped down her back and between her breasts, making the snug bulletproof vest wet. No one had warned her about the bugs. She was used to mosquitoes in the north, but these little black bugs the size of a pinhead were unreal. She could feel them biting behind her ears and down the back of her neck.

Rick smiled again. “Bug spray man, you need some spray. They don’t really bother me too much, they mustn’t like Cuban blood. We call them no-see-ums.”

Lani frowned, scratching the back of her hand. She was the Florida Department of Law Enforcement’s expert on religious and cult activity. She was the only one in the department who had any background, having studied religious history in college. She’d fallen into the position backwards and had since been called out to more of these cases than she could remember. She’d been brought in from the state capital and assigned to work with Rick when the Walker story first broke. Routine homicides, domestic violence cases, and robberies were left to the local authorities; missing killers connected to Satanic sects and senators were another matter. Tallahassee wanted a lid on this case ASAP. Her presence often helped ease inter-county police department tensions. Lani and her new partner were one of three units assigned to the Clewiston killings.

Rick stopped for a moment. “This guy’s on the run, but where?” Rick went over the report in his head. “The sheriff’s department found Walker’s rust-colored Ford Taurus last night. They found an envelope containing several dozen one dollar bills sandwiched between two one hundred dollar notes.”

Turning to face her, he felt sorry for his new partner. Her blonde hair was matted down by sweat. “Here, drink some water.” He handed her the bottle of water he held in his hand. “I’m surprised that the Charlotte and Lee County Sheriff departments didn’t shut down the roads through Clewiston the other night. Too late now. They’ve screwed things up so far. The crime scenes have been poorly controlled and whatever evidence that’s been gathered is probably contaminated.”

“Different counties, and easy for you to say working in Collier County. They couldn’t get things together quick enough. Can’t blame them, though. If there was more manpower, we’d have better control. This could be a mess; the people we might be dealing with will be organized, and we’re not.”

“How do you know that?”

“Just done this enough times and I’ve been dealing with these Satanic sects for years now.”

“So you’re a fucking veteran.”

"Could say that. I've paid my dues."

"A man was found dead one block from where Walker's car was found. There's no evidence to link the two. I'm waiting on the forensics from Lee County. The man died under suspicious circumstances. His neck was broken, as was his nose; no evidence of any other wounds. A pool of blood was found on the cement floor of the stairwell, which did not match the dead guy's." Rick shook his head. "I have a gut feeling that the two incidents are connected, though. It's time to put up a pin board on this one. I think we have enough information to start mapping."

"You're probably right."

"So what's your story, Green? Are you some sort of *X-Files* specialist, aliens and all that shit?"

"No such thing as aliens, Ramirez. Roswell was made up. What I do believe in is religion and the ability of some people to warp the minds of those who are susceptible to being brainwashed. That's a cult in a nutshell."

"Heard you spent time undercover?"

"You could say that. I am baptized as a full-fledged Satanist. I was in deep. I know how these sick people work. It's usually the innocent who end up doing the bad things, while the ringleaders get off scot-free. If I showed up in one of their church meetings now, I'd be strung up. I helped bring down Jimmy Broughton ten years back in Jacksonville. He was one deceptive, sick bastard. I ended up living with him for a year before we could gather enough evidence against him. I still get the shivers thinking about it."

"So you were having sex with him?"

Lani shot Rick her best eye dagger. "None of your damn business, Ramirez."

Rick shrugged off the affront. "So . . . are you insinuating that Walker might be innocent?"

Lani turned, placing her hands on her hips. "I'm just saying that we need to keep our minds open to every possibility. He could be innocent. He may have been coerced into doing something against his will. But if he cut up those people, he's still guilty of murder."

Ramirez nodded. "If Walker headed north, we'll have to wait for him to make a mistake. His face is all over the local and state news. Someone will see him at a gas station, or he might be careless and use a credit card."

Lani shook her head. "If he's headed north, we have to trust in the system. Plus, his banking capability has been cut off. We must assume that the young man is still in the area. It's likely he didn't have much cash on him, no one does anymore. The Bank of America put a freeze on his accounts. He made one call on his cell phone after the killings."

"Yep, and we have a tag out on the recipient's cell phone. It was registered to a Perry Masterson. Huntley and Edwards are tracking him down."

"John White and Bill Reyes are working on his close family. Walker's mother is deceased and his father hasn't been seen in years. The only others in the area are his maternal grandparents, both Seminole. The grandmother lives in Ft. Lauderdale. Someone from Miami is checking that lead. She seemed to have no idea of her grandson's whereabouts, and in fact has not seen him in seven or eight years. She's under surveillance." Lani swatted at the bugs that were nibbling at the back of her wrist. "This fucking swamp was a bad idea."

Rick shook his head.

"He has family in Georgia. His father's sister Rebecca flew into Southwest Florida International Airport this morning from Atlanta, and she's booked on a return flight this evening. Her rental car is marked and she's being followed. She visited a lawyer's office, Robertson and Robertson."

Rick paused. "So the family has been in contact with Walker and are determining the legal parameters available to him."

"Hopefully the lawyer will talk some sense into him."

* * * *

The drive to Big Cypress Reserve, southeast of Fort Myers, halfway across Highway 41 toward Miami, had been fairly short—roughly three quarters of an hour. Rick parked their car off a quiet road at a place called Shark Valley. Walker's grandfather lived in a small village close to the popular tourist site that sold native souvenirs and airboat tours of the Everglades. After inquiring at the welcome center, they were told that the old man lived a short walk into the bush. Unless you knew the back way in, it was inaccessible by car.

Lani pushed ahead of Rick as they finished the short trek along a well-kept wooden walkway. She jumped as a small gator slipped from the side of the pathway into the murky water. Rick chuckled. "They don't want anything to do with you, man."

"Easy for you to say, Ramirez. You've grown up with these stupid reptiles, and these bugs."

"Just because I grew up in Florida doesn't mean that I wrestle gators. I don't think I saw my first one until I was a teenager, on a school trip or something. I was raised in a shithole neighborhood in West Miami. We spent most of our time hanging out on street corners and getting in trouble—not messing around in the swamp. I read somewhere that gators don't want shit to do with you, but the snakes are another matter. Don't be grabbing any branches or sticking your hands into any dark bushes and you'll be okay . . . Heads up, there's some buildings up ahead. Remember, we're not supposed to be here. Reservations have their own laws, and we have no authority."

"Let's just see if we can get a nibble."

The small native village that appeared in a large clearing was a throwback in time, quite primitive to Lani's eye. It was made up of twenty or so small wooden buildings with reed-thatched roofs. Many of the buildings boasted a few modern touches here and there, which indicated that the outside facades might be more for show. ATVs were parked beside most of them, and there was a sprinkling of satellite dishes mounted on outside walls.

Their attention was drawn to three men sitting outside the front door of the only conventional looking house, on old beach chairs. Two were younger, in their mid-twenties; both sat with hunting rifles propped up beside them. In the middle of the two sat an older, tall, native man wearing blue jeans and a Florida Marlins T-shirt. They remained seated as the two approached.

Lani didn't waste any time with formalities. She removed her identification from her coat pocket and flashed it in front of the men. "Lani Green, Florida Department of Law Enforcement. I am looking for Nathaniel Portman." She paused, waiting for an answer.

The young man to the left grinned. "Hey Gramps, they're callin' you Nathaniel. Nobody calls you Nathaniel except Grams."

The old man glanced at the man beside him.

"You are Nathaniel Portman?" asked Lani.

The old man answered in perfect English. "Blaze just told you who I am. Don't mess around with formalities. I know exactly who you are, and in fact I knew you were coming, that's why I am sitting here waiting for you."

Lani flinched ever so slightly. "Jackson Walker. Do you know of his whereabouts?" She flashed him her badge again. The old man didn't bother to look.

"Of course I do, I'm his damn grandfather, which you obviously already know. He's out there." He pointed towards the swamp. "You won't find him, though. Remember that jet that went down a dozen years back? Needed our help to find it, didn't you? Now if you guys needed us to find a plane, you ain't gonna find the boy. Matter of fact, I don't know exactly where he is. He's with his cousins and they'll be moving around. You go out there, you'll get lost. There's other folks lookin' for him, better equipped too. Not the kind of people you want to be messin' with—bad people. They won't find Jack, but they will sniff you out within hours. Shoot you dead and feed you to the gators. Never . . . see . . . you . . . again." He emphasized his words clearly, as if Lani might not understand English. "I'll tell you this as well. Jack spoke to a lawyer lady. He'll be headed for the hills now. For what it's worth, I know my grandson. If he says he didn't do it, he didn't."

Lani pondered the old man's words. It's true, Walker could be anywhere between Naples, Miami, and Lake Okeechobee. He could also be lying, though she had a sense he was telling the truth. "Do you mind if we look around?"

"Nope, look all you want, lady. He's not here though. He was here, but now he is gone. I'll tell you exactly where he was and how he got here. Don't be poking around after dark, though. I can't guarantee your safety."

"Is that a threat? Threatening an officer of the law is an indictable offense."

"No, I'm just sayin'. He came here by taxi and spent a few hours talking with me, then left by airboat," Gramps lied. "If you walk down that path over there, you might even be able to see his footprints. Do you no good, though."

"Look, Mr. Portman. I could have you brought in for aiding and abetting a known felon. You are being coy, but the fact is you have taken part in hiding the young man."

Gramps stood up and stared into Lani's eyes. She backed away, not being able to meet the man's gaze. It was like he had put a hand on her forehead and pushed her backward.

"Like hell I have. I am not hiding him; in fact, I have told you where he is. I don't have to remind you, I am sure, that you have no jurisdiction over this place, or any other reserve in the United States of America. You can have a look through our little village, but it will do you no good, Miss Green. If I were you, I would call the Reserve Police. The chief's name is Benny. I can give you his number. I will promise you one thing—if you can bring me evidence that clearly indicates my grandson's wrongdoing, I will turn him in to Benny. However, I will not risk him being indicted without that evidence."

Lani knew they would have to walk the place. It was field operations 101, even if it was a waste of time. If Walker had been here at some point, there could be evidence to corroborate the old man's story.

Rick spoke up. "Who are these *other people*?" He was agitated when the old man mentioned them earlier.

Gramps responded calmly. "Devil spawn." For the first time since their meeting began, the old man seemed at a loss for words. He stood and turned to go into his hut. "Take a look around. Again, I wouldn't be hangin' about after dark." The old native man pushed the front door open, and with a few shuffles he started to shut the door.

"Wait, Mr. Portman. The devil spawn that you mention. Do you know if they are connected with the Satanic cult your grandson was rumored to be a part of?"

He turned back toward Lani looking quite irritated. "There is a connection, Ms. Green, and Jack is not part of their outfit. He made the mistake of falling for the wrong girl, and now he is paying the price. Love is blind, so they say."

Lani put her hand on the door to stop it from closing. "Can you tell me more?"

"Look lady, like I said, you're on our reservation. I don't have to tell you anything."

"Then let's hope that you have no need to leave . . . the reservation."

"Touché." The old man smiled and closed the door in Lani's face. As they moved away from his home, Lani said to Rick, "Either he is the best poker player I've ever met, or Walker is not here. Still, we'd better take a look around."

"I'm thinking the same thing, and not getting a warm fuzzy feeling here. It's getting late though, and that talk about the devil gave me a shiver." Rick crossed himself.

11

HENRIETTA LEPLEY

IT WAS A QUIET afternoon at the Remington Golf and Country Club. The dining room was less than half full for lunch. Three well-dressed women sat at a table in the back corner of the stately room, which overlooked the 18th green. Tables were set with fine white linen, bone china, crystal glasses, and polished silver. A server delicately placed the entrées in front of them. The eldest of the three, Henrietta LePley, offered a toast to the other women. Sarah and Jasmine raised their wine glasses.

"To your fine work, Sarah. You are a true disciple of the left-hand path. Your diligence will not go unnoticed. Satan is all-seeing and he does not forget those who perform his work so beautifully."

Jasmine did not have a last name as far as Henrietta knew. She was High Priestess and was held in great esteem within the Church of Set. Her anonymity was important to her and it was a rare occasion when she was seen in public with other members of the church. However, Henrietta had asked for her attendance and no one crossed the matriarch. The old woman was the true head of the congregation and its principal benefactor.

Jasmine agreed. "It's good to have people like you, with your extraordinary talents. Your profession may be held in ill repute, but it is the oldest known to man, and the devil does not look at it with ill regard."

Henrietta smiled. "You will be handsomely rewarded. Please take this as a token of my appreciation." The older woman handed Sarah an envelope. "This stipend should keep you afloat for some time. Now, the priestess and I have some other business to discuss. Thank you, dear. I would try to stay out of sight for the time being. You are due a long holiday."

Sarah nodded, looking down at her untouched entree. "I did find the experience thoroughly enjoyable. He was a nice boy and my favorite trick to date. Most don't last for nearly half a year. I trust the amount that was agreed upon is in here?" She raised the thick envelope.

Henrietta smiled, her numerous wrinkles melding together beside her mouth. "And then some. Your work for Set and his praise should be more than an added bonus, but we have paid off your local debts and credit cards. Thank you, darling." Henrietta gave Sarah another one of her patent smiles, which meant she was finished with her. "A car will be waiting for you out front and will take you wherever you wish."

"Ladies." Sarah pushed her chair out and stood up, acknowledged Henrietta, and bowed slightly to Jasmine.

The two women watched as she left the restaurant before they began talking.

"What will you do with her?"

Henrietta fussed over her Cornish hen for a moment and smiled before taking a bite. "She will be dead within five minutes. Her wine was poisoned."

Jasmine looked at her glass, a slight frown forming on her exotic, beautiful face.

"No need to worry, dear. The church has great need of you, as do I. The driver who will be picking her up is a useful man. He will feed her to the alligators tonight." She finished her mouthful. "I read the Tarot cards yesterday and they indicated a weakness in the girl. She may have developed a soft spot for the young man. We cannot risk any indiscretions at this time. She won't be missed.

It's funny how the law turns a blind eye to missing strumpets. Besides, I can find better uses for the money at this point in time. Make sure to drink from the correct glass, priestess."

Henrietta sat in thought for a few minutes as she picked at the bird in front of her. She was in her one hundred and fifth year, but did not look a day over eighty and felt even younger. She believed it to be a benefit of her faith. She'd sold her soul to the devil early in her youth. She inherited her role within the church from her mother. Early in her youth, she had discovered a taste for women, and thus never bore children of her own. She didn't worry too much about ascendancy to her position. She felt strong, and the cards told her that her genes were such that she might live several more years. Lucifer would provide.

"The boy must die." She picked up a bone, stripping it of flesh with her perfect teeth.

"That may prove to be difficult. He's gone into hiding and the police are tracking him."

"Yes, and the damned Indians again. They have been a thorn in my side for decades. We must keep true to the purpose of our gambit."

"What of the man who was killed at Sarah's apartment complex?"

"A shame, he was useful. He was the eldest of three brothers within my employ, as was their father before them. Their name is McFadden. Jimmy and Isaac remain. From time to time, we need the help of those who are truly bad. The McFaddens are true to our cause. Their family has been useful to the church since the beginning. I fear very little, my dear, but I do respect the badness of these men and have done my best to harness and coddle them as my mother and her predecessors did. They are a family of serial killers who have, from generation to generation, learned to hide their tracks perfectly. Every now and then I let them off their leashes; boys must play."

Jasmine shuddered slightly.

"I sent Eric to Clewiston to intercept the Walker boy, he lost track of him and found him again at Sarah's. I thought he would be sufficient to handle the task. I dare say that if he had gotten his hands on Walker, the lad's soul might still be in torment as we speak. Unfortunately, Walker is resourceful. But the

McFaddens live in the Everglades; they know it like the back of their hands. They will find Walker and we can then move on to finishing our play.

"Now, let's finish our lunch. I look forward to spending a leisurely afternoon with you."

12

THE SWAMP HOUSE

WHEN IT WAS BUILT one hundred and four years earlier, the McFadden house rivaled the homes built by Edison and Ford, all grand statements of Southern wealth, Fort Myers-Naples landmarks. The old home sat on twenty manicured acres. The homestead was located fifteen miles south of Immokalee Road on the edge of the Everglades, skirting the edge of Big Cypress Reserve. It backed onto a small river that was fed by the great swamp. The house was no longer what it had once been, its current inhabitants not as appreciative of its grace as those in the past. The old dwelling was used from time to time when the McFadden brothers were not getting along, or were entertaining a willing or not so willing guest. The grounds were now overrun with large trees, shrubs, and tall grass. Old rundown vehicles were scattered here and there with no apparent plan. Isaac resided in the manor house, and Jimmy lived in the back shop which sat directly on the edge of the river. The boys lived their lives on the edge of the Everglades, as had their ancestors before them. They were poachers, hunters, and efficient killers.

It was a bad day for the McFaddens. Eric, the eldest of the three, had died the night before. The police indicated that he'd cracked his head open falling down a flight of stairs. Jimmy and Isaac didn't believe it was an accident for one minute. Their eldest brother was as surefooted as a mountain goat. Eric had been killed, and the boys knew who'd done it—Jack Walker. Eric had been sent to kill him, but somehow things had gone wrong, and the McFaddens intended to find out what happened and finish the job.

Jimmy was pottering around in the shop, emotionally oblivious to the sudden change in his life. He turned his head slightly to the sound of Isaac pulling up next to the building in his big black Lincoln. He knew the sound of the car and the way Isaac drove it; he was abrupt, and always in a hurry.

The boys ran a limousine service to and from the Southwest Florida International Airport. Isaac had received a call from the old lady saying that she had a girl who needed to be taken care of. Isaac complained, stating that he and his brother needed to grieve their brother's death. She would have none of it, claiming that there would be time enough for sadness, now was the time for retribution. Isaac put his nose to the grindstone, knowing that he would have to pick up the slack created by his elder brother's death. He was shell-shocked by it. His passing opened up deep-seated emotions, including one that he discovered he did not like. Was it empathy? He knew there wasn't a chance in hell that Jimmy felt such emotion. His younger brother had been diagnosed in his youth with severe autism. He was incapable of empathy. Instead, he was methodical and fixated on routine. He ate the same thing for breakfast every day: eggs and bacon, white Wonder Bread, untoasted with a dab of orange marmalade. He liked ham and cheese for lunch, again on Wonder Bread, and for dinner he rotated between steak and fries or hot dogs, rolled up in a piece of white Wonder Bread. He was a creature of habit.

****

An hour earlier, Isaac was picking the girl up at the country club, which normally would have been Eric's job. He tried not to look at her too closely, as he knew her imminent, unpleasant future. Isaac, possibly for the first time in his life, felt sorry for the attractive girl who sat in the back of the car. He'd been told by the old woman that she had been Walker's whore and that her purpose in life had been served. Still, he wondered why this one needed to die.

"Southwest Florida International Airport, please. I don't really know where I'm going. Kind of exciting. Just going to grab a ticket somewhere."

Isaac nodded. He knew where she was going. Her eyes looked like they were getting heavier and she had begun to nod. It wouldn't be long now. If there was a silver lining, the poison preferred by Henrietta was humane—no pain, just a gentle drifting off into sleep and most likely death, if she was lucky. The girl slumped down to her side, her breathing shallow to nonexistent.

* * * *

When Issac arrived at the plantation, he decided that he didn't feel much like talking to his younger brother. He stopped the car abruptly beside the back garage.

Jimmy walked out to the driveway as his brother opened the car door. The day was unusually hot, and a sulfurous smell emanated from the swamp. He wiped his hand across his brow. Isaac stepped out of the car and opened up the back door. He reached in and pulled the body of a young, attractive brunette out by her feet, her head bouncing off the bottom edge of the door frame and then again on the gravel driveway. He doubted Eric would have been so clumsy. He hoisted her over his shoulder and walked purposefully to the shop door. Jimmy followed like a puppy, trying hard to get a look at the girl. "Take it easy, Jimmy, let's get her inside first, you emotionless bastard."

Jimmy looked at Isaac curiously, but only for a moment, then once again was intent on getting a look at the girl. He reminded Isaac of a dog waiting to get at the scraps from a steak dinner.

The shop was large and made of tin and timber. The back side faced the river with two large bay doors which were left open, except in bad weather. A bass boat sat in a cradle hoist connected to the dock, as well as a prop boat. There were several Sea-Doos, kayaks, and canoes littering the bank beside the shop, all in various states of repair.

The interior was damp and smelled of oil and mold. The walls were covered with numerous exhibits of taxidermy: gator heads and skins, bear heads, shark jaws, a stuffed panther, snake skins, various small animals, waterfowl and assorted fish. Jimmy, as had his father before him, used a large wooden table close to the back doors to perform the rites of his hobby. Various tools and wicked-looking knives hung from it. A mortician's metal table stood a couple of feet to the side. It was slightly canted to one end, at which there was a drain. A makeshift bedroom and kitchen with two cots lined the opposite wall. The rest of the large shed was filled with scattered clothing, dismantled pieces of small machinery, recliners, and televisions from many eras including an old black and white from the 1950s with rabbit ears on top.

Isaac placed the body on the wooden table. "There's one for you, Jimmy. You don't even have to buy her flowers."

Jimmy ignored Isaac's jab and walked over to the table. He stroked the girl's hair with one hand as he checked for a pulse on her neck with his other. "Do I have time to keep her for a bit?" he said with a deadpan voice and expression. "We need to bury Eric and all."

"Is that emotion I detect, little brother? The old lady said not to mess around with this one. Cops might be up here asking about Eric. I'd chop her up and feed old Bessie and her young ones tonight."

Jimmy became slightly less calm, almost agitated. "That doesn't leave me much time. You know I like to get to know them a bit. And Bessie's full, I fed her the gator scraps this afternoon."

"She's in the water tonight, period. We got another job from the lady. We need to hunt Eric's killer, says he's with the Indians, they're probably hiding him out in the swamp. I want to be up before daybreak."

"We'll kill 'em, Isaac, we'll kill 'em. Do we get to shoot Indians?"

"The devil will have his way, Jimmy. The only good Indian is a dead one."

"When we gonna bury Eric, or can I stuff him?"

"You're not fucking stuffing him. Even your sick mind must see the wrong in that. I said we'd pick him up from the morgue in a few days. County says we need to clear up some legal details. Before we do that, we'll kill Jackson Walker. Maybe you can stuff *him.*"

Jimmy hopped up and down a few times and then put his hand on the girl's neck again. "Oh . . . there's still a pulse, Isaac. She ain't dead."

Isaac looked away in disgust. "Lucky her." He turned to head toward the old house. "I guess I'll leave you alone. She's in the water tonight, you hear?"

Jimmy shrugged. "She's awful pretty."

"You heard me. We're off at first light tomorrow. Make sure you get some shut-eye."

Jimmy waited for Isaac to get settled in the big house before he went back to the girl. She was good looking, but Jimmy needed to see more. He started to remove her clothing but then stopped.

"Don't need you makin' any noise, little girl." He stroked her hair.

He went to the other side of the room and brought back a spool of thick, black thread and a long, curved needle. It took him a minute or two to thread the wicked device. He pinched the girl's lips together with the thumb and forefinger of his left hand and sewed them shut with his right. It wasn't a tidy job, but it would be effective. He strapped her arms and legs down to the corners of the table.

Jimmy was pleased that she was alive. That was the way with poison. She could revive quite nicely, or remain in the induced coma until her vital signs slowly died away. He had a feeling about this one, though; he could tell that she was a fighter. He sat down on a reclining chair and stared at the young woman. After an hour she started to move a little bit, her head slowly rolling from side to side. He stood, wanting to see the look in her eyes when she awoke—that was his favorite part. She would be thirsty; he saw the impression of her tongue probing the sides of her mouth. He'd left a tiny hole through which he could insert a straw.

Her eyes flashed open, her head darting every which way trying to get her bearings. When she noticed that she was tied down she tried to scream, but all that came out was a muffled wail. Then she saw Jimmy. Her eyes bulged in their sockets as she tried to free herself from her bonds. She struggled for a couple of minutes, but soon realized it was in vain.

"It's all right, darlin', the more you struggle the worse it's gonna be. In the end, if you're a good girl, I promise that I'll finish things quick."

Once again she started to struggle frantically.

Jimmy picked up a long fillet knife that hung at the side of the table.

Sarah tried her best to scream again, and she tried to poke her tongue through the stitches, all to no avail.

"I'm not gonna split you open right here. That would make too much of a mess. Calm down now." Jimmy slipped the knife under her dress and slit the front slowly. Sarah lay motionless, her breath pushing in and out of her nostrils, straining for oxygen. He slit open her bra, exposing her small, firm breasts. He let out a slow moan. Once again, Sarah tried to scream.

"I hear you're a right little whore. Only thing is, I'm the one gittin' paid now. Kinda ironic, isn't it? Now we got a couple hours to get friendly here and then I'm gonna put you back to sleep. You'll not remember anything where you're going, so don't fuss."

He slit open her panties.

* * * *

Isaac opened his eyes groggily, then sat bolt upright. Jimmy stood over him with a hunting rifle in the crook of his arm. At times it could be disconcerting living with a psychopath.

"Y'all said the break of dawn."

"Knocking on the door would've been sufficient, and don't ever poke me with a fucking rifle again. Thing could go off." He didn't know exactly what he'd do to Jimmy if he poked him again, but he had to keep the upper hand with his little brother. It often unnerved him to think what Jimmy might do if Isaac was deemed unnecessary. "Why don't you get the boat ready, I'll be down in a few minutes."

Jimmy smiled like a praised puppy. "All done, Isaac, I made breakfast too."

"You dumped the girl last night, right?"

"Yep, that's all tied up."

"What do you mean, tied up?"

"Just what it means, Isaac. Don't worry, she's been taken care of."

Isaac got up, shaking his head, his morning wood poking out of his boxers in Jimmy's direction.

"Better put that way, Isaac, might shoot someone." Jimmy bent over laughing.

"Get the fuck out of my room, you stupid shit. I'll be down in a minute." He kicked Jimmy playfully in the backside as he exited the room.

Isaac dressed himself in proper safari attire, complete with a wide-brimmed hat. When he arrived downstairs, Jimmy had a fairly decent breakfast ready for him.

"I figure we should take a look in the reserve. There's a dozen or so spots where Walker might be holed up, but you would know better, Jimmy. They'll not be too worried about the authorities. Authorities won't go on Indian land without a judicial order, they'll most likely wait for him to try and leave. If the Indians see us, they'll shoot, so let's be careful. Our airboat's new and we can count on going faster than anything they have. If we shoot one, we have to shoot them all, got that?"

"Shoot the fuckin' Indians, I got it." A puzzled look came to his face. "Why haven't we shot 'em before this?"

It was a perfectly logical question to ask, but Isaac didn't attempt to respond. It would be too frustrating to explain.

The McFaddens loaded up their gear into the boat. They carried loads of extra gasoline, stored in jerry cans at the front. Several high-powered rifles sat in a rack behind the steering console. A small canoe lay across the bottom, along with clothing and food supplies.

"Looks good, Jimmy. Let's get out of here."

13

STORM

SUMMER STORMS ARE A part of life in southwest Florida. The state's southern tip sits under a tropical depression from July until mid-October—hurricane season. The storm that was building over the Gulf turned inland. It was not classified a hurricane, but it carried winds in excess of ninety miles per hour, strong enough that evacuations were recommended on the barrier islands that surrounded Fort Myers and Port Charlotte. There would be few casualties, but it was still a time to hunker down and stay indoors, much like a winter storm in Buffalo or the Midwest. There would be wind and there would be rain, and lots of both.

Jack looked to the west as Janie was helped into the old airboat. He walked over and put a hand on the gunnels as Josh, Bobby and Nate prepared to depart. "Think it's wise to be heading back with that storm moving in? I don't like the look of that sky."

"Not my call, Jack, supposed to get the lady back before nightfall." He looked to Janie.

She nodded. "If you want me to get you out of this mess, I need to go."

"Agreed, but I was thinking if I stay here, I can't do anything to help myself. If I'm going to break for it, I can't think of a better cover. It'll be dark in an hour and a half. What if I come with you, Janie?"

Josh folded his arms. "I don't know, you could hole up out here for years. Gramps said as much."

"I think he might agree with me. It's an omen, this storm. I'm coming with you."

"The police know they can't get you here, but they're going to be watching for you coming out . . . guaranteed."

"You're right, but there's no way they'll be able to cover every inch."

Josh cut him off. "Not on my watch, cousin. I'm taking Janie like we planned. They'd have you in leg irons and an orange suit faster than you could skin a possum. I'll come back for you once we get her safely back to Myers. Hold tight and maybe we can get you out to the Caloosahatchee later tonight. We have a boat out there along the river just in case, but it's gonna be a hell show with the weather. Sit tight, bro."

Jack shrugged, his head lowered. "Suppose you're right, but I sure want to go. I'm starting to feel like a caged pigeon."

"We'll be back soon. I'll leave Bobby to watch over you. Bobby, you see anyone you don't know, unless they show you government ID, put a bullet in their forehead."

Bobby grinned, nodding his acknowledgment.

Josh looked to the sky and chuckled. "You'll be okay, cousin. Like I said, he's a good shot."

Josh pushed the boat out into the lake as Nate fired up the noisy engine. Within minutes, they were lost to sight. The wind was really building, but for the time being, the rain held off. The boat crashed and banged against the waves. As the craft reached one of the canals that ran into the small lake, things smoothed out a bit.

After a fifteen-minute run, Josh motioned for Nate to slow the engine. He pointed to a plume of heavy smoke rising from a point a mile away to the south, riding the wind eastward. He yelled. "It's rainy season, fires don't just start out here. I gotta see what's up.

There's a small village on an island over there. It has me worried. Only take a few minutes."

"I'm counting on you guys to get me out of this place, not to get sidetracked," yelled Janie.

Nate pulled a rifle out from under the driver's bench, cocking it to make sure it was loaded. "True enough, lady, but there are things happening out here right now that are out of the ordinary. Sit down and be quiet until we've taken a look."

Janie was not used to being told what to do like this, but the look on the young Seminole man's face forced her to bite her lip.

As the boat neared the small island, they could see that several small dwellings sitting in the middle were ablaze. The lack of movement was even more alarming. The small enclave housed two Seminole families.

"Put 'er up on the beach, Nate," yelled Josh over the sound of the howling wind and rumbling engine.

The men dragged the boat up on the shore. Janie felt uneasy and remained seated on the middle bench. What was supposed to be a fairly simple meeting had now changed into something more sinister, and she didn't like it. She made a mental note to increase her fee.

"I'm gonna take a quick look. Stay here and keep an eye on Janie."

Nate nodded his head and cocked his rifle.

Josh carefully made his way into the small group of buildings. The flames had devoured most of the small wood homes. Five minutes later, he returned at a jog. His face was drawn, his eyes welled up in tears.

"Whoever fucking did this is gonna pay." He slumped down, catching his breath, his rifle resting across his knees. "Four of them shot dead, one of them a kid . . . " He started to hyperventilate. "Hector was one of our friends growing up," he told Janie.

"Man . . . Hector?" Nate exclaimed.

"Yeah, him and his old lady, could be his kid, too. The other one is one of the old-timers, I can't remember her name. I think it's Peggy, the one with the bum leg."

"Fuckin' hell, she's friends with my mom."

"The rest of them must have got away, all the boats are gone except for Hec's. The place is gonna be cinders within minutes.

I saw shells everywhere, there must have been a firefight."

Janie could see the pain on both men's faces. Nate looked particularly shaken up, his lower lip quivering. "Who would have done this?"

"I have a pretty good idea—one of the old families."

Janie cut off Josh before he could finish. "Jack told me about them. But he said there had never been any violence . . . ?"

"Josh will tell you, if there was a good enough reason, it wouldn't take too much. It used to be pretty brutal in the old days. These people took their liberties during the Seminole wars. It was bad enough that our people fought off the US Army, but the fuckers tried their best to finish us off after the war was all said and done. There's a few who know the grass flats pretty good."

"Nate's right. There's no doubt in my mind that this mess is tied in with Jack and whatever the hell he's done. Maybe the whole situation was created so the fuckers could start a brawl in the first place. I wouldn't put it past 'em."

Josh and Nate stood in silence for a time. Janie didn't want to interrupt; she could see that they were distraught. After a time, Josh spoke up. "We can't do anything with the bodies right now. I pulled them into a clearing. We don't know if there are any more dead in the huts. I'm calling the Reserve Police. They're gonna have to clean this mess up. Now let's get you out of here, Janie. Whoever did this can't be too far away."

14

SENATOR HUNTER

SENATOR HUNTER ROLLED OVER onto his back in near exhaustion, his heart pounding, sweat rolling down his temples, his penis still erect. He looked back at Phyllis, her golden hair flayed out on the pillow. She was hard to resist, her perfect body nestled up beside his. Their relationship had begun innocently enough: an innuendo, subtle touches and looks. They'd shared a suite in Orlando at last year's Republican convention, separate bedrooms. He'd walked into her room to ask a question and caught sight of her coming out of the shower. He'd backed out of the room, but his lust was aroused.

A month later, after a late night at work and a few drinks at a lounge, the privacy of the back seat of his limo provided ample room for transgression. He could not restrain himself and she did not back away from his kiss. The smell of the woman had become enough to drive him crazy. He knew that what he was doing could bring him down politically, yet he did it. When he was with her, he could think of nothing else. When he was not with her, he was truly remorseful, realizing it would be the end of his twenty-five-year marriage if he were caught. It was like the woman had some sort of power over him; there was no other way to explain it.

"You are too young for me, Phyllis. You're going to give me a heart attack. Wouldn't that look good on the evening news."

Phyllis looked at Jim for a few seconds and smiled, her eyebrows narrowing. "We can stop this thing if you're worried about scandal. I'm thirty-five, you're fifty-five. You should go back to your wife, we can move on from this, no harm done. We have to be able to face up to the consequences. They're small for me, but for you, it's your life."

Jim lay his head back on his pillow, looking up at the ceiling. "Too late for that, my darling. This could end my political career, but I still have my law degree and I can't see us getting caught. The fire is gone in my marriage. I'm bored." He patted his flabby belly and smiled. "Besides, look what you'd be missing. Let's not go down that road just yet. Look, you evoke something within me that I can't explain. I want to be with you no matter how wrong it is."

As any good politician would do, he redirected the conversation. "What do I do about Jack Walker?"

Phyllis lit a cigarette. "Tough one, lover boy. You gave him a second chance. I would make a public statement as soon as possible, and keep it as close to the truth as you can. You are a benefactor of the University of Florida. You took in a past superstar, down on his luck, who had a history of drug abuse. You had no knowledge of his affiliation with this devil church. Disassociate yourself from him. Do it now before people make their own inferences."

"What about Sarah Courtney? She's on the Republican payroll."

"It stinks, but you have two more years in your term. Hopefully it will all blow over by then. Plus, there has been no word of the girl since the murders." She smiled.

"I find no humor in this nasty state of affairs, and I don't know why you would be smiling. Two people are dead, and there is a link to my office."

Phyllis pulled away, sitting up. "If you're so concerned, why were you not working on the Walker problem instead of fucking me? This could've waited. You men are able to fuck at the worst of times, I don't get it. If I were you, I'd be back at home with my wife doing a photo shoot showing your devotion to family and religion. The Southern Baptists would eat it up. Instead you're lying here with your prick in the air smelling like pussy."

Phyllis rolled out of bed, pulling the sheets off with her, casually wrapping them around her. She stepped toward the bathroom. "You have a two o'clock with the opposition to the Clean Water Bill. Crotchety old lady, so I am told."

"Henrietta LePley. She knew my parents. She's old Florida blood. What harm could come from listening to both sides of the argument? Maybe it will be enough to listen. Some people just need to be heard, and she has been persistent."

"We'll see, Jim. I don't get that feeling after my conversations with the woman. You're going to have to make a decision and keep to it. These people will not be happy with anything less than a strong rollback on your policy. They will be a thorn in your side."

Hunter planned on putting forward the legislation, taking the necessary steps to do what was right to save the watershed, to save the state's precarious ecology. But the old cronies who had lived in the state for more than a century had strong pull within the Republican Party. He needed to listen to them at least, or there would be backlash. There was big money in cattle, oranges, and sugarcane, and he understood that those people would be hurt economically. Some would even lose their livelihoods.

The people who paid state taxes and voted for him could see for themselves the changing ecosystem. Freshwater was being dispersed through the larger river systems in massive quantities and not allowed to find its traditional slow route through the Everglades, allowing for more arable farmland. The discharges carried pesticides and fertilizer, which in turn killed the brackish saltwater estuaries along the Florida coastline. Some species of wildlife were being pushed to the point of extinction, the Florida manatee being just one example. The once-pristine beaches, the heart of Florida's vacation industry, no longer had the crystal clear waters they were known for.

* * * *

Phyllis and Jim sat at a table at party headquarters, waiting for the meeting. Hunter didn't know what to expect. He knew little about Henrietta LePley, other than that she pulled a lot of strings in South Florida.

The senator stood as the old lady entered the room, accompanied by her lawyer. She stood erect and walked without a hitch or hint that old age was affecting her. She was dressed immaculately in a tailored pantsuit with flat, sturdy shoes, very businesslike. She approached Hunter with her hand outstretched. Her face was almost flawless, though he could see that her skin was thinning. Her handshake was firm, unrelenting, yet what caught him most were her eyes. Emerald green, piercing. He was caught speechless for a moment but recovered quickly, catching the faintest of grins on the corners of her old, thin lips.

"Senator Hunter." Her voice was very appealing—motherly. It had been ten years since his mother passed away and he felt comfortable with the woman, a comfort he had not felt in some time. He felt a sudden need for her approval, and fought off the desire to give her a hug.

Phyllis snapped him out of his trance. "Senator, may I introduce Henrietta LePley."

He shook his head ever so slightly.

"It is a pleasure to meet you, James, if I might be so forward. I have heard good things about you, son."

Son . . . "Nice to meet you as well, Ms. LePley." He gestured toward a seat across from his.

Everyone sat down.

"I will not waste time, James. You are a Southerner, just like I am a Southerner, like my mother before me. We are both good Republicans." She gestured to Hunter with an open hand. "My family has supported the Grand Old Party since its inception."

Hunter found himself leaning closer to the woman as she spoke. "Your support is greatly appreciated, ma'am."

"Thank you." She sat in thought for a moment. "We have to protect that which is inherently ours, James. We can't let the Northerners control our state, but that is a topic for another day. As you know, I am opposed to your legislation. I have voiced my displeasure with the Governor."

Hunter gestured in understanding. "In the end, Ms. LePley,

it is a legislation that is essential to the welfare of our state. Our wetlands need to be protected so that our children's children might enjoy what we've been able to enjoy."

She seemed to grow larger. "I don't ask that you kill the bill, James, only that it be somewhat softened. That the reclamation of farmland be delayed over time, so we can properly prepare for the losses we will incur."

Hunter looked her in the eye and became lost in her bewitching gaze. He mumbled, "That would be a significant change, Ms. LePley. We have the natives to consider as well. We are changing the watershed and how it sustains their lands."

"You are enabling the natives. They should be subordinate, not controlling. The government tap dances around the Indians like they are royalty. They own some of the sugar cane, the oranges, and now the gaming. They play both sides nicely. I come to you now to make a proposition to help us gain control of the state's economy."

"And what would you propose?"

"It's simple. Do not support the new bill. I can promise the state of Florida a 5 percent tax on the revenues derived from the farming activity."

"How can you promise that? What authority do you have?"

"James. Five percent of something is better than 5 percent of nothing."

His grandmother had called him James, and the way she said his name warmed him.

Phyllis cleared her throat. "Can I offer you some tea, Ms. LePley?"

"Henrietta will be fine, and yes, that would be lovely. I prefer black tea, from a bag, nothing loose."

Hunter motioned to one of his aides to serve the woman. "Ms. LePley, I appreciate your sentiments, and I understand what you are saying. However, there are greater stakes at hand. The ecosystem is dying and the Seminole people are on the front line to see the changes that are coming. They are pleading with us to keep our house in order, as are our constituents."

"Unlike your own house, Senator . . . The *Walker* boy."

"He is of no consequence to this discussion."

"Is he not? He worked for your office, James. He is Seminole.

Let's not be coy, Senator. This looks bad for your office. All things considered, including a possible conflict of interest, it might be prudent for you to soften the proposed bill as we have asked."

"You are over the line here, Ms. LePley. The Governor and I have been discussing the matter and are in accord. Our meeting has come to an end." He began to stand.

"James."

The way his name rolled off her tongue froze him. He slowly sat.

"We are not finished, James." She smiled. Her breath, or maybe it was her scent, smelled gloriously of lavender, or maybe it was honeysuckle. He wanted her to continue talking. "That's better."

Phyllis sat quietly with her hands neatly resting on the table, her eyes vacant.

"I would like to invite you, James, to a dinner tomorrow. It would be nice for you to meet our consortium. I think you will find what they have to say quite . . . enlightening."

"It would be my pleasure."

"I would like you to bring Mrs. Hunter." She glanced at Phyllis and smiled slightly.

"She would be happy to come."

Henrietta stood up, and Hunter followed her lead. "My people will contact yours with the arrangements."

15
CLUES

RICK RAMIREZ AND LANI Green sat in the Lee County Sheriff's offices off Ben C. Pratt Parkway, close to Highway 41.

"Not a word, nothing," said Lani. "Since we lost Janie Callahan's tail there hasn't been a peep."

Rick shook his head. "You're the one who told me the fox always comes to ground. He's holed up with his relatives and, if he is guilty, he might just stay out there for a good long time. It's only been a few days." He ran his hand through his hair. He stood to look at the map pinned to the corkboard wall. "What now?"

Lani moved to stand beside him, likewise observing the map. "Let's review our progress . . . or lack of it. We didn't get much out of the cultists. Every lead we've followed thus far has turned out to be an alias or red herring. No one in any alleged position of authority has turned out to be solid."

"Is this typical?"

"It's a little bit more hush-hush than what I've seen. Most Satanic cults are quite visible, they have agendas, they need to be seen. This one is different. Nothing is registered. We're doing background checks on all the names we've uncovered. We've interviewed five couples who check out. None claim to have any interest in the Brotherhood of Set beyond casual participation. They claim that the leaders of the cult never use their real names. There is a High Priestess, several Deacons, and an old lady known as the Matriarch, whom we assume is Henrietta LePley. From what they say, Walker is fairly new to the congregation."

"Kinda spooky if you ask me."

Lani stared at the map of southwest Florida. "Nothing to be spooked about. Most of the stuff these whackos claim to do is just crap with no substance behind it." She traced a few lines on the map with her finger. "We don't have much information besides the route that Walker must have taken that night. We know that he was likely behind the death of Eric McFadden. The blood samples match those taken during his drug rehab in Cincinnati."

"Both of these guys show up at Walker's girlfriend's apartment. McFadden lives in Saint James City out on Pine Island. He has a brother who's an accountant in Naples. The family owns a lot of property. Have we checked out the brother?"

Lani picked up her coffee cup, taking a sip. "I've left a few messages for him, asking for an appointment to see him. His secretary says he will not be at work for the next week due to the death of his brother."

"Where does he live?"

"Inland somewhere. Remember, I'm not from here, you'd know better. Quite a ways south off Immokalee Road, right in the middle of the Everglades. Can't get an answer at the home."

"We'll be going to that funeral."

"Nothing in the papers, and I've called all of the local funeral homes. They normally know where these things will be held, theirs is a competitive business. The body is still at the morgue. No arrangements made to date."

"And no affiliations with the Satanists?"

"Dead end there."

"I've got a friend out on Pine Island. I'll give her a call and see if she knew this guy, or his family."

"We've contacted other notorious cults in the US and Canada to see if there are any affiliations. There are none, though a high-ranking member of the Church of Satan indicated that there is a sect of Satanists from South Florida that correspond with them from time to time, but they are secretive, which we already know."

Lani paused for a moment, pacing in front of Rick's desk. "What nags at me is the fact that Walker doesn't fit the profile. What if he was just chasing a pretty girl? What if he's not guilty? He will try to clear himself. The law firm will have met with him by now—no doubt it was Jane Callahan. She will resurface. You still have the law office under surveillance?"

"What do you think?" Rick huffed.

"I didn't mean that, of course you do."

Lani's cell rang. After a short conversation she hung up. "There's been a shoot-up at one of the Seminole villages, at least four dead. The Reserve Police are asking us to come in and have a look, they don't have the forensic equipment to handle the situation. We might have to wait for this nasty storm to pass first. It would be okay if we could get there by road, but evidently it's on an island."

16

THE HUNT

"THE FUCKER'S CIRCLED THE island three times now," Bobby said as he stood on the beach, his long, black hair blowing sideways in the wind of the heavy storm. He held his rifle cocked in his right arm; Jack stood beside him. They watched the airboat as it bobbed in the same place out in the middle of the small lake. Rain pelted them in the face, making it hard to see, much less focus on the distant craft.

Bobby yelled, "I don't recognize that prop boat. Not one of ours, or the other companies'. One of those fuckers who live on the edge of the swamp," he said, his teeth chattering.

Jack nodded. "There's two of them. These the assholes Gramps was talking about?"

Bobby reached behind his back and pulled out a handgun from his belt. "Could be. There's lots who live in the swamp, but not many who have money. Take this." He showed Jack how to cock the weapon. "Just point and shoot."

Jack was surprised at how heavy it felt. He'd never held a real handgun, only the rifles Josh and he had used to hunt small animals in his youth. He felt empowered by the shiny silver weapon.

The boat's motor roared and the craft lurched toward the island.

"Fuckers are comin' in."

Jack's heart skipped a beat and his mouth felt uncomfortably dry.

The man at the front of the boat dropped down to a knee; it was hard to see exactly what he was doing. Jack thought he saw a few puffs of smoke, then heard the whistling of bullets past his head. He'd never been shot at before, and it was surreal enough to stun him, but only for a moment.

"Yeah, and they're fucking shooting at us," he yelled at Bobby. He heard a dull thud beside him and the clatter of Bobby's rifle hitting the roots of a nearby tree. The young Seminole lay motionless on the beach. Not knowing what else to do, Jack dropped to the ground and rolled beside Bobby. As he did, he put his hand into something mushy and hot. He looked at his hand, it was covered in a mess of brain matter, blood and shattered bone.

"Fuck me," Jack yelled as he jumped back.

The top of Bobby's head was gone, gore from inside spilling out onto the sand. Jack felt his chin start to quiver. The airboat was getting very close to the island, so he forced himself to move. After grabbing the rifle that lay on the ground, he rolled behind an old rowboat that was half-buried in the sand. He pointed the handgun at the boat, brushed his hair out of his eyes and squeezed the trigger. The recoil of the weapon numbed his wrist. He'd expected one shot, but it kept firing, his hand progressively pulling upward. The first three bullets hit the water in front of the boat. The next three pierced its bow. He could see wood and metal flying back into the boat. The driver veered sharply to the left. He wasn't sure if he'd hit either of the men, but his effort deterred their attempt to beach. He pulled the trigger again. Three more bullets went in the direction of his attackers, all of them missing their intended mark. The magazine was empty. The prop boat raced to the left of the tiny island.

Jack moved to Bobby's body, half-crawling half-stumbling, and searched through the dead man's pockets. He found a full magazine for the handgun and several loose high-powered rifle cartridges. He wasn't sure how to load the weapons, but he knew that he was better off having them than not.

"Poor bastard," he blurted as he turned and ran for the chickee hut. He knew that the men were searching for him, and he also knew that they were a lot better at this sort of thing. He calmed himself and thought about his options. They would expect him to run to the huts. He would have to get out quickly. He anticipated they might run the boat up on the other side of the island. "Okay, what next?" he mumbled. He stuffed a couple of bottles of water into his pockets and went out the back door. Looking around, he saw a large stand of trees off to one side of the small island, and he ran for their cover. Once there, he slumped down behind three large palmettos, trying to catch his breath. He fumbled with the handgun with shaking hands. He'd seen enough action movies to know that there should be a catch or something similar at the top of the handle. He pushed a small lever forward and the empty magazine popped out. He jammed the full one in and it clicked into place. He nodded to himself, encouraged that he might not be totally useless. The wind and rain were becoming nearly unbearable; the warm pellets stung his bare skin and eyes. He peeked around the tree and scanned the immediate area. He couldn't see anyone.

He decided to skirt the edge of the island to see if his attackers had landed their boat. Halfway to where he anticipated they might be, he found four kayaks turned upside down on the beach, most likely used for fishing by those using the camp. He ducked behind them. He could hear the low growl of the airboat from up ahead, but he couldn't see any movement. He looked to the line of sawgrass which formed the north and east shores of the small lake, then back toward where he guessed the idling craft to be.

He flipped one of the kayaks over, grabbed a paddle and pushed it out into the lake. The sawgrass shoreline was a few hundred yards away. It wouldn't be easy in this wind, but he had no choice. His attackers appeared to know what they were doing, and he had to be honest with himself—he didn't. He would be paddling crosswind, so it wouldn't be too bad, and though visibility was poor, that would aid in his escape. He was fortunate to have spent a lot of time in a kayak as a kid and when deploying shark bait in the sometimes rough and windy gulf. He smelled the exhaust from the boat once he was downwind from the island. He could hear the low rumble of the boat's motor; the hunters couldn't be far away.

Each stroke of the paddle was desperate. He needed to get to the line of tall grass before his pursuers returned to their boat. He would easily be spotted if they returned and looked out onto the water. The corner of the island provided a bit of cover, but once into the middle of the lake he was vulnerable. He reminded himself that rhythm was just as important as brute force. *Use your legs.* He quickly settled into a steady groove and he made good time crossing the short expanse of water.

A surge of adrenalin ran through him as he remembered the woman he had been looking after. It was too late to go back for her now; her fate would be sealed. Or maybe not: maybe she would be able to find a nook in the island in which to hide.

Each yard passed in what seemed like slow motion. He drew a heavy breath when the back of the kayak cleared the edge of the grass, hopefully hiding him from his pursuers, but his relief was short-lived as the wind whipped the sharp edges of sawgrass against his face, neck and arms.

Jack knew he needed to go west. If he went east, he would end up hopelessly lost in the Everglades. The storm was coming from the west, which meant he needed to head directly into its teeth to get out of the swamp. The reality of the task ahead hit him like a cold slap; he might have to paddle for hours, maybe through the night. The reeds were being blown in his direction, making it nearly impossible to push the blades of the kayak forward. His skin was being whipped raw from the grass. He decided that he would have to go sideways to the north and hope to find a canal before it became dark.

****

The prop boat's engine roared and Jack felt his stomach rise in his throat. He sat motionless. They must have seen him; the craft was coming in his direction. He pulled the handgun out of his belt and sat as low in the boat as possible, waiting to fire if he had the chance. He feared that the boat might run him over.

If he survived the collision, the thought of snakes and alligators and how difficult it would be to swim in the grass scared the daylights out of him. The boat passed behind him, missing the point at which he'd entered the sawgrass by several yards. He hunched down as low as he could, and was lucky not to be seen. The larger boat needed to keep up some momentum to push through the tall grass. It headed north. He turned the kayak around and moved to the crude path forged by the prop boat. He gambled that they would not expect him to follow them. The paddling was much easier and he made good progress.

The airboat stopped; Jack guessed it must be several hundred yards ahead of him. He hoped that his assailants had found a canal. He heard the engine rumble again and the boat came back in his direction, but three hundred yards to the west. He pushed hard and within a few minutes he paddled into one of the east-west canals he'd been hoping to find. His assailants seemed to be sweeping the area, searching for him using the canal as a point of reference. He would have to take baby steps. When the airboat was searching the tall grass, he paddled down the canal towards the west and the setting sun. When the boat returned to the flat water of the canal, he hid in the sawgrass.

The backs of his hands were ripped raw and his face was an open wound from the sharp reeds. Jack played cat and mouse with the airboat for what seemed ages. The sun was starting to get low. The game appeared to end when his assailants doubled back to where they had started the chase. He thought he could hear the motor open up, possibly heading back into the lake. For now, it appeared he had evaded the hunters.

* * * *

"Goddamn it Jimmy, I told you he went in farther to the left."

Jimmy puckered up his face even more than was normal. "I had the f-fucker, he musta moved."

"We've been going back and forth for more than an hour now. Walker could be heading toward Okeechobee. But I doubt it; that would be a death trap for him, he'd be doing our job for us. He'll head for dry land, to the west. That's what I would do, and it's his only chance to get out of here. There's a levee seven miles to the west, runs north-south. We'll wait for him there.

If he doesn't show up, we'll know that he's dead. No way he's surviving if he heads east."

Jimmy nodded.

"Let's go back to the island for a bit, just in case he doubles back. It'll take him a few hours to reach the levee; we can wait there for an hour or so, just in case he wants to make our lives a little easier. Then we head for the south end of the levee. The northern edge is a dead end."

Jimmy threw down the throttle and headed out of the sawgrass.

* * * *

The canal ran toward the west. If it didn't veer, it should lead Jack to safety, to a road or possibly one of the rivers that meandered through the Everglades. He was twenty miles too far to the south to find the Caloosahatchee, which was the biggest watercourse in the area. He paddled for at least an hour; the sun was just about to set in front of him, which meant he was still heading west—the right direction.

Jack was falling into a semi-stupor, his strokes now shorter and less effective. The bases of both his thumbs were worn raw, and hurt with each stroke. A movement to his right startled him. The reeds shifted and a large alligator moved out of the grass and swam slowly towards the kayak. He was not sure if the creature was interested in him or if he was simply in the way as the gator went about its normal business. He'd seen many smaller gators thus far, but none that would have posed any danger. If this creature decided to turn on him, he would be in trouble. Its head was massive and its back broad. He guessed it to be at least ten feet long. He stopped paddling and watched the beast swim towards the kayak. The gator was definitely aware of him, but didn't appear aggressive; its cold, reptilian eyes just watched him. He pulled the rifle off his back and made sure that it was cocked and ready to fire. He leveled the weapon, trying to keep his aim between the middle of its eyes. He wasn't sure how far the report of the gun would carry in the wind, but he waited for the last possible second, not wanting to take a chance. As the beast neared the kayak, it submerged. He held his finger on the trigger following the dark figure as it swam under the boat. It took an eternity to pass. He drew a heavy breath as the gator broke water near the other side of the canal, quickly disappearing into the long sawgrass. He sat motionless for a few minutes and drank the last of his precious water. He thought how ironic it would be to be eaten by a giant gator after surviving multiple attacks by a bunch of bloodthirsty Satanists.

The paddling was monotonous, his back was aching, as was his wounded leg; the driving rain stung his eyes. He started thinking about what he would do if and when he made it back to civilization. Perry had been right, he was a bloody fool. Now retribution was all he could think of. *I'm going to put a bullet right between that bastard Buck's eyes*.

He was jolted back to reality as he nearly ran aground on the bank of the canal as it abruptly turned to the north. Ahead of him was a large embankment running north to south along the canal. He pulled the kayak up onto shore and scrambled to the top. The slope was treacherous from the mud created by the heavy rainfall. Once on top, he could see that a dirt road ran along the narrow strip of land as far as he could tell in either direction. He sat down in the mud for a moment half in thought, half in exhaustion.

He retrieved the guns and shoved the kayak as deep as he could manage into the tall grass. He slung the rifle over his back and started walking to the north. He walked for at least half an hour before the levee ended in a large reservoir. *Damn*. He would have to swim across. *No way. Who knows what's in that water*. He turned and went south.

It took him about an hour to reach a tall, wire mesh fence blocking his path. In the darkness he could see a roadway on the other side. In the middle of the fence was a doorway, chained and padlocked. He rattled the lock; it was firmly in place, but really old and rusty. He took out the handgun and fired a shot into its center. It took three more shots to shatter the lock, sending the pieces falling to the ground. He opened the mesh door and walked towards a wooden bridge that traversed a small drainage ditch. As he neared the other side of the bridge, a figure stepped out from behind a sign. Even in the heavy wind and rain, Jack could see the rifle pointed at his chest. He thought about reaching for the handgun he'd just put back in his belt, but he heard a man's voice from behind him.

"I wouldn't try that if I were you, Walker. My brother is the best shot in the county and there's nothing we'd like more than to shoot you and leave you in this ditch for the gators. Put the rifle on the ground. Slowly."

Jack slowly pulled the gun over his head. and placed it onto the wooden floorboards of the bridge.

"Kick it into the water."

Jack followed orders and nudged the rifle over the edge. The wind was howling too hard to hear the splash. He got a good look at both men as they rounded him off the end of the bridge. The man with the rifle was five or six inches shorter than him, chubby, dark hair and had a sour look on his face. Jack got the feeling that he would not hesitate to pull the trigger—there was something in his eyes that told him so. The second man was nearly as tall as he, maybe an inch shorter. He was blond and wore some sort of safari outfit. Both men, like Jack, were drenched to the bone.

"Put your hands on your head."

He obeyed the order.

The man with the hat reached behind him and removed his pistol. He gave him a little pat down and shoved him toward the end of the bridge. The shorter man backed up with the rifle pointed at the center of Jack's chest.

"You gave us a good run, Walker," said the taller man. "But I was right: nowhere else for you to go. You see, we know these parts better than most. Either you end up as alligator food out in the middle of the Everglades, or you break for the coast. Pretty simple, and this is the only way out for miles. It would be a lot easier to put a bullet in the back of your skull right now and drag you back into the swamp for the gators. But . . . " his face became clenched with fury. "Seems you killed our brother Eric."

"Eric?"

"Don't be so fucking stupid," yelled the sour-faced man. "You broke his fucking neck."

Jack tried to hide his sudden understanding.

The taller man pushed him forward again. "We're not going to give you the satisfaction of a quick death."

They herded Jack back toward the swamp on the other side of the fence. As they neared it, Jack felt the blow of something hard on the back of his head. The last thing he remembered was falling face first into the mud at the base of the walkway.

17

ALL IN

JANIE STEPPED OUT OF the cab in front of her house, leaned in, and paid the driver. It was late and she needed a bath, a stiff drink, and some sleep. Her hair was pasted to her head and she was sure that she smelled bad. She lit a cigarette and glanced over at the car that sat parked across the street a couple houses down—cops, most likely. She stood halfway up her driveway and stared at the car. She may as well give them a good look.

She unlocked her door and headed straight for the freezer where she found a lonely bottle of Grey Goose vodka. She poured three fingers into a tumbler and tossed in a few ice cubes, then sank down into her favorite couch and turned on the television. Her first sip was like the nectar of the gods. It had been a stressful few days and there was a lot to mull over. She lit a Marlboro for good measure. She flipped on the evening news, hoping to find Jack Walker's mug plastered across the screen. It was big news, but evidently not as big as some turbulence in the Middle East.

"Do you really want to do this, Janie Callahan?" The sound

of her own voice gave her some comfort. She needed to believe in a case to be able to pour her heart into it, and she wasn't sure she did here. Digging deeper into the bowels of a Satanic cult was not to be taken lightly. A shiver ran down her spine. There was something evil going on and Walker was part of it, but just how much? If she bailed on the case, he would eventually be caught and most likely rot in a prison cell. Maybe he belonged there.

On the other hand, she was inclined to believe Walker. More to the point, she was nearly broke and if she dropped the case Peter would fire her. She downed the vodka in one long, delicious sip and stood to pour herself another. She decided to call Peter and ask for more money. If he balked, she would call it quits, but she knew he would pay. Money took care of a lot of things. She wasn't going to risk her life for chump change.

She pulled one of the new cell phones out of her purse and dialed Pete's number. "Hello, Pete."

"Janie, where the hell are you? This case is rolling into something big. I just heard an Indian village was burned. Bodies were found."

"I was there."

"What?"

"I swear . . . it was a mess."

Pete continued, "Two more bodies were found close by on another island, a male and a female, both killed by gunshot."

"Christ, Pete, is it Walker?"

"I don't think so."

"I don't know about the female, but Walker was on one of the islands with a Seminole man and woman. You say there are only two dead. Either one of them is Walker, or he is on the run again, or captured."

"Well, I'm sure that if Walker was shot, we'd know by now. It came from a good source with the Collier County Sheriff's Department. Who would capture Walker?"

"The Satanists."

"Oh . . . I don't know what to say about that. The Reserve Police must figure this thing is getting too hot. The natives are allowing the local police to go onto the reserve and they'll be after Walker, assuming he's not one of the deceased. How did the interview go?"

"Christ, Pete, he could be dead, and if I'm going any further, I need more money."

"If he's fucking dead he's dead, and we make nothing. We have to assume that he's alive. You didn't answer my question."

"You haven't given me a damn chance and you didn't answer mine. You're always cutting me off. It went as well as it could under the circumstances. I was lucky to get back alive. This storm is brutal. Three hours in a bloody airboat. I've got a lot to think about. I need to make notes, formulate a plan of action. But I want more money. I'm putting my life at risk if I go any further."

Peter hesitated. "I'll give you 10 percent of the firm's fees on top of your normal stipend."

"Fifteen."

"Not a dime more, Janie. Can I help?"

"Yep, you gotta be there when the rabbit comes to ground. Walker's going to need representation. There's only a few ways this thing can go: he's on his way out of the Everglades, he's dead, or he's captured. I've got a few good leads on where he might be if he's not dead."

"Does that mean you're accepting my offer?"

"Possibly, maybe."

"Careful, darlin'."

"Always. I'll call you in a bit once I go over my notes." She hung up and didn't give him a chance to argue.

She needed to believe that Walker was alive. If he wasn't, the case was over. If he was captured, The Brotherhood of Set must be responsible. There were too many coincidences to ignore. She had three leads: Buck Henderson, Henrietta LePley, and Jack's grandfather. Janie decided that the grandfather would be the best bet; she needed information immediately and she knew where to find him.

* * * *

Janie stepped out her front door after taking a short nap and a shower. This time she was better prepared. She wore a long rain coat over her sturdiest clothing. The rain and wind were still strong, but seemed to be dying off during the past hour or so. Over her shoulder, she carried a duffle bag filled with extra clothes and her handgun. She looked over at the unmarked car;

there were now two people sitting in the front seat. She calmly walked in the opposite direction. After she turned down a cross street, she looked back to see if the car was following her. Sure enough, it was.

She kept walking until she reached the entrance to a neighboring condominium complex. Once inside she ran as fast as her smoke-damaged lungs allowed until she reached the electronic gate. She had a friend who lived there so she knew the gate entrance code. Her pursuers would be able to get the code easily enough, but it would take a minute or so for them to call dispatch. She ran through the pool area towards the back fence. There was another pedestrian gate that exited onto one of the main roads. Directly across the street was a 7-Eleven where she was a regular customer, mostly buying cigarettes, and a Bank of America. She called a cab as she labored across the street, out of breath, asking to be picked up in the rear parking lot. She entered the bank as calmly as possible.

Keeping an eye on the street, she took some money out of the ATM. After a few minutes, she saw the unmarked car pull up in front of the pedestrian exit to the condo complex. One of the officers got out of the car and began walking across the street toward the 7-Eleven. She was more than happy to see the taxi pulling into the parking lot behind the bank. As the cop went into the convenience store, she slipped out of the bank and got into the cab.

The driver, an older, balding man, turned to look at her over his shoulder. "Where you headed?"

"Go south," she said, which was the opposite direction the police car was headed. "I'm in a bit of a hurry." She slouched down in the seat as she saw the police officer on foot heading into the bank. The driver pulled out onto the street and she was in the clear. "Take 41 to Naples, then towards Miami. We're going almost halfway across." The driver looked pleased, as that was a fair distance and would cost at least a one hundred and fifty dollars—plus tip.

She called Peter, who was quick to pick up. "Hey, it's Janie."

"Where are you now?"

"On my way to see Walker's grandfather. Look, there's a lot to explain in a couple of minutes, so listen carefully." Janie recounted the facts that she had discovered. Peter listened patiently, making the occasional comment.

"So you think there is a connection to the Satanist Church?"

"Absolutely. Contact the police and let them in on things."

"Okay, I'll follow up with James Hunter, Buck Henderson, and Henrietta LePley. Listen, you be careful. I don't want you getting hurt . . . or in trouble. You're going to the reserve in case Walker shows up there and to question the grandfather, nothing more. Call me in four hours."

"Trouble? Come on, Pete, you're sending me into a Satanic rat hole. Talk to you soon." She hung up and put the phone back into the duffle bag.

18

HELL

JACK OPENED HIS EYES. His mouth was very dry and his lips were somehow stuck together. To his horror, he realized they were sewn shut; the stitches dug into his flesh like tiny daggers. His hands were trussed close to his feet with a zip tie. His back felt as if it were being bent in two, and his head ached where he'd been struck. It was a small, dark space, and he didn't like to be confined. Slivers of light sliced from around the outline of the closed door. He tried to wiggle but couldn't move. He was wedged between something and a wall.

The place was damp and musty, smelling of oil and feces, maybe blood. He pushed against whatever it was that held him against the wall. It was heavy and rolled to the right. It rolled back against him once he stopped pushing. The object moved slightly. He let out a startled scream that was muffled by his sewn lips. The thing beside him was alive. *Holy fuck.* He tried to push the thing harder, in utter panic. With the last limits of his pain tolerance and strength, he was able to roll the object over. Settling back, he could see that the object was a human body, which was moving slightly. He was lying head to foot with it. The ends of both legs were bloody, footless stumps, sewn up to staunch the flow of blood. Jack calmed himself as best he could and pushed back the sensations of nausea. If he were to vomit, he would choke to death.

He tried to remember what had happened. He could recall being hit from behind. He could see his assailants' faces. He couldn't remember getting to where he was now. He'd been knocked cold a few times in his life, mostly playing football. He recalled the doctors' warnings about further concussions. This last knock was the second such blow in the past few days. He closed his eyes as his head began to swim and he slipped into unconsciousness for a time.

Footsteps coming toward him . . . the door opened. A rough set of hands grabbed him by his shoulders and dragged him into the light. It took some time to clear his vision. He was in some kind of garage filled with stuffed animals. Televisions blared from all corners of the room. The man stopped as he reached a clearing in the shop's floor. He slit the tie that bound Jack's hands to his feet and Jack sighed a moment's breath of relief. His back cramped as it was allowed to straighten. The man sat him up against an old sofa, and he was thankful for its support.

"You're lucky I haven't let Jimmy feed you to the gators. Way too simple. Hold still now." The man pulled out a camera and snapped a few photos of him. Jack could see the sun shining through the windows and a large bay door that was open to the outside. He could see that the building backed onto a water course, he could smell swamp. His captor was dressed in a light grey suit and tie. He remembered his face from last night, very pale with a hawk-like nose, tall and lean. Behind him stood another man, shorter, stockier, with a slightly deformed face. "Yes, if I had my way, you would be at the bottom of the swamp, chopped up into a hundred pieces. Jimmy here is itching to cut you up. He's a remorseless bastard. But even if he weren't . . . you did kill our brother." The man brushed his hand through his nearly white hair. "I don't know why she wants you alive. Never argue with a witch, I always say. It's bad for one's health." He chuckled.

"I hear that you're a sports hero, Mr. Walker. Well, there will be no heroics from you on this occasion. You see, we have a vested interest in your imminent misery. It's all very fair. You kill our brother Eric, we make you suffer for as long as we can without letting you drift into the peacefulness of death."

He turned back to Jimmy. "Throw him back in the cupboard. And I told you to get rid of that whore two days ago. I mean it, you sick bastard."

Whore? Jack felt his face staring to flush.

Isaac saw the look on Jack's face. "Ah, so you have seen my little brother's plaything. You were fucking her for a while, were you not? Maybe I'll let her live a while longer. Jimmy does appreciate an audience, and as I like to say: he is remorseless."

Jimmy shuffled over and grabbed Jack by the twist tie that bound his feet. He yanked hard, allowing Jack's head to bounce off the wooden floor. Pain wracked his already tender, pounding skull. He had never felt so helpless as Jimmy dragged him along the rough floor towards the open doorway. He was at the mercy of his captors. Once in the closet, Jimmy laid him on the floor in the opposite direction and he was able to get a quick look at the form that had been next to him in the dark.

It was female. Her feet and arms had been cut off, the ends sewn and cauterized. She was naked, and her body was soiled from her own defecation and blood. Her lips were sewn shut like his. *Sarah.* He had hoped the hawk-nosed man had fabricated the tale. Before the door was shut, he wasn't certain but he thought he saw her eyes open slightly. Then there was darkness, except the slivers of light that peeked through the edges of the doorway. After a few moments his eyes adjusted and he was able to see the details of her face.

No matter how badly he had been betrayed by the woman, no one deserved this fate. He shuddered to think what had happened to her, and what was still planned for her he could only imagine. If he were to get out of this mess, he would take retribution against those two men. He had a sinking feeling, however, that retribution would never come. The men knew what they were doing and looked as if they'd done this many times before.

He was being kept alive for a purpose. He could only assume it was someone related to the Brotherhood of Set. *The Priestess? Henrietta?* The latter was most likely. He looked back to Sarah. *You poor soul; this is no way to die.*

He slowly inched himself forward to the point where his hands were level with Sarah's throat. He slowly flipped himself over so that his back was facing her. He felt for her throat. Once he had it in his hands, he squeezed with what strength he had left. He felt her struggle slightly, her breath straining through her nostrils for a moment. He pressed harder, pushing himself on top of her as much as he could to gain leverage. He kept the pressure on until he could feel no more movement. He slumped back to the ground with a thump.

He lay motionless for a few minutes catching his breath. *Who was Sarah Courtney? Was that even her name?* Jack doubted it. If he'd asked himself six hours ago if he cared if she jumped off a bridge, the answer would have been easy. In fact, he might have even pushed her if he'd had the chance. She'd been a conniving, lying bitch and knew what she was doing all along. But it was obvious now that they'd both been pawns, caught up in some warped scenario. Though there was a part of him even now that wanted to leave her in this cruel state, the only humane thing to do was to put her out of her misery. Deception or no deception, she had been a proud person. You get to know someone after four months. He was sure that she would thank him when they met up in hell. Or were they already there?

Jack dug down deep into his inner resolve. It would be quite easy to give up; death awaited him in short order. But he was not ready to die.

19

SWAPPING STORIES

PETER WALKED OUT THE front door of his office building. He pondered calling the authorities, but figured it would be much easier to flag down the men in the black sedan sitting in front of his office. Janie was right. It was time to feed some information to the good guys. He assumed that they knew a lot more than he, but the case was in damage control at this point and he would give them what information was required to help promote the safety of his client.

Within half an hour, officers Ramirez and Green were sitting across from him at his desk. Ramirez pulled his hand through his thick black hair. He moved from side to side in his chair, unable to find a comfortable position.

"Mr. Robertson, you realize that withholding evidence from an ongoing investigation is illegal?"

Peter stared out the window for a moment. "Don't patronize me, Officer Ramirez. So is revealing a client's confidential disclosure." He turned to stare at the man. "Look, I called you in to offer some help. I fear my client is in grave danger." He paused for a moment, turning again to look out the window at the rain pelting down against the glass. "I believe that Jackson Walker is innocent and I am trying to piece together his story. Frankly, there are too many holes at this point. This whole thing could be bigger than my client and his involvement. I was hoping that together we might be able to trade information and get to the bottom of it all. I know you want your arrest, but wouldn't you like to crack open something really big?"

Lani nodded.

"We made contact with Walker two days ago. He was staying on an island. One of my assistants interviewed him."

Lani moved forward in her chair, her brows furrowing. "We're listening, Mr. Robertson. Do you mind if we record this conversation?"

"No, not at all. My sources indicate that there have been attacks on a number of Seminole villages within the watershed, including the island where Walker was located. We believe he is on the run. He was on the island where a Seminole woman and a younger man were killed, both by gunshot wounds. Can we agree that this is accurate?"

Lani turned her head to the side, not committing.

"It is no secret that a local Satanic cult may be involved. I am going to give you two names: Buck Henderson and Henrietta LePley. My client believes that he is being framed. We believe him, though we do not have enough evidence to put together a slam-dunk case. Both of the individuals whose names I have given you are associated with the Brotherhood of Set. We haven't had enough time to locate these individuals." He paused, rubbing his hands slightly.

"I believe you have the resources. Our biggest fear is that he has been abducted. His body was not found on the island. Since he hasn't shown up dead or arrested, and he isn't with his family anymore, I can only assume that he may be in bad hands. We need to get him in before anything terrible happens to him."

Lani looked at Rick, then turned back to Pete and lied. "Is that it? You haven't told us anything that we didn't already know."

"Don't be coy, Agent Green. We can work together. I will tell you if I hear anything new, if you would be so kind to give me your number."

Rick pulled a business card out of his wallet. "I appreciate your position, sir. You're in over your head. I think you know this or you wouldn't have called."

Peter let out a long breath. "Ramirez, it's all about making deals. Jackson Walker is my trump card. Who's got the second ace? You or me? You wouldn't be here if it was you."

Lani smiled. "You let us know if anything else comes up. I will promise you one courtesy—if Walker shows up, you'll be one of the first to know. For your sake and his, Mr. Robertson, I hope that your assumptions are correct. It won't be the first time that a suspect claimed he was innocent."

20

HENRIETTA LEPLEY

HENRIETTA SAT ACROSS THE massive oak desk from her father. She had stacked papers on it neatly into symmetrically perfect piles. Her hair was styled in the tight bob that was fashionable for the 1920s, and she wore a white dress, long and starched with a short black jacket covering her shoulders. It was her choice to dress as she did, just like it was her choice to accompany her father in his daily activities. She'd gone to work with him every day since her tenth birthday. It could be no other way.

Henrietta watched as an older man dressed in a pinstripe suit viewed a set of documents her father had placed in front of him. Roger Edgar, her father's real estate broker, had made the long drive down from Tampa to Charlotte Harbor for the meeting. Her father looked at Roger over the top of his glasses, as was his way.

"Looks good in principle, Mr. Edgar," he said in a deep southern Floridian drawl. "It will allow us to link up those other parcels we bought two years back. We made a pretty good deal on the other two. What is the resistance? Do these people think they have us over a barrel?"

"Maybe they do, Mr. LePley. They know that you need the land." Edgar crossed his arms over his paunch of a belly.

George LePley dropped the papers to his desk briskly, disturbing one of the perfectly placed stacks of paper. "Nonsense. I may be the only man who has any interest in that land, but we can let them stew on the deal for another year for all I care, make it two years." He hesitated, meeting Henrietta's eyes for the slightest of moments. "Unless you know more about this deal than you are telling. You wouldn't have an interest with the other party, now would you, Mr. Edgar?"

There was an uncomfortable silence. Henrietta turned her eyes off to the side, as if looking at someone and nodded. Henrietta's father had found it unnerving when the girl did this, but after a time learned not to question the peculiarity.

"Mr. Edgar," Henrietta stated in her sweetest voice, "the Booths have been wanting rid of this property for some time now." She stood, glancing to the side once again. "It is common knowledge that they want in the neighborhood of twenty thousand dollars. Now you bring them an offer of twenty-four. My father is paying you handsomely with a two-thousand-dollar commission. You wouldn't be looking to double your fee, would you, Mr. Edgar?"

A bead of sweat formed on the man's brow. "Yes, of course I am being paid well. I always am, Miss Henrietta."

George stood slowly, having made a slight change to the document. "Take this back to the Booths. I will not pay a dime over twenty grand. Don't come back without the papers being signed. If you do, I'll be looking for another broker and you will be out your commission. Good day to you, sir." He handed the papers back to the man.

Roger Edgar extended his hand. "Of course, sir. I'll do my best to get the papers signed." He quickly shuffled out of the office, happy to escape the LePley scrutiny.

"You were correct as usual, my darling girl."

Henrietta's face beamed with pleasure at the praise.

"Now be a good girl and go get yourself a soda." He tossed

her a couple of coins. “Allow me the privacy of a cigar.”

Henrietta nodded. She knew that her father needed to be left alone from time to time and there were no more meetings slated for the day. She left the building and made her way down to the wharf, where the fishing boats were bringing in their daily catch. The place smelled of fish, salt air, and sweat. The docks and surrounding streets were crowded with laborers, loading and unloading cargo ships. Old whipping posts remained as a stark reminder of times when these men were not paid for their work. She was fascinated with the place.

Henrietta moved along to the stretch of jetties, observing every detail. She sat down on a piling and watched as a large black man oared his skiff into its crude dock. He tossed a thick rope to the young girl with a broad and welcoming smile. He spoke with a thick Spanish accent. “This is no place for a little woman.”

“You will tire one day of saying the same thing, Mr. Cortez. What did you catch today?” She stepped down into the boat. Fish covered the deck with a large net strewn across them. “Snook, redfish, mullet and what is that beast?” She pointed to a large shark strewn across the bow of the boat.

“Blacktip shark. Miss Henrietta. You gonna get that pretty white dress dirty, and your papa will have me skinned.”

“I doubt that, Mr. Cortez. Maybe just tied and whipped.” She glanced at one of the posts on the shoreline.

The man’s broad smile disappeared. She had inadvertently crossed a line that he did not like. “Get you home now, Miss.”

“Aw, I’m sorry Mr. Cortez. I really didn’t mean it.” She glanced back at the large shark. “How’d you catch that thing?”

“Free line.” He picked up a long coiled cord. “Mano a mano.” He flexed his massive biceps. “Today I am the fish’s master. Tomorrow . . . maybe not.” He laughed, his broad smile returning to his wide face. “Take some fish home to your mother.” He put two large snook into a burlap sack.

“Thank you, Mr. Cortez. I will see you tomorrow?”

The man smiled and lifted her up to the dock. “It is not wise to say such things, little woman. One day you will say it to someone who is not as nice as me.”

She smiled. “I will remember that, Mr. Cortez.” She turned

and headed towards home.

Henrietta turned sharply to the right, stumbling for no apparent reason, she gathered herself and nodded, whispering. "Yes, the dark people are proud."

Henrietta walked slowly for a few minutes back toward the town center and to her father's office building. Henrietta decided to leave him alone for the rest of the day. She didn't think he would appreciate the smell of fish in his office. Her father's driver took her home in one of the company's Model T Fords.

Her mother, Cecilia LePley, welcomed her in the kitchen of their large ranch style home in North Ft. Myers, happily accepting the fresh fish. She was a robust, pleasant woman with large hips and breasts.

"Would you like some tea?" her mother asked.

"Yes please." Henrietta's relationship with her mother was strong. There wasn't a lot of talk between the two, but there was a bond, more powerful than blood. The two bore a common talent—they were spirit whisperers. Her mother, like her French ancestors. liked to call it voodoo or witchcraft. Cecilia LePley was not as powerful with the spirits as her little girl, but made great use of the gift by making her everyday life, and that of her families . . . easier. Henrietta, on the other hand, saw the gift as a source of power, which needed to be exploited. A whisperer could see spirits. A witch's strength lay in the clarity in which they could see the apparitions and their ability to interpret the intent or message put forward from the being. A whisperer with little power often fell to insanity, as they did not have a strong enough will to filter or block the lesser and sometimes stronger entities from their normal daily lives. The stronger witches, like Henrietta, even at a young age, could interpret and at times bend the will of a stronger entity.

George LePley was different from her mother. Henrietta had watched her father conduct his business with the utmost scrutiny. There were those who questioned why George allowed his daughter to follow him during his daily work routine, but most wrote it off as an idiosyncratic Southern custom that the LePleys had not discarded at the turn of the century. If you wanted to do business with millionaire George LePley, you accepted the presence of his daughter.

Henrietta would watch the men that George met during his meetings. She unnerved some of them, but long-time associates grew accustomed to her. She had the knack of stepping in with a quiet comment just at the right moment, as if she knew what they were thinking. Henrietta would take her father aside and offer her understanding of the matter. In time, George understood that she was always correct in her assessments. Ultimately, he accepted her as part of himself.

* * * *

George LePley was wealthy. His ancestry was long and well-ensconced within the hierarchy of wealthy Southern families. His father had been a captain under General Lee in the Civil War. His ancestors had fought the Indians in the Seminole wars. Though he could not prove it, Henrietta's father claimed roots back to the 1500s, when Ponce de Leon had used the west coast of Florida as an outpost for pirating. It was an old family story that a LePley had buried treasure on Estero Island, later called Ft. Myers Beach. Henrietta knew the myth to be reality, though the knowledge of its specific location had been lost in the telling.

As far back as their ancestry went, so did the link to the Church of Set. The LePleys had been blessed with strong occult awareness. They learned to use their power and their links to the venerable church of Satan to forward their aspirations. The LePleys were one of the original benefactors of the grand old Republican Party. The family's wealth expanded slowly through generation upon generation of prudent investing and management of the estate. The LePleys had a keen eye for profitable advantages. George believed that there would be money in sulfur, of which there was an abundance in the area. Henrietta agreed. He was working on a project to bring a rail line in from Miami and the Port of Tampa. Port Charlotte and its deep harbor would be the perfect location to export to the rest of the world. He and his business partners bought hundreds of acres on the coast, as well as on Gasparilla Island. The venture would bring prosperity to southwest Florida in the early- to mid-1900s.

* * * *

Henrietta sat at the same table as she had all those years ago, where her mother had served her tea. The decor had changed; the house had all the modern amenities one could want, except televisions. Henrietta didn't like noise and distractions; it disrupted her ability to connect with the spirit world. Heavy machinery and people talking had the same effect.

Henrietta had never taken a man. She had decided in her twenties that they were not to her taste. For a time she dated men in hopes of becoming pregnant, but by her thirtieth year, a strong and impetuous entity had declared her infertile. "So mote it be," she stated. Henrietta did not bat an eye.

Henrietta settled in to running her estates, and over the next several decades created an even bigger financial empire. She aged abnormally slowly. Her fingers were into everything from oil, sulfur, sugar cane, and turpentine to gambling, and that is where she found herself today. It was a major disappointment that a Republican senator would have the gall to suggest that her rights be subdued in her home state. She had overcome a lot in her hundred-plus years and would not see her legacy compromised. Republicans were supposed to behave responsibly, not like the damned Democrats who could not think four years ahead to the next election.

She feared the Chinese, who could plan and look ahead more than any respectable Republican. If Americans were not careful, China would own the country within fifty years.

* * * *

Henrietta looked forward to the evening ahead. She had invited the good senator to dinner, where she would introduce him to some of her fold. The Walker situation was under control and she would now need Senator Hunter to change his mind. Mason Matye, president of the American Branch of the Church of Satan, a good friend of hers and a powerful witch of his own accord, would be there tonight. Some extra muscle might be required.

Henrietta had arranged to be picked up at six by Isaac McFadden. The tall, blond man opened the rear door to the limousine and took the old matriarch's hand to ease her into the back seat.

"Good evening, Isaac," she said as he released her hand.

"Ms. LePley, it's always a pleasure. It's been a long time since I've had the privilege of driving for you. Eric would have had the privilege, but as you know, he's dead."

"Forget the pleasantries, Isaac, this isn't the time. Get into the driver's seat so we can talk."

Isaac raised his eyebrows as he turned away and smoothly slipped into the car, closing the door behind him. Eric had been her normal driver, and he was not used to being so close to the woman and so subservient. He blamed her more than Walker for Eric's untimely end, but decided it was best to placate her until he could find a sensible retribution for the incident. He left the privacy partition open and pulled out of the driveway.

"The Walker boy, is he still alive?"

Isaac paused for a moment, choosing his words carefully. The old woman had a penchant for knowing whether or not you were being truthful. She was the only person he'd ever met who could unnerve him with a few subtle words. "Yes, but uncomfortably so."

She sat for a few minutes, fussing with her lipstick and hair. "If he is to serve his purpose, he must remain . . . so." She smiled, showing her teeth, her eyes meeting his in the rear view mirror. He couldn't hold her stare. "If we were to need him tonight, could he be prettied up?"

"Yes ma'am." He supposed that Walker could be made to look passable. "No worse for the wear."

"Good. Once you have dropped me off, I would like you to make sure he is presentable. I may call upon you to . . . present him. We may need to let the senator know that we have detained him."

"'Present' him? We don't entertain many visitors out here, ma'am."

"Don't be coy, Isaac, surely your degree from Cornell provided you with the brains to figure out this complicated request. Have him presentable for me when I call."

"As you ask, ma'am, just give me some lead time if you can." *Bitch.*

Henrietta didn't say another word until they reached Remington's. She looked Isaac in the eye as he helped her out of the car. "This is important Mr. McFadden."

He nodded as he let her hand go.

****

Tables and chairs had been cleared out of the large, well-appointed dining room except for one long table with place settings for twenty. The sun was low, sitting in the middle of the large windows that filled the western wall of the room. The light reflected off a massive chandelier that hung from the center of the room's vaulted ceiling. Several of the dinner guests, in black tie and formal gown, milled around the service bar next to the room's entrance. Henrietta had hoped that she would arrive after the senator, but the politician was late. One and all turned to acknowledge her as she entered.

Buck Henderson was the first to greet her, trying to flatter her with his Southern charm. "Why, Henrietta, you look ravishing tonight, and not a day over fifty."

Henrietta bared her perfect teeth. "There is no need for the bullshit, Buck. I haven't looked fifty in more than thirty years. I see that everyone is here except our esteemed guest."

Buck backed away one step. "No harm intended. No, we just received a call saying that the senator was tied up in a late meeting. He'll be coming with his wife and secretary."

"That should be interesting. He's screwing both of them, and one more than the other. I do enjoy watching for subtle innuendoes. You have the photos, of course?"

"Yes."

There was a commotion in the grand entrance. Hunter was being escorted through the two massive front doors. He was followed closely by his wife, Debra, and Phyllis. Henrietta turned and walked toward them. They intercepted each other at the entrance to the ballroom.

"Ms. LePley. Thank you for the invitation."

"It's my pleasure, Mr. Senator."

"Let me introduce my wife, Debra."

"Ms. LePley." She shook the matriarch's outstretched hand.

"My personal secretary, Phyllis McRae, you met the other day."

Henrietta met the woman's eyes and shook her hand. Phyllis lowered her eyes. "You have been very diligent in making the senator available tonight. I know that you manage his affairs very closely."

Debra's eyes shot quickly to meet Henrietta's, then turned away.

Phyllis responded, her voice wavering ever so slightly. "Yes, Ms. LePley, we keep a close eye on the senator. He is a busy man, as you most certainly know."

"Yes he is." She grinned, showing her perfect teeth. "Let us get a drink."

She walked toward the bar, guiding Hunter along. A thin, bald man in his mid-sixties turned as they approached. He was impeccably dressed in a brown summer blazer and white pants.

"Everett, I am so pleased that you could make it." She turned to Hunter. "Senator, let me introduce you to Everett Oelze and his wife Annemarie." An attractive, plump woman of Italian descent and similar age turned upon hearing her name.

"It's nice to see you again, Everett," Hunter said. "Correct me if I am wrong; you are a member of the Tea Party and a benefactor of the GOP. We've met a few times before." He extended his hand.

Oelze grasped Hunter's hand enthusiastically. "Yes, Mr. Senator, may I call you James?"

Hunter nodded smiling. "Mrs. Oelze, it is a pleasure."

"We met in Jacksonville last year," Everett said. "We had one hell of a time at that golf outing."

Hunter nodded. "Yes, they do know how to throw a party. I wish the golf, or at least my golf, had been better. That TPC course tore the heck out of me. You want to know where your game's at, take to the big stage."

"Yes, I had a hard time myself." He paused for a moment. "I supported your candidacy in the past two elections."

Hunter forced a smile. "Yes, of course. I thank you for that."

Oelze nodded, taking a sip from his bourbon. "One hand needs to wash the other."

Hunter's smile disappeared. "I see where this is going, Everett. I am a firm believer in walking the company line, but I am also a man of conviction. If you are referring to the Clean

Water Bill, it is my legislation and I plan to have it passed; my constituency demands it."

"Your legislation is good for the birds and fish, but will kill the backbone of the Floridian economy. You are starting to sound like our President. If we continue to give away tax dollars, our great country will be bankrupt."

"Is it America's bankruptcy or your bank account not being as full as you might wish that you're most concerned with, Everett?"

Henrietta put her hand on Everett's arm. "We haven't offered the good senator a drink yet, Everett. There will be time to talk about these things at dinner."

Everett nodded. "Of course, where are my manners? What would you and Mrs. Hunter like?"

"Honey?" James turned to Debra.

"A mojito would be divine, thank you darling."

"Make that three, please, Everett." He turned to Phyllis. "Mojito?"

She nodded. "Yes, please, I need a drink."

Once they had their cocktails, Henrietta guided them to an outside terrace. "You see, James, it is more than the whim of an old Southern woman. I will benefit if the bill is squashed, there is no question. But this runs deeper. It is about Americans remaining in control of America. America owned the world after World War II. Since then, it's been in steady decline. We have mortgaged our future. As a people, we don't plan—we react. Our politicians—please accept my apology, James—are only interested in the next election. There will be another debt crisis in the next 10 to 12 years. I'm not so sure that we will be able to crawl or buy our way out of that one."

She put her finger on his chest. "It's time to start taking back our country a piece at a time. It will not happen in one fell swoop. Strong local policies will snowball. Other states will see what we have done by looking after our own backyard. It's not just about your bill." She smiled her toothy smile as one of the people on the terrace approached.

The man was not tall, perhaps five-foot-eight, but he had a presence. His eyes were nearly black, his hair dark and closely shaved down to his scalp. He wore a black pinstriped suit with a white shirt, open at the collar. It was the way the man looked at him that unnerved Hunter, and his cologne was strangely intoxicating. Both Henrietta and this stranger had the same effect upon him. He didn't like it, yet he felt compelled to meet him.

"Senator," the man said with a slight French inflection. He offered James his hand.

Henrietta interjected. "James, let me introduce an old friend of mine. Mason Matye. How long have we been known each other, Mason?"

"It seems ages, my dear." His eyes never left Hunter's. "So this is the esteemed senator that I have been hearing so much about?"

"So much about?" Hunter scrunched his eyebrows. He turned to Henrietta. "I didn't come, Ms. LePley, to be broadsided." He turned to Phyllis. "I think I have heard about enough for this evening, Phyllis."

Mason interjected. "Of course, Mr. Senator, it was not our intention to gang up on you. We simply wanted an opportunity to give you our side of the issue which has been the source of our, shall we say, impasse. Your office has not responded to our communications, which is not very . . . democratic."

A large, older gentleman turned from his conversation and moved in beside Mason. "Buck, have you met the senator?" Henrietta interjected.

He spoke in a loud, deep voice. "Why, no, I haven't had the pleasure. Buck Henderson."

Hunter shook the man's hand. He did not say a word, but nodded his acceptance of the man's introduction. He turned back to Mason.

"Sir, if I responded to everyone's whims, we wouldn't accomplish much. We did in fact send a letter to Ms. LePley's office that we could not recommend your position. I think that was pretty clear."

Henrietta smiled, her perfect teeth like tiny little daggers. "Then it is your final position that you are backing the legislation?"

"If you want to phrase it that way, then yes. That is my position and I don't plan on changing it anytime soon. Now if we don't have any other issues to discuss, I think I will be rude and decline to stay for the dinner. I find the conversation of little interest, and I have made my position quite clear." He turned to Debra, who was visibly on edge, as was Phyllis.

Henrietta placed a hand on his shoulder. "And which of these two women will you be fucking tonight? Mr. Senator?"

Hunter's face turned dark red. "I've never heard such—"

Buck cut him off. "Such what? Come now, Mr. Senator. We know that you have been having an affair with Ms. McRae for some time now." He pulled an envelope from his jacket pocket. "We have ample proof."

Debra Hunter burst into tears. Phyllis didn't say a word.

"Let's all sit down at the table now like proper Southerners. I think there might be more to discuss than anticipated."

The small group moved into the dining hall where the other guests sat in their seats waiting for the remaining guests to be seated. James Hunter looked like a caged animal. His face was red and he didn't try to mask his anger. Debra walked beside him in shock. As they sat, Hunter noticed that Phyllis was no longer with them. Buck showed the Hunters to their seats. Henrietta sat at the head of the table, and Mason sat beside her. There were two empty seats beside each.

Henrietta tapped her glass with a small silver spoon. Servers poured wine and served a spicy squash and prawn soup.

"Esteemed brethren, I have asked you here under circumstances that our guest, Senator Hunter, might find . . . uncomfortable. So mote it be." She stared at one of the empty chairs directly to her right and nodded ever so slightly. "Senator Hunter, as you know, has declined to support our stance with regards to our farming rights, rights that we have enjoyed for generations. It is with funds generated from our enterprises that we support the Republican Party. Senator Hunter's election campaigns have profited from our support. Our church has supported the Grand Old Party since its inception."

Hunter raised his head, aborting his second attempt to text his driver; *he needed to get out of here*. "Your church?"

"The Brotherhood of Set. Come now, James, don't be so naive. There has been talk of Satanism in the papers, and where there is smoke, there is usually fire. Yes, James, there is such thing as Satanism. It is very powerful and can be persuasive. Our church has been here since before our great nation was formed, since before the birth of your Christ. Different names, but always present. We always get what we want. Now I need to make sure that you will comply with our wishes. I am not asking you. I am telling you to make sure that the bill is softened. We want our proposal, which has been presented in Tallahassee, to be accepted. The state will profit. It is a good deal for all. We are offering tax dollars for land."

Hunter looked around the room. He couldn't help but notice everyone staring at him intently. He tried not to look at his wife, but he sensed her eyes upon him. "Where is Phyllis?"

"Quite dead by now."

His heart flipped for a second, and he could feel the rush of blood in his temples. He felt the scrutiny of everyone at the table, including Debra. "What if I don't agree?"

"You won't do that now, James. Let me outline your options. I will admit that from time to time we have to rely upon some hocus-pocus, if you will, but in this case prudent planning will suffice. Your little whore of a secretary was on our payroll. We know everything that you have been doing and planning for the past two years. You have no secrets, not even your pillow talk." She held up a small recording device.

Debra slumped down in her chair. Hunter turned to her and forced her to sit up, pulling her up by her shoulders.

"Your scandalous behavior should be enough to ensure that you never get re-elected. However, I know you to be a man who values his reputation. We will withhold these pictures, should you comply. Your intern, Jackson Walker, is implicated by participating in the rites of Satanism. He has been framed in cult murders, of which I am sure you are aware. Your picture has been taken with my other most esteemed guests, many of whom," she paused and motioned towards Mason Matye, "are leading members of the Church of Satan's American Chapter. Unlike me, they are well-known by the FBI. One of my associates will be pleased to give you copies of the photos. We could easily establish a link between Walker's participation and yours, of course. Jackson, I will assure you, is alive, but in our custody should we need him."

Buck stood and placed his iPhone on the table in front of him and made a FaceTime call. Hunter could see Jack, who could also see him. Hunter was taken aback by the color of the young man's face and the thick black stitches that criss-crossed his lips. Buck ended the call.

"We shall call Walker . . . *leverage*. Your political as well as personal life will be destroyed."

Mason stood. "Mr. Senator. We know where your children go to school. We won't hurt them at first, only if necessary. It would be a shame if unfortunate accidents were to befall their little friends. Such things can be traumatizing at such a young age. If you try to do anything to our members, we have the means to cause distress. Such are the benefits of strong associations with a devil." He smiled, reading the defiance in the senator's eyes. "Mr. Hunter, we will kill everyone dear to you, your wife, your mother; we know that you have a springer spaniel named Chocolate."

Debra Hunter collapsed in distress, her breath coming in short gasps. Hunter tried to calm his wife. No one at the table moved. Facial expressions around the table were calm; no one appeared to be concerned with Debra Hunter's discomfort.

"Senator Hunter." Henrietta rose to her feet. "I think that we have made our position clear. Please help Mrs. Hunter out to your car. We will be in contact with you to make sure that you are in line. We will expect you to do what is necessary at your soonest convenience."

The guests returned to their dinner as James Hunter helped his wife walk toward the exit.

* * * *

Jack closed his eyes to focus on what had just occurred. The televisions around the room were loud, each on a different channel. The Tampa Bay Devil Rays were playing the Toronto Blue Jays on a large flat screen mounted on the back wall. Another smaller screen featured the World Fishing Network, and a third, an old black and white RCA, played a rerun of the *Iron Chef* program.

It had become crystal clear to Jack that he was a small pawn in a bigger game. He had been framed to force Senator James Hunter to do something against his will. No doubt it was the legislation he was working on. Jack couldn't imagine that his personal situation would be enough to change the mind of the politician. He knew that the man wouldn't bend to change important policies because of what he represented in terms of leverage to his captors. He didn't know exactly what his use was, but he made up his mind to do whatever it took to get himself out of the equation.

Jack dug down deep to find the fortitude to move forward. The bastards who held him wouldn't blink an eye to kill him. But he thought about Gramps and his cousins. They'd bailed him out when he had needed help the most. He owed them his best effort. His mind flashed back to an image of the young Seminole, Bobby, lying dead on the beach with the top of his head taken off, his blood washing away in a torrent of rain from the tropical storm. One of the men standing in front of him had pulled the trigger. *Fuckers.*

Jack could barely maintain his kneeling position, his hands once again bound to his ankles by a stout cord. He was sure that at least one of his ribs was broken, along with the severe bruising to his arms, face and abdomen. Jimmy had lost his mind when he found Sarah strangled next to Jack and had kicked him to the point of near-unconsciousness. If some of the stitches that bound his mouth had not pulled loose, he would have suffocated.

The blond man, Isaac, stood over him, looking at him with distaste. What made Jack nervous was the calmness with which he spoke. Isaac was in control, and there was nothing that could be done about it. Jack was helpless.

"Be a lot easier if we could just kill you." He put his phone back in his jacket pocket, then hauled back with his foot and kicked Jack in the gut. "She'll let us kill you soon enough. I'll have Jimmy put you up on the meat hooks and we'll hang you out over the water. Jimmy will cut off the tips of your toes first, so there's a nice flow of blood. Sharks are pupping upriver right now. Won't take long for the gators. We'll let them eat you alive. Eye for an eye, Mr. Walker, an eye for an eye. There's lessons to be learned in life, but unfortunately, you're not going to get the chance to learn from your mistakes." He leaned down and pushed the convulsing prisoner over onto his side. "Jimmy, put that down and help me get this son of a bitch back in the closet."

Jack couldn't see the other man, but he knew he was there, as he could hear the sound of a saw cutting through something hard. He grimaced as he contemplated the probable source of the sound. He was roughly dragged and stowed in his now familiar prison. He couldn't move. His bindings were tight and cut off the circulation to his left hand. His ribs hurt too much to try anything more than a wiggle to a more comfortable position. He closed his eyes and tried to rest. When and if his chance came, he would need every ounce of energy he could muster. His face had been pushed into a pile of rags that smelled of kerosene and mold. He tried to push them away as best he could, but it did little to fix the problem. The pile was simply too large. He could hear the two men talking and then the sawing started again, its high-pitched whine much like the drills used in a dentist's office. On and on it went, then it stopped abruptly.

Jack found sleep somehow, only to be awoken again by the sound of two male voices arguing. Squeaking wheels, sliding doors, the sound of a boat motor moving away until it couldn't be heard. Sleep. Pain. Despair.

21

CARLY HENDERSON

RICK RAMIREZ AND LANI Green pulled into a swank condo complex on Vanderbilt Beach Road in North Naples. Buck Henderson was registered under five addresses in the United States: Naples, New Orleans, Atlanta, New York and San Francisco. Rick called the Naples address and was surprised to get an answer. Carly Henderson, Buck's wife, said she would be happy to answer any questions they might have.

Rick pulled up to the front of the multi-story building and looked over at Lani. The two of them were tired. Neither had taken any real downtime since they had been called in on the case. Everything had moved quickly since the killings six days earlier. Lani was starting to look haggard; dark pockets had formed under her eyes and she was moody as hell. "Say, you okay?"

Lani sat up in her seat. "Yeah. Just getting worn down. Can't wait to get this thing wrapped up."

"You look like hell. You always get wrapped up like this?"

Lani didn't answer.

"All this cult stuff. How much credence do you put in it?"

She sat for a moment gathering her thoughts. "A lot, actually. This one's not in your face like Ocala a few years back. It's subtle, the players are deep-seated. The Church of Set is well-run. I think we're looking at a good old-fashioned, well-backed Satanic cult, textbook. I can't find any links to any national Satanist churches. They don't advertise. They don't have an agenda that I can pick up on, besides the possible link between Walker and James Hunter."

"I think we should pay the good senator a visit once we're done here."

Rick checked in with the doorman and they were shown to the elevator. "Floor eleven, unit 1104, Mr. Ramirez."

* * * *

Lani and Rick offered their identification when Carly Henderson answered the door. Rick took the lead. "Mrs. Henderson, thank you for taking the time to talk with us."

"Certainly, please come in. What seems to be the problem? I've never talked to the police before. Now the IRS, that's another issue." She laughed. Her cheeks were flushed and she kept moving her hands back and forth from her hair to her lap.

Rick watched her closely before speaking. Most people being questioned gave away the answers before the questions were asked. They were usually the innocent, the jilted lovers, the neighbor, the spouse. She knew why he and Lani were here, he could sense it. He forwarded his line of questioning. "Mrs. Henderson, your husband is implicated in the cult slayings of two people up on Lake Okeechobee nearly a week ago. We would like to know his whereabouts so we can question him."

Carly Henderson did her best not to flinch. She swallowed a couple of times before responding. "I assure you that he's not part of anything like that. Buck's off in Atlanta. You know he's a part owner of the Braves?"

"No, I didn't. If he is, it didn't show up in our searches. We're told he was seen in Naples earlier today. He drives a black DeVille, license plate KT41 33Y?"

"Yes, that's his car." She hesitated. "He must have come back early."

Rick took a chance. “His car was followed last night traveling north on 41 at about five.”

“Oh . . . ”

“Mrs. Henderson. We know he’s still in the Tri-City area. Is there anything else that you want to tell us?” He let her hang on his words.

Carly’s voice wavered ever so slightly. “I assure you that he is in no way connected with any cults. It was just dreadful what happened to those people. We’ve been watching it on the TV.”

“You didn’t answer my question, Mrs. Henderson.”

Lani interjected. “We’re not insinuating that you have done anything wrong.”

“If he’s here, I don’t know anything about it. Maybe he’s out with a floozy from Handsome Henry’s and doesn’t want me to know about it.”

Lani smiled at the woman. “Be that as it may, it doesn’t answer our question.”

Lani looked at Rick. The woman wasn’t going to give them anything else, but her nervousness backed up their hunch that Buck Henderson was still in the area. “Mrs. Henderson, if you can tell us anything else, please give us a call.” He handed her his card.

After the door shut behind them, Rick turned to Lani. “So, what do you think?

“He’s still here.”

“Obvious.”

“She wasn’t shocked when you implicated him. I was glad that you jumped ahead. You didn’t give her time to get settled. Peter Robertson’s intel was correct. We can assume that Buck Henderson is connected with The Brotherhood of Set.” They stepped into the elevator.

“Let’s head up to North Ft. Myers and see what Henrietta LePley can tell us.”

“It’s not worth it. Let’s put a watch on both places. I don’t think we will learn more there than we did tonight. We might set them off. Can we get a phone tap on Henderson’s line? LePley’s as well?”

“Might take a bit for the warrant, but I’ll call it in.”

She pulled out her phone and made a note. “We have a hell of a lot of ground to cover. If we can get a tag on the old woman, we can make a decision then. The reserve is under surveillance and the Seminoles are now co-operating with us. Where the hell is Walker? We should be able to get this case closed. What I don't get is the motive. Robertson's holding something back."

"Doesn't want Walker snagged before he can get something tangible in his defense."

"His assistant, Janie Callahan. If we tag her, were going to find Walker. We've had a watch on her for five days, but she keeps slipping us. She's elusive."

"Or we're bad at keeping tabs on her. She slipped Jenkins yesterday in five minutes. But then again, he's a lazy bastard." Rick cracked his neck, placing his hand on his chin. "We get a lock on her again, I want someone holding her fucking hand." He stepped out of the elevator and turned to Lani. "The Seminole village, she'll have gone there. I'll call in to get the Lee County traffic chopper ready. After we talk to Hunter, I want to get straight down there."

They got into their car and Rick fired up the engine. Lani adjusted the seat, tilting it back.

Rick guided the car back to the city center. He pressed the feed button and spoke to the in-car computer. "Call Senator James Hunter." Five possible numbers came up on the screen. "Call office."

The call was answered by a male. "Senator James Hunter's office, Jaime speaking."

"Hello Jaime, this is Detective Rick Ramirez from the Lee County Sheriff's office. I would like to speak with Senator Hunter ASAP."

"That might be difficult. The senator has just gone on a leave of absence."

"Is anything wrong?"

"Personal issues, sir. We're not to book any appointments or forward any calls."

"Can I speak to his assistant?"

There was a pause on the other end. "She's no longer with us."

"No longer with you. I spoke to her three days ago. Phyllis is her name, correct?"

"Sir, she passed away last night."

Rick nearly swerved off the road.

"Is the senator still in Naples? You realize that I can get a subpoena for this information."

"Sir, I am just following orders. I would suggest you do what you need to do, and I mean no disrespect. I'm doing my job."

"Okay, Jaime. Just do me a favor and mention that the sheriff's office called. If the senator contacts you, or if he's actually there, please give him our number."

"I'll do that for you."

Rick hung up.

"What's that all about?"

Rick relayed what he had just found out.

"Christ, he is involved. I'll get a warrant ordered."

Rick stepped on the gas. "See if you can get Hunter's address, and let's find out if there's an autopsy ordered on the assistant Phyllis."

"On it." Lani started dialing.

Rick guided the car back to the city center. He tapped the control button on the computer. "Senator James Hunter, Bonita Springs, Florida. Cell phone." Hunter's cell phone was private, but had been linked to an earlier call this week, allowing the Florida Department of Law Enforcement's central computer to grab and store the number.

"Dialing the number." The phone rang five times before the voice mail clicked in. "You've reached James Hunter on my private line. Please leave me a message and I will be pleased to get back to you as soon as possible."

"Good evening, Mr. Senator. This is Detective Rick Ramirez of the Lee County Sheriff's Department. Please return my call at your soonest convenience, you have my number." He didn't think he would get the man on his cell, especially if he didn't recognize the number.

"Office."

"Dialing the number."

The phone rang through to an automated answering system. "The office of Senator James Hunter is currently closed and will reopen on Monday. Please dial one for a company directory." Rick hung up, muttering to himself. "Closed on a Thursday and I just spoke to them. Yeah, the bastard's involved."

Lani nodded. "Though maybe not of his own volition."

“Maybe. He didn’t answer his cell, either.”

“Hmmm. Certainly fishy.”

“Yup, gotta talk to this guy, and fast. Let’s go to his house. Start route guidance.”

“Starting route guidance,” the car responded.

Rick turned to Lani. “Call in that warrant. I’ve got a feeling that the senator won’t want to talk.”

22

GRAMPS

"YOU'RE LUCKY YOU DIDN'T get shot comin' in here late at night. The reserve is buzzin' like a swarm of hornets." The old man appeared to have aged since Janie had seen him last. He looked tired and frail, his eye sockets dark and sunken. Janie gazed down at the old Seminole, who was flanked by the two men she'd met before—Jack's cousin Josh and his friend Nate. Both carried high-powered rifles.

"I couldn't think where else to go. I need to find your grandson."

"Now isn't that a revelation. Half of South Florida is looking for him. You were most likely followed by the police."

Janie smiled at the man's sarcasm. "True enough, but I was careful. If anyone knows where he might be it will be you."

Josh interjected. "We know where he was, as do you. He is no longer there. The people we left him with are dead and there is no sign of him. We thought he might show up outside the swamp. Jack would have tried to contact us. We think he's either dead or captured."

"Captured? Captured by who. The swamp people he was telling me about?"

"We have some ideas, and yes, they are on the top of that list."

"Do you plan on doing anything about it?"

Josh hesitated. "Yes, but this doesn't concern you."

"Listen. Don't give me any of that Indian bullshit about looking after one's own kind. I've got a stake in this and I'm going where you're going. You're going to have to tie me up or shoot me if you want to stop me."

Gramps put a hand on his grandson's leg. "I have seen her involvement in my dreams. Their paths are connected."

"I don't believe in any of that voodoo crap, but you heard the man. Our paths are connected." She turned to Gramps. "You've seen him in your dreams?"

"Thought you didn't believe in voodoo, Janie?" He smiled for the first time since she had arrived.

Janie leaned down and grasped his wrinkled, calloused hands. "I don't, but I need at least a glimmer of hope in order to build up enough courage to go any further. Look, I saw it in his eyes. Your grandson is not guilty."

"I told you that when we met days ago."

"No one we meet is guilty, right? I work for a criminal lawyer. Ninety percent of our clients are guilty. This is different, and it is high profile. Do you mind if I smoke?"

Gramps gestured approvingly.

Josh walked into the kitchen and soon returned with a six-pack of Coors Light. He handed one to Janie, who exhaled a thick stream of smoke from her wrinkled lips. "Liquid courage. Do you have anything stronger?"

"Nope, just light beer, it's Gramps' favorite, and he pays for it." Josh grinned.

Janie accepted the beer.

Josh handed one to the other men. "We leave a few hours before sunup. There are three possible groups that could be behind this mess, all of them old families. There's one that we'll call on first. I don't think it's them, but they might just give us some information. Are you still packing?"

Janie patted her handbag. "Always."

"Good, you may need it. You get shot, we're not slowing down. Understand? We'll have to dump you in the swamp."

Janie grimaced. The prospect of her lifeless body floating in the swamp as gator food sent a jolt of reality through her.

"Why do you want to come so badly? This is dangerous. You can wait here with Gramps."

"I can look after myself." She paused for a moment, thinking of a good response to Josh's question. "Maybe I'm just reckless." *And I need the money.*

* * * *

Janie didn't sleep and got up on her own accord. She heard Josh and Nathan milling about by the airboats out back of the huts. She grabbed her bag and hurried down to the dock. She wouldn't put it past them to leave her behind.

"Janie."

She was startled and turned to see Gramps sitting in a rickety wooden chair beside the back door. "Gramps?"

"The boys are just worried about you. I told them not to dump you."

"That gives me some comfort," she said, smiling slightly. She took a moment to light up a cigarette. "I don't care much what happens to me once I'm dead. Let them dump me, just let my boss know. He'll tell my family."

"Take this." He handed her a necklace with a woven pendant. Three glass beads hung from the bottom. "It's a talisman. It was given to me by my father to ward off evil spirits. I want it back if you return."

Janie accepted the gift. "If? Like I said, I don't believe in voodoo, but I will take it if it makes you feel better."

The old man met her eyes with his, holding her in place. Janie shivered. "I don't believe in trickery, but I do believe in spirits and the power they can convey upon the living. Take this advice and heed it well: you are dealing with sons of the devil. He is real, and he is powerful."

Janie took the relic and placed it over her head, tucking it under her shirt. "I will remember what you said."

"Hey, girlie," Nathan shouted. "We're leavin'."

Janie bent down and kissed the top of the old man's head. "I'll be bringing it back." She turned and hurried down to the airboat, which was being fired up, blue smoke pouring out from its exhaust.

23

HUNTER

SENATOR HUNTER SAT BEHIND the mahogany desk in his home office. His wife was still in bed. He expected that the Lorazepam she had taken would keep her knocked out for the rest of the day. He took a shot from the tumbler of bourbon that sat on his desk. He loved his wife, but no longer in the way that he had loved Phyllis. But now Phyllis was dead.

He pulled open the right hand drawer and looked down at the revolver. He picked up the cold, heavy, antique gun. It had been passed down from his grandfather and still worked impeccably. He tapped the barrel in the palm of his left hand and opened the magazine. Six rounds sat in their individual slots. He snapped it shut with a loud clunk. The feeling of the gun in his hand gave him a sense of power. He could bring about resolution with the weapon. He contemplated putting the barrel of the gun in his mouth and pulling the trigger, but he wasn't a coward. Cowards killed themselves. He was pissed off. He didn't like being pushed into a corner. This was more than a corner, it was the end of his career and the end of his family. It was murder . . .

He shook his head and returned the gun to its resting place in the drawer. He was a politician and would not resort to violence to solve his dilemma.

Hunter looked across at his one remaining intern now that Jack Walker was gone. Mike Perkins sat in a large leather chair by the door rubbing his head between his hands. He'd been with Hunter for a few years. Hunter used Perkins when he went to various functions. Since Walker had disappeared, Perkins had served as his driver. The senator and his family had grown quite fond of the young man, but the present situation had pushed the boundaries of any niceties.

Hunter placed the gun on the table. "Let's go over this again, Mike. How did they manage to sedate you? Your negligence has put me in an awful situation. I sent you a text partway through the evening telling you that I needed an excuse to leave."

Mike shook his head. "Last thing I remember I had parked the car and was talking to one of the serving girls. Wait . . . she did offer me a bottle of water. That's when I blacked out. Next thing I know, I'm lying here on your couch."

Hunter pursed his lips angrily. "I drove you home. You were sleeping like a baby in the back of the limo." Hunter paused for a moment, panic welling up in this throat. "The lady we went to see is trying to blackmail me."

"You didn't contact the police? I mean, what the hell happened, sir?"

Only he and the Satanists knew what had happened thus far. They were playing extreme hardball. If he'd contacted the police, he would be implicated in the mess even worse than he already was.

Mike stood up, nearly falling over. "I would like to offer you my resignation, sir. I take my job seriously and I messed up."

"Bullshit, Mike, you're a good man. We've all been fooled. I'm being pressured hard by the bastards who did this. Look, I need you to get my family out of here. Book a hotel up north. Savannah, the Hamptons, maybe Canada. Have my brother Robert take them. I'll give him a call if he asks you any questions."

"What about you?"

"I want you to stay with me, I need your help and I can't talk to anyone else. You know what's going on and that's bad enough.

These people we're dealing with are dangerous. They have made threats. If I contact the police, the game is up. I have to play this out for a day or so to see if I can salvage something."

"Where's Phyllis?"

Hunter's head dropped, his eyes closed. "I'm assuming that she is dead."

"What!" Mike shook his head, clearly shaken by the last comment. "This is out of hand. We have to call the cops. If you don't mind me saying, these situations don't usually work out for the best. There are experts who know how to deal with this type of situation."

"I know. I just need some time to think it out."

"Sir . . . I'm a bit scared here. It's kind of freaked me out being knocked out and all."

Hunter stood up and looked down at the young man. "Son, I need you to keep things together for a couple of days. That's it, that's all I'm asking for."

Perkins dropped his head for a moment, then met Hunter's eyes. "Okay. I will see to your family. How is Mrs. Hunter?"

"Mad as hell. She's going to want blood. Thankfully, she took a sedative. I need you to get her away, *now*."

Mike moved toward the door. "Got it."

Hunter slouched back into his chair and drained the last of his drink. He reached down beside his desk and lifted his leather briefcase, opened it, and placed the old revolver into it. He eyed the half-empty bottle of bourbon for a moment, but thought better of it. He needed a clear head.

His cell phone rang. He didn't recognize the number, but the same number had rung through earlier in the day. He'd given orders that he was not be disturbed. He wanted to hit the decline button, but something told him that the call just might be important.

"Hunter."

"Mr. Senator, this is Detective Rick Ramirez of the Lee County Sheriff's Department. Do you have a minute?"

"Detective Ramirez, who the hell gave you this number?"

"I understand your agitation, sir, and I apologize in advance. There is no such thing as an unlisted number for the State of Florida. We have our ways."

Hunter paused. "Fair enough. You've got one minute to tell me what you need to tell me. I am a busy man."

"Absolutely, sir. This won't take a moment. I believe, Senator Hunter, that your intern, Jackson Walker, has been set up in order to get to you. My partner and I believe that he is innocent. We would like to talk to you about some of our findings. Maybe you can shed some light on what's taken place over the past week."

Hunter paused. "Well, Ramirez, you're lucky that your timing is good. I'd like to hear what you have to say about Jack. I can't meet you at my home; I think I'm being watched. I'll call you back at this number in half an hour and tell you where we will meet."

"I appreciate it, Senator."

* * * *

Rick pulled up behind the idling Town Car. He turned to Lani. "He said that he wanted to go for a drive with us, that there were things happening, that he didn't trust anyone, that he was afraid someone would see him. We've got half an hour with the guy, then we're to bring him back to this same spot where his driver will be waiting."

"Okay Rick," Lani said as she placed the digital recorder under the seat. "I don't know how the hell you pulled this off."

"I'd like to say that it required skill, but I have the feeling that we just might have lucked out. The department wants to know what he has to say as soon as possible." He looked at her. "Is everything all right? You look a bit pale."

"I've just got a few personal things on my mind. I had a call from someone in my family last night," she lied, "and it's put me into a bit of a mood."

"You can't pick your family . . . Look, he's getting out." Rick hustled out of the front seat to greet the senator.

Hunter stepped out of the car and walked to the back of the cruiser. Rick helped him into the back seat. "Watch your head, sir." He smelled of alcohol, but he didn't appear to be drunk. Rick turned and flipped open his wallet to show the senator his ID and badge. Lani did the same from the front seat.

"Thank you for meeting us, Senator Hunter. I'm Detective Lani Green from the Florida Department of Law Enforcement.

This is Detective Ramirez from the Lee County Sheriff's department."

Hunter looked Rick in the eye. "Like I said, your timing was good. Please drive."

Rick pulled away from the curb. He saw the senator's car pull away at the same time and make a U-turn in the opposite direction.

Lani turned to face Hunter. "Mr. Senator, I won't beat around the bush, we are pressed for time. We are investigating the killings that took place nearly a week ago in Clewiston. As Detective Ramirez mentioned to you on the phone earlier, and as I'm sure you know, your intern Jack Walker is the prime suspect in those killings."

Hunter nodded. "Go on."

Rick interjected. "Like I said earlier, we don't think he did it."

"What makes you think that?" Hunter said.

Lani spoke. "He doesn't fit the psychological profile of a cultist. We intercepted one of Walker's cell phone calls to a friend and tracked down the recipient. The call came shortly after the killings occurred. His friend, after we threatened him with incarceration for aiding and abetting, indicated that Jack was seeing a girl who was a Satanist."

"Sarah Courtney."

"You know this woman, sir?"

"If you'd done your homework, you'd know that she worked out of the Republican office down in Naples . . . Of course I knew Courtney."

Rick spoke. "Lani is a cult specialist, sir. And yes, we have done our homework."

"Good to know. You now have twenty minutes."

Lani continued. "His friend Perry indicated that his infatuation with Courtney led him to attend some of the regular functions of the Brotherhood of Set, of which she is a member. The church has deep roots in South Florida, at least from what we can tell. There are similar sects throughout the country and around the world, and they exert influence in places that you would never suspect." Lani paused. "When I say that Walker doesn't fit the profile, I mean the profile of a Satanist. He does, however, fit the profile of someone the Satanists might target in order to press their interests. His friend Perry indicated that he was about to split with Courtney, as things were going a bit too far for his liking. They are clever when they bring you into their fold. Jack was probably asked to do something on their behalf and has been framed in doing so."

Rick interjected. "Do you know why the cult would have wanted to frame Walker? I suspect that it's tied in with your political dealings, Mr. Senator." Rick pressed his point. "I believe that they are putting pressure on you for some reason. I haven't been able to piece together the whole puzzle, but I suspect that you might be able to help us out."

Hunter was quiet for a few minutes. His face had turned grey. When he spoke, his voice seemed hesitant, slightly shaky. "My better instincts tell me that what I am going to say . . . is the correct thing to say." He looked out the window for a few moments. "I hadn't planned on doing this for a few days." He hesitated. "Can I take you into my confidence?"

Rick quickly replied, "Of course."

Lani deftly moved her hand under the car seat and turned off the digital recorder while Rick navigated through a left hand turn.

"I was told not to contact the authorities."

Rick inadvertently let the car slow down and the driver in the car behind them lay down on his horn. Rick sped up. "Mr. Senator, I assure you that you are doing the correct thing. Now. I am going to pull over so we can take some notes. Do you mind if we record what you have to say?"

"No I don't, but I have some conditions. I am telling you only because you are closer to the truth than you might think, and I don't know how to move this thing forward without creating an even bigger fiasco. I don't want to jeopardize the safety of my family. These people have made threats."

Rick pulled into a side street and stopped the car in front of a large furniture warehouse. "You're being blackmailed?"

Hunter nodded.

As she pulled a pen out of her jacket pocket, Lani slipped off the safety on her Glock semi-automatic pistol.

"If I confess to the authorities—and this of course means you—they have threatened to kill my family, and let the cat out of the bag about my affair with my assistant Phyllis." Hunter let his head fall back against the headrest. "I don't mind confiding in you as long as nothing is said until I have the chance to resolve matters in my own time." He looked down at his feet. "Yes, I have been implicated in the Jackson Walker mess, but that's only the tip of the iceberg. They have pictures of me openly socializing with the national head of the Church of Satan, Mason Matye. They have pictures of me having sex with Phyllis. The other night I was invited to a dinner where I was broadsided by the Satanist bastards. They have killed Phyllis and threatened to implicate me unless I back off on the Clean Water Bill."

Rick exhaled loudly. "Christ!"

In one swift motion Lani pulled the Glock from its holster and placed the muzzle of the gun against Rick's head. Rick was too shocked and caught off guard to react. "You were told not to contact the authorities, Senator Hunter." Lani squeezed the trigger as Rick moved to knock her arm away. The bullet exited the back of Rick's head, shattering the side window of the car. He slumped against the door. She turned and pointed the gun at Hunter. "Don't make a sound!" Hunter put his hands up.

Lani pushed the security locks, making sure that Hunter couldn't get out of the car. The back seat, once locked down with the security mesh between the front and back seat, was impossible to get out of. She decided that cuffing him on her own might be risky; she decided to leave him be. She then reached over Rick's body and opened the car door. With some difficulty, she unbuckled Rick's seatbelt and pushed him out the door, his body falling in a heap beside the car. She pulled herself out of the passenger's seat. With her jacket, she removed as much blood, bone, and brain matter as she could from the driver's seat and side door panel.

Lani didn't have much time; soon someone would pass by. Ramirez's body lay in a fetal position wedged under the side of the car. Lani pushed him up against a chain link fence next to a large clump of tall weeds. Using some road debris, she hid the body from anything but close inspection. She knocked out the rest of the glass and slipped in behind the wheel. Within minutes, the car was headed south down Highway 41 toward Naples.

"What the hell have you done!" Hunter yelled.

Lani lost it. "If you had just done as you were fucking told, we wouldn't be in this mess."

"We?"

"Yes, *we*. You realize they most likely won't let either of us live."

"Who are they?"

"The Satanists, that's who. The goddamned devil worshipers, remember? The ones we have been talking about."

* * * *

The call she'd received the night before ran through her head again, his voice calm and measured with its French inflection:

"Lani, it has been some time since we last talked—years, in fact. You made a deal with the devil, my dear, and it is time to pay up. I made sure that you were the one who would be called in on the Walker case. We need you to keep an eye on Senator Hunter. We have been applying some pressure on the man. We need to know that if he decides to speak to the police, he will be intercepted and silenced. Like you, I am doing an old friend a favor. I need to know that I will not be disappointed . . . Lani."

Hunter broke Lani's trance. "Whatever it is you think you have to do, it doesn't have to happen. You can drive us back to my house We will sit down and talk this through."

Lani sat quietly for a moment, concentrating on the road. If she did what Hunter was proposing, the Satanists would hunt her down. They had their ways; they still had their claws on her. She feared what they might do to her even more than incarceration. She wished that she hadn't had to kill Rick, but it had to be done. Rick was a straight shooter, a by-the-book cop. He would have reported what he'd heard from the senator. She'd hoped and prayed that Hunter would hold his silence, that she wouldn't have to do what she'd just done.

"Mr. Senator, I don't think your situation puts you in a position of power anymore. You have been implicated with the Satanists, and in fact, probably had an affair with one of them. You're just as screwed as I am." As the words left her mouth, she wished she hadn't said them. She wasn't thinking clearly.

"So you're one of them?"

Silence for a moment. "Yes, I guess so, yes. I spent some time in deep cover with them many years ago. I had no intention to participate in their practices, but they have their ways of drawing you in, even if you don't want to, much like what probably happened to Walker. They are like the Mafia. Once you're in, you're in for life."

"So you're going to take me to them and they're going to kill both of us. That makes a hell of a lot of sense."

"Nope, I've done what was asked of me, so hopefully they will still have some use for me. You . . . you should have kept your fucking mouth shut. They were only asking for more time before you flood their farmlands. Something could have been worked out. Now be quiet. I'm not in the best of moods. I just killed a police officer and kidnapped a state senator. Nope, just don't say another fucking word or I'm going to turn around and put a hole in your forehead."

Hunter was a caged animal, his face a deep shade of red, his arms folded across his chest. "You are delusional if you think they're going to let you off the hook. You've been manipulated as badly as I have, as badly as Jackson Walker."

24

THE DELIVERY

JACK STIRRED. HE'D BEEN drifting in and out, but this time something was different. There was a weight upon his chest and a tickling sensation. Was it sniffing? *Christ*! He tried to push whatever it was off of him, but his numb hands were painfully tied behind his back. He could feel its claws digging into his chest as he struggled. He rolled to the left, away from the smelly pile of rags that his head rested on. The animal fell off him, its long skinny tail slapping him in the face as it scurried off into the recesses of the dark room. There were spiders and cockroaches, but it was the rats that scared the hell out of him. He feared falling asleep to awaken to his flesh—or worse, his eyes—being eaten by the hellish creatures. He'd been able to fend them off, but they were becoming bold and he didn't know how much longer he would be able to keep up the battle.

Jack had lost track of how long he'd been captured. It might have been two days, maybe three. He could hear the crickets, and there was a sliver of moonbeam threading its way through the cracks between the planked walls of his cell. He could hear snoring from the adjoining room. He shook his head to stay awake. He didn't want to go over the events of the past weeks and months as he'd been doing for the past few days. Worry was beginning to drive him nuts. He had to let go of what he could not control. For now, he would try his best to stay alive.

He cursed his naiveté. He'd been too trusting of people. Sarah, Buck, Henrietta, his father. He began to shake with fury. *Damn them all.* If he were to somehow survive, he would change. He laid his head back down on the kerosene-scented rags and closed his eyes for a time. Without intending to do so, he fell into a dreamless sleep.

"Wake up, you lazy bastard." Jack was ejected from his slumber by the hard end of a boot to his ribs. His body clenched in agony. He looked up. It was daytime, he could see the silhouette of the pucker-faced Jimmy standing over him.

"Wake up, you lazy bastard," Jimmy repeated. "It's time to feed you to the gators." He pursed his misshaped lips. "The woman phoned. Says she has no need for you. Lucky bugger, time to put you out of your fucking misery." Jimmy laughed. "Yep, time to put you out of your fucking misery." He reached down and dragged Jack by his feet.

Halfway out of the room, Jimmy reached to his belt and pulled out a fillet knife and cut the rope that tied his hands to his ankles. "Can't drag you that way, you bugger . . . you lucky fucking bugger." His face formed that horrible pucker that Jack had learned to dread. He resisted the urge to struggle—just yet. Jimmy dumped him in the middle of the large room. To his right he could see the blond man sitting at a small table, impeccably dressed, reading a newspaper and sipping from a tea cup. He turned casually towards them. "Just leave him there for the time being. We'll have to wait until nightfall. We have another one coming in, a senator no less. Special instructions to follow, my dear brother. They should be here in half an hour."

Jimmy frowned and nodded toward Jack. "Thought you said we're gonna kill him?"

"Patience, little brother. We must follow the demands of the old woman. She's the one paying us, and she wants him alive for the moment. Leave him there, I want him to look lively when she gets here."

Jack's fury continued to mount. His eyes found the metal mortician's table a few feet to his right. How many people had they tortured and killed? They needed to be found out. No, a prison cell would be too good for them. He would kill them both if he got half the chance.

****

Jimmy and Isaac stood out in front of the shed, its wide, sliding door open to the hot, dusty driveway. They watched the black sedan roll into the yard. A blonde woman stepped out of the driver's side door. She was probably in her mid-to-late 40s and had a gun holster strapped across her chest. As she moved toward them, they could see bloodstains on her shirt and the left side of her face; her hair was matted.

"Mr. McFadden?" Her voice was gravelly with a hint of shakiness.

Isaac stepped forward, offering her his hand. She shrugged it off.

"Isaac McFadden, ma'am."

Her eyes held a wild look, darting left and right as if she were looking for something or someone. "They said you might have another car for me?"

The car began to rock slightly from side to side. They heard muted yelling from within.

"You'll have fun getting him out of there; he's been going nuts in there. He's not tied down but he is locked in. Here's the keys." She handed them to Isaac.

"So this is the fucking senator?" Jimmy said in a gleeful burst.

She nodded slightly and turned away quickly.

Isaac motioned towards the shed. "Would you like some tea? It might take some time to get another car." He motioned toward the sedan. "We can let him bake in the sun for a time. It will make him more docile."

"I didn't get your name?"

"Green, Det—" She interrupted herself. "Lani Green."

"How do you take it? Or would you prefer coffee? I can make some in the house."

Isaac guided Lani into the garage by her elbow and offered her a chair at his table. She moved along with him like a ghost.

The room was ablaze with radios and TVs. "I have to apologize for the noise, Ms. Green. You see, my brother has a mental issue, and the sound allows him to concentrate on being normal. Otherwise he would be . . . difficult to be around."

"Oh." As she sat she noticed Jack lying on the floor, his eyes focused upon her.

She recognized his face, having looked at pictures of him a hundred times over the past few days. "With sugar, please, tea is fine." Her eyes darted back and forth from Walker to Isaac.

"Earl Grey, you might find it calming."

With shaking hands, Lani accepted the fine china teacup, rattling it ever so slightly on the matching saucer. "So this must be the infamous Jackson Walker?"

Jack's eyes bulged as he shook his head vigorously from side to side. He tried to groan a word through his sewn lips.

"Indeed. He's in a cranky mood this morning, please just ignore him. He is normally quite congenial."

Lani shook her head slightly and sipped some more of the flowery but bitter black tea, her eyes flowing back and forth between Isaac and Walker again. She couldn't resist; her years of training got the better of her. "Aren't you afraid of being found out, Mr. McFadden?"

"Why the concern, Ms. Green? And by the way, I know all about you, how you became a member of the church." He sipped his tea, delicately holding the handle of the thin china cup between his thumb and forefinger. "I also know that you are a cop. You might just have sold yourself too cheaply. I hope that what you received in turn was worth dying for." He smiled, looking at her, his brows pushing down ever so slightly.

"Dying, Mr. McFadden? Is that a threat?"

"Take it for what it is. You are dealing with a bunch of devil worshipers. If you play with fire, you are bound to get burned . . . that's all."

"You are on the prime suspects list. I redirected Ramirez—my partner—away from your file more than once. I did the same for Henrietta LePley. Ramirez is dead," she said with a slight quiver to her voice. "But still, it's only a matter of time before the police are onto you." She shook her head.

"My brother and I are cleaners, Ms. Green. Do you know

what a cleaner is?"

"Of course." Her hands grew heavy. She dropped the tea cup on the floor; it shattered into dozens of pieces. She tried to stand. "Christ, I'm sorry." She fell back into her chair.

Isaac stood and stepped to her side. He could tell that her body was now numb, and her eyes slowly turned to meet his. "Removing bodies and any evidence of their existence is our family business. We have been doing it for more than a century. The Church of Satan, The Brotherhood of Set, or whatever you choose to call them, they pay their bills quite lavishly. By tomorrow, your remains will be nothing more than a trace of protein floating in the vast river of grass. The Everglades are very efficient at cleansing; it is a good partnership. Your DNA will be spread between here and Florida Bay within a week. You see, I have poisoned you, Ms. Green. You will be able to see and feel what is happening to you. Your mind will be unaffected. You know that by now, don't you? Your motor skills have left you. By nightfall, your heart will slowly stop beating. It really is a terrifying way to die, fully aware of it all. Yet, even so, young Mr. Walker will wish he had the same fate as you by the time we are finished with him." He removed the handgun that hung at her side. She was helpless to resist. Isaac watched as she slumped to the ground, her body limp as a rag doll.

"Pity. That was Mommy's favorite cup, Jimmy."

"She will have to fucking pay. Right, Isaac?"

"Yes Jimmy, she will have to pay. She is a cop who knows too much. We will have to put her on the hooks and wait for nightfall, then you can bleed her out."

Jimmy chuckled. "Yep, on the hooks for you, girlie."

The brothers picked up Lani, each by an arm, and carried her to the back corner of the building. A series of tracks lined the ceiling, leading to various parts of the large room, as well as leading out over the back dock. On the track were numerous large metal hooks that were used for hanging cattle carcases ready for butchering. Jimmy moved a small footstool over so that he could guide two of the hooks to either side of her neck and under both of Lani's collarbones. Isaac lifted her up as Jimmy drove home the sharpened hooks with a small mallet.

"I do wish Eric wasn't dead, Jimmy. This is work unbefitting a gentleman." Her weight was released and she was left to hang. Blood trickled out of the wounds to wet her shirt.

"She'll last until midnight, I bet," Jimmy chortled.

Lani's eyes stood out on her face like perfect little circles, her pupils dilated black holes in the whiteness.

Jimmy looked at Jack, a horrible smile forming, his yellow teeth clenched together. Jack started to struggle for all he was worth. Jimmy went over to him and kicked him in the back of his head, temporarily stunning him and making Jimmy giggle. "Once they're on the hooks, they don't struggle."

Isaac moved between Jimmy and Jack, putting his hands on his younger brother's shoulders. He looked him straight in the eye. "The old woman said she wants him alive, at least until tomorrow." Jack calmed down, hearing Isaac's words. "Leave him out, he's not going anywhere trussed up like that. Tie him to the couch."

* * * *

Isaac and Jimmy went outside to the car. Isaac pondered how they would get Hunter out of it. "Sometimes a simple plan is the best. Brute force and a bullet," he muttered under his breath. "This should have been Eric's job, little brother. We'll just have to make do, won't we?" Isaac looked through the window, measuring up what he thought the senator would do when the door opened. "Grab his legs as soon as I open the door, Jimmy. If he backs himself in, you'll have to go and get him." Isaac took Lani's handgun out of his pocket and fiddled with it for a moment, taking the safety off.

Jimmy opened the door and as he did so, the senator tried to kick him in the chest. Jimmy grabbed on for all he was worth, pulling him halfway out of the car. Isaac aimed Lani's handgun and fired one shot, blowing off half of Hunter's knee. He stopped struggling instantly. Jimmy dragged him out of the car and into the driveway. Isaac meshed his hands into the man's hair, getting a good grip, then whacked him on the back of his head with the gun. Hunter was more than adequately subdued.

"That's a nice piece of work, brother. Once we take care of our visitor, I want you to take this car to that sinkhole out past the Freel's place. We haven't used it in years, been saving it for a special occasion."

Isaac's phone rang. He pressed the answer button and held the device up to his ear. "Yes, Henrietta . . . I understand. We'll be ready and waiting."

"One more for the fucking hooks?" mumbled Jimmy. His smile was wide as his puckered mouth would allow.

"I'm not sure about the hooks, little brother." Jimmy's smile evaporated. "Tie him up and gag him. The old woman wants this one alive as well."

* * * *

Henrietta put the cell phone back in her purse. She could see Buck watching her in the rear view mirror as he drove. Henrietta liked to sit in the back. She sighed and muttered as if talking to someone beside her. "Yes it's a damn shame."

Buck turned his head towards the back of the car, doing his best to keep his eyes on the road. "What did you say? What's a shame, Henrietta?"

"Keep your eyes on the road, please. You are getting too old to drive like that. You know by now that I talk to myself. It is a witch's prerogative. It's not wise to questions a witch's prerogative, Mr. Henderson."

Mason Matye, who was sittiing in the front passenger's seat, chuckled.

"We have the senator. That was Isaac McFadden. We have to clean up this mess, it's time to kill them all, Buck. It's time to cut our losses. The senator, Walker, anyone else that we deem to be a loose end, must die."

"And the farmland?"

"Plan B," said Henrietta.

"That doesn't sound promising."

"Subtlety has always been our strength, Buck. That which has transpired has not been subtle. We have orchestrated assassinations in the past that still garner attention. Politicians are not immune to being killed. We are nowhere close to achieving what we want, and events have spiraled out of control. It's time to regain control. We have lots of money, more than we know what to do with. It is time to step back. How far is it to the McFadden estate?"

"Estate?" Buck said. "I'd say an hour with this traffic. What about the senator? How the hell are we going to dispose of him?"

"I think we need to find an untimely end for Hunter. Have we found out where his family is? We shouldn't have let them out of our sight,"

"We have her under surveillance. Hunter's wife has gone north." Buck returned his gaze to the road. "I didn't think Hunter would defy us."

"These things happen. Have Mrs. Hunter poisoned at your soonest convenience, she knows too much." Henrietta folded her hands behind her neck and stretched. The day's events had given her a headache.

"As you wish." Buck turned his head back to the front of the car as they neared a stoplight.

"We will use Walker. If we set it up correctly, it will work nicely. His hands will be all over the Hunter assassination and the killing of the rest of his family. The Clewiston deaths will disappear. Then we will have Jackson Walker come to some fiendish end. The Georgia Satanists are devilishly good at such things, aren't they Mason?"

"Indeed they are, Miss Henrietta. If there is any way that my people can help, we would be more than happy to lend a hand," said Mason.

Henrietta smiled. "Thank you, Mason, but it won't be necessary. I have a dear friend who is associated with the church in Savannah. You see Buck, people want to believe in evil and the things that evil people do. It makes for great press. Nobody likes to watch pleasant news; it's boring. In a couple of days, we will leak the news that Walker has been spotted in Georgia. It's messy, but I think it will work out just fine. I will need you to deliver him."

Buck hesitated for a moment, not happy with her last sentence, but he knew better than to argue. "You have never been wrong, Henrietta."

"Not in over a hundred years. We will have to try and bend the governor's arm. I feared that it would come to this. Some of our people know some of his people. We'll save our farmland yet, Mr. Henderson. Now, concentrate on the road. Get us there in one piece, if you will."

25

THE EVERGLADES

"STAY LOW, JANIE. THESE folk don't take kindly to people trespassing on their land. Old Pete has more bluster than a trussed-up gator. I want to ask him a few things."

Nate navigated the prop boat up against the rickety dock. Josh jumped up to tie the boat down. As he turned to grab the bow line, he was greeted with the muzzle of a double-barreled shotgun. An older man wearing overalls and no shirt spit a black gob of tobacco juice into the water next to the dock. His voice was heavily accented in Floridian drawl.

"You got no business here, Injun. Back your sorry ass outta here."

Josh could tell instantly that the Lee brothers were not their quarry.

"No harm done, brother. Any idea where the Walker boy might be?"

The man lowered his gun. "I've heard what I've heard and the swamp don't give up its secrets. Get off my property."

"The McFaddens?" Josh probed.

The man smiled. "I don't know nothin' about that. They're a bad lot, them. Wouldn't surprise me. Stay away from them, and you ain't heard nothin' from me. Y'all hear?"

"What about the Peters, up on Okeechobee?"

"Like I said, I don't know nothin' about them either, so get outta here." He raised the gun again.

Josh knew better than to press the matter. "Thank you, sir." Josh turned to Nate. "Back 'er out."

Old Pete fired back a parting comment. "Y'all don't come back here. We stay off Injun lands. You stay off ours."

Josh nodded, slowly backing his way into the boat, not taking his eyes off the man. He motioned for Nate to back away from the dock. Once they were a good distance away, Janie nudged Josh in the shoulder. He turned his head to the side so he could hear her.

"So why did we go there?" she shouted over the loud engine.

Josh yelled back. "I didn't think it would be him, but he as much as told us that the McFaddens might be involved. There could be a few others, but I figure they're one of the closest possibilities. Whatever is going on, or whoever is responsible, has its roots in the southwest. Now I know there are a few other families located on the East Coast, but we have to deal with the obvious."

"Are they one of those devil-worshiping families Jack was talking about?"

"I don't know about devil worship, but they're notorious for doing dirty work for the old families. I think they might know what's going on, if they're not involved. We'll need a plan if we're to get close to them."

Janie took a moment to think. "So . . . you have no goddamned plan?"

"Sorry Janie, I do have a plan, but things don't always happen as you expect them to. I've never been to the McFadden homestead. I don't know the lay of the land."

"You're fucking kidding me. I'm no expert, but if we roar in there and we hit pay dirt, the bastards are going to shoot us. I would if I were them. Pull this goddamned boat over and turn off the engine. I need a fucking cigarette. You guys are goddamned lucky I came along. You can't just go into some devil's hole like the Lone Ranger and Tonto. Christ, I'm no munitions expert, but I have a handgun and I see two hunting rifles. That guy back there, Old Bart?"

"Pete."

"Okay. Old Pete could've blown off your head in two seconds and done some serious damage to Nate and me. We need a machine gun or something."

Josh motioned for Nate to slow the boat. Nate left the boat idling in the middle of the channel. Janie didn't take twenty seconds to light up her cigarette, taking a long drag.

Nate spoke up. "She's right. I've been thinking the same thing. What if we pull up some way from the place and sneak in?"

"Pull up and sneak in? This is getting better by the minute." Janie pulled her hand through her blonde hair and shook her head. "I think we should call the cops. This has gone too far. Why haven't the cops checked out these people?"

"Hey Janie, calm down. I don't know that they haven't." Josh put his hands on her shoulders. "All I know is that we've waited around for a few days now and there's a good chance my cousin is in that place. If we wait any longer, he might be killed. This is swamp justice, darlin'. It's been going on for a hundred years."

"Fucking great. Don't you guys have a tribe or something? I'm not up on my native culture bullshit, or whatever you want to call it. It's just the two of you and me, shouldn't we have some backup?"

"Yes, we do have a tribe, but it's not called that anymore, and there's not many of us, and even fewer who would risk their lives for Jack."

"What about the poor bastard who had his head shot off on that island? Didn't he have some cousins we can call?"

"Good point," said Josh.

Nate punched Josh lightly in the shoulder. "She's right. We could call up Blaze and Robbie and tell them to cover the front of the place so we have some backup." He looked Janie in the eye.

She exhaled a plume of grey smoke. "Blaze and Robbie? Great, they sound like action heroes."

Josh let go of her shoulder. "Got any better ideas?" He waved the smoke from his face. "Here's what we're going to do. We'll get the boys to watch the other side of the place. It'll take some time for them to get here. Then we'll scope the place out. We can pole the boat up close. It's a big estate, if what Gramps says is true. We'll check things out the best we can. I don't trust the cops not to fuck this up and get Jack killed, but we'll call them if things look dicey. Fair enough?"

Janie tossed the half-finished smoke into the water. "It doesn't sound like a great plan, but at least we're not heading in there like a bunch of idiots. Are we going to ask these McFaddens anything if we're greeted like we were by Old Pete?"

"Not sure." He looked to Nate. "I think we're heading to the right spot. We don't need to overthink this. If they are the bad guys, they'll be shooting and asking questions later. I'd like to get a look at the place up close. Nate, call those guys up. Never know, they could be high as kites at this time of the night. Janie." He put his hands on her shoulders. "I just want to see if he's there. We may not be able to tell, but I have to try. You can stay in the boat if you want."

Janie contemplated the offer. "Nope. I'm not sitting out here on my own. What if something happens to the two of you? I don't know how to run this thing," she patted the side of the boat, "and I don't know where the hell I'm going. I'm coming with you."

* * * *

"The old woman's here," Isaac shouted into the shop. Jimmy didn't answer. He stepped further in. "They're here, Jimmy. You'll have to turn down those televisions a bit."

Jack was propped up against one of the easy chairs, his hands and feet still bound. From time to time he would look at the woman hanging from the ceiling track. She'd long ago lost consciousness. He shivered. It was only time before he suffered the same fate. He worried about his feet and hands. He couldn't feel them anymore, and he feared that he might have suffered irreparable damage.

Isaac's words came to him in a haze as he drifted in and out of his stupor. *The old woman?* He craned his head toward the door.

* * * *

Buck guided the Town Car down the long stretch of driveway that lead to the back of the McFadden property. He was greeted by Isaac McFadden, impeccably dressed in white pants, a grey jacket, and a paisley tie. He shook Buck's hand as he got out of the car. "Mr. Henderson, always a pleasure."

Buck opened the back door and helped Henrietta out of the car. "I wouldn't call this a pleasure, Isaac. It's a bit of a balls-up if you ask me."

Isaac moved to kiss Henrietta on the cheek. With apprehension, he greeted the matriarch. "Miss LePley, it's grand to see you again so soon."

Henrietta returned the gesture with a feigned smile, her thin lips stretched across her perfectly straight teeth. "Isaac, I trust that you have tethered our prisoners appropriately? We cannot afford any more . . . " she looked to the ground, "disappointments."

"Yes ma'am. I'm sure that they will both be pleased to see you on this fine evening."

"Don't be so ingratiating, Isaac. I'm not in the mood for it."

"Please come inside." Isaac led Henrietta and Buck into the workshop. Henrietta winced at the sound of the televisions and the stale-smelling air. "These devices must be turned off."

Isaac shook his head. "If you want my brother Jimmy to remain in a pleasant mood, they must remain on. We must keep him focused on the task at hand. If we turn off the TVs, his mind will wander. We don't want that."

An evil look spread across Henrietta's face, her mouth drawn back in a snarl. "Let's make this quick then." She turned to Lani Green, hanging on the hooks. There was no movement other than a shallow rising and falling of her chest. "There can be no sign of this one, Isaac. Have your brother dispose of her now, while we discuss the fate of the other two."

"But that will take time, Miss LePley. We were taught by our daddy not to rush things. It is delicate work to dispose of a body properly. The bones must be broken up, the teeth ground, the body parts scattered. The Everglades must be allowed time to do its thing."

Henrietta's face drew in upon itself, projecting a menacing stare. "Do it now," she said with an eerily level voice. Isaac didn't argue.

"Jimmy, it's time to get rid of the girl, and do kill her first so we can save some time. This might prove to be a busy night."

Jimmy looked up from a knife he was in the process of honing to a razor's edge. "Do I have some time with her?"

"No time, Jimmy. I said kill the girl now. Straight to the swamp."

Jimmy looked at Henrietta. He didn't like the woman. He imagined drawing the blade across her thin, wrinkled throat; it would be like cutting butter. But then he quickly changed tack, as he remembered that she paid the brothers well. "H-help me get 'er off the hooks, Isaac."

"Buck, please give the boys a hand."

Buck didn't seem all too pleased at the prospect, but nodded. Within a couple of minutes, Lani was lying on the silver mortician's table, her head lolling from side to side. The surface was protected with a large plastic sheet that hung over the edges and covered six or seven feet of the floor. Jimmy went to the back of the shed and returned with a circular saw, the kind surgeons used for amputations. He plugged it into a socket on the wall beside the table and placed the tool on the table beside the woman.

Henrietta shook her head. "She sold her soul to the devil, poor girl." Her face broke out into an even smile. "Everything has its cost."

Jack closed his eyes, resting his head against the back of the chair. He didn't want to draw attention to himself. For the first time since he'd been taken captive, he saw a chink in the McFadden armor—they deferred to Henrietta. Had he been left to the brothers' whims, he would be dead by now, he was sure of it.

Jimmy started to dismember the body. Jack watched out of the corner of his eye as a line of red ran its way down a plastic tube and then into a large metal bucket. He shuddered. These bastards knew what they were doing. Jimmy saw Jack watching and grinned. "Gonna be you soon enough."

Jack could hear Henrietta, Buck and Isaac talking just outside the shed. The discussion seemed a bit heated, but he couldn't understand what was being said over the roar of Jimmy's power tools.

The sound of the electric saw continued. Every now and then it would labor, followed by a burning smell, like cooked meat. There was a thud. He could see one of the woman's hands hit the floor—very little blood.

It didn't take Jimmy long to chop up the body. Soon there was a pile of body parts on the floor on top of the large plastic sheet, and the saw was turned off.

Jimmy emerged at the side of the table holding the head of the woman by the hair, its mouth hanging open, the tongue protruding farther than Jack would have thought possible. Jimmy saw Jack looking.

"This is gonna be you soon enough, you motherfucker. Yep, gonna be you soon, your tongue will be hanging just the same, no muscles to hold it in. Grind up the head and get rid of the teeth. No records then. Rest goes t' the gators." He picked up a plastic bag and put the head in it, along with the woman's hands. He tossed the bag and it landed on the bench with a soft thump. The rest of the body parts were wrapped up in the large plastic sheet that had covered the table and floor.

Jack watched as the chubby little man took both the bag and the wrapped-up body parts out to the dock. Jimmy came back and carefully retrieved the large bucket that contained the woman's blood. Jack didn't bother trying to hide the fact that he was watching; he stared, giving his best evil eye, but it had no effect upon the demented villain.

* * * *

Nate cut the boat's engine half a mile from the McFadden property. He and Josh paddled the boat the rest of the way. "It's just around the next bend, according to the GPS," Josh whispered.

Janie didn't like the feeling in the pit of her stomach. She tried to remain calm but found herself moving this way and that, tapping her foot on the floor of the boat. Nate put a hand on Janie's shoulder. "Have to stop that; sound carries over water." She nodded and wrapped her arms around her front, just under her breasts, trying to squeeze her restless body into submission.

As they rounded the bend in the river, the light from a structure that sat on the river's edge lit up a small bay in front of it. They neared, and saw a long dock with a light on the end of it, thousands of bugs swarming around it.

"This is it," whispered Nate, looking down at the GPS again.

The boys edged the boat into the tall grass near the shoreline. Both men got out into the waist-deep water and pulled the boat further into cover, quickly jumping back. A well-equipped bass boat sat tied up to the dock. Josh whispered as he checked to see if his rifle was loaded—for the third time. "Let's lie low for a bit and have a look." Janie wasn't sure if Josh made the suggestion more out of indecision than prudent planning, but she and Nate nodded at the same time, relieved at the short reprieve.

There was life within the boat house. Janie could see shadows moving. After ten minutes or so, a short chubby man walked out to the end of the dock and placed a couple of bundles down into the fishing boat. He retreated and returned with a bucket of something that he poured over the side of the dock. He leaned down and swished it out with water, then returned to the building. Within a couple of minutes, Janie saw some movement on the top of the water beside the mooring. She was too far away to make out its cause. "Gators?"

Nate nodded. "Or catfish, who knows. We get bull sharks up this far and it's breeding season."

"Nice," Janie said under her breath.

"Yep, they can live in fresh water for a time. What the heck is that guy up to?"

Janie ducked as the man reappeared on the dock. She looked over to see that Josh and Nate had done the same. The chubby man jumped down into the boat and fired up the large black Mercury outboard that hung off the rear, tossed the mooring lines onto the dock, and then backed into the channel.

Josh began to fidget. "Crap, if he comes this way, he might see us."

* * * *

Jack was relieved when Jimmy left the building. He heard the boat's engine fire, and listened as it idled away from the dock. His attention turned to the four figures returning to the building. As they entered the light he could see Isaac, Buck, Henrietta and a swarthy-looking thin man whom he'd never seen before. The man had a very distinctive, menacing face, one that he would have remembered.

Henrietta frowned. "Can you turn off these televisions? Your brother is gone."

Isaac put his hands together and made a slight bow. "Of course, Henrietta." He moved from set to set and soon the room was eerily quiet.

"When you're finished, could you please escort in Mr. Hunter."

Henrietta seemed a bit more at ease with the televisions turned off. She walked up to Jack and hovered over him with narrowed eyes. She reached down and held his chin, forcing him to face her. Her breath was like honey and strawberries. He had the strangest urge to kiss the old woman. Then it struck him—Sarah's breath had been the same. He couldn't take his attention off the woman long enough to ponder the possibilities.

"You have been a useful tool, young man. We have one more request."

Isaac interrupted Henrietta as he dragged Hunter into the room. He looked terrible—his face was drawn, and his normally perfect hair stood up every which way. His knee was wrapped in a towel, the blood from the gunshot wound seeping through. Isaac heaved Hunter down onto the couch beside Jack. The senator looked Jack in the eye, his face riveted in pain.

Henrietta stood looking at the two helpless men. "As I was saying. We need Mr. Walker for one last job. You see, Senator Hunter, we must kill your family and who better than an on-the-run Satanist? Everyone knows too much to remain alive. You became an associate of the Brotherhood of Set, as did your intern. People will believe it. Mr. Walker, you remain the drug-using crazed cult killer. We'll concoct a devilish scene for your death, James. The public will love it." She turned to Jack. "We will make sure that you are shot in the act of killing the Hunters. Perfect."

"Buck, you and Mason please take Mr. Walker to Savannah and personally oversee the slaughter of the good senator's family. They are under surveillance?"

Buck nodded.

"Good. I'll call my pilot and make sure the jet is fueled and ready for take-off."

Buck didn't look happy. His cheeks were slightly flushed and he hunched over just a little. It was a lot to ask of a man nearing eighty.

Mason interjected. "Madam, you have the full backing of the Church of Satan. We can help to ease the load." He made an accepting gesture with his hands.

"Thank you. I knew that you would see things our way. So mote it be."

Buck walked over to Jack and picked him up by the shoulders. "Isaac, give me a knife so I can cut Jack's feet loose. I'm getting too old for this horseshit. He won't be running after being trussed up like this for days."

"I wouldn't do that. Let's get him into the trunk of your car first. Once you're gone, I will bury the senator out back beside the hogs. Jimmy has an old wooden casket he uses for this purpose. He'll last a day or so in there if we put a piece of hose in the ground."

Henrietta put a hand on Isaac's shoulder. "I do like the idea of the box, it's simply terrifying. Yes, bury him out back until we can figure out what to do with him, Isaac, but do . . . just keep him alive. You see, James, I will allow myself the pleasure of your torment. None of this had to happen, but you made your choice."

Jack couldn't hold in his fury any longer and started to struggle. Isaac, Buck and Mason moved to get a handle on him. Isaac cursed: "Okay, we'll do this the hard way." He took out Lani's handgun from his pocket and raised it to strike him.

Jack stopped and shook his head. He'd been hit too many times in the head, one more might be the end of him.

"Now that's better."

Isaac helped Buck and Mason stow Jack in the trunk of Buck's Caddie. Isaac let out a sigh of relief as he said his goodbyes and the vehicle made its way off the property. Jack Walker's departure meant one less thing to worry about. The situation was teetering out of control. There were too many loose ends. He feared that Jimmy and he were going to get caught. He feared that Henrietta was going to let them take the fall for everything—he wouldn't put it past her. It took a great deal of skill and know-how to dispose of a body. It had to be done methodically. He'd told Jimmy to take his time dispersing the cop's body. Without the expertise of their older brother Eric, they would be hard pressed to dispose of multiple bodies without getting sloppy. Their eldest brother had been good at fixing these sorts of messes. Isaac wasn't used to working in the trenches, and his hackles were on end. He walked slowly back into the shed where Henrietta stood, having a conversation with herself. He shook his head. *Would he have to kill her?*

Isaac drew a heavy breath. Henrietta sat on the large couch that lay misshapen in the middle of the room. "Henrietta, I'm going to truss him up and gag him in the closet until I have a chance to dig his grave. I'll need Jimmy's help."

"You know best, Isaac. When Jimmy gets back, take the time you need to clean things up. Bury the senator so that you can pass close inspection if the authorities show up. I will give you instructions as future events bring some clarity to the matter."

"Things are a bit messy for my liking, Henrietta. We pride ourselves on being meticulous."

"Don't worry, Isaac. McFadden Inc. will be well-compensated."

* * * *

"Christ, he's coming this way," whispered Janie. "What now?"

"Just keep below the gunnels. Nate, get ready to fire up the engine." Josh got down on one knee and leveled his rifle towards the oncoming boat. The driver didn't seem in too much of a hurry, and was busy moving things around below the deck of the boat as he navigated the dead calm waterway.

Janie was sure that the man would see their airboat. The protective frame for the prop and driver's seat stuck partway up above the grass. Janie turned to look at Josh as he cocked his rifle, his eyes narrowing as he took careful aim. As the boat sat down to plane, it suddenly slowed down, pushing forward a wave that rolled out towards the near shore.

"Fuck," growled Josh. The boat slowly edged closer to their hiding place. The motor slowed to an idle, the boat barely moving. Then the boat accelerated, passing their hiding spot, disappearing into the night.

They all looked at each other at the same time, then toward the boat that sped away from them to the south.

Janie pulled out a cigarette, which Josh promptly swatted away into the water. “Nope. Think about it, Janie, we gotta move. We’re going to get a closer look at those buildings while that guy is gone, but we have to move fast. He could come back at any time.”

The two Seminoles pushed the boat to the shore, the aluminum bottom eventually grinding on dry land.

“You first.” Josh tossed Janie off the front of the boat. She landed on the half-mud half-clay shoreline, her shoes sucking as she pulled them forward, each step a struggle. Nate followed and pulled the boat up farther with a frayed bowline.

Janie turned to confront Josh. “What if that guy comes back?”

Josh looked up at the star-shrouded sky. “Jesus, you’re like my old girlfriend. Look, I can’t stop to tell you about shit every time something fucking happens. Let’s just get a good look and get out of here. Maybe we’ll find my cousin.” He paused, looking at his phone. “Just got a text from Blaze. They’ve arrived at the front of the property. Come on, let’s get moving and don’t say another fucking word.” Josh pushed her forward, and Janie reluctantly complied.

She turned. “So these are the McFaddens?”

Josh nodded. “Be quiet and move,” he said.

Once on dry land, they were overcome with mosquitoes and no-see-ums and the reeds bit into Janie’s face. She didn’t like being manhandled and shushed; her temper simmered just below a boil. But it soon cooled as they neared the metal building that hung out over the water a hundred yards away. Josh pushed her up the low mud embankment to the shore. She swatted his hand away, then promptly slid hands down into the mud. Josh pushed her up again and she paused for a moment, bracing herself on her hands and knees looking at the shed in the distance.

* * * *

Henrietta grew nervous as she contemplated where she was and what had happened. Isaac was right, this had gotten messy.

"You must take me away from here immediately. Our business is finished for the night."

Isaac looked back at her as he peered from the double open doors out to the water. The old woman looked spooked. "Is something wrong?"

Henrietta moved towards Isaac and raised her hand. Isaac moved to get away, but Henrietta quickly grabbed his chin with her long fingers. His eyes were captured by her gaze. Her breath was like berries and cream. He swooned. "The senator?" she asked.

"He's trussed up good."

"Jimmy?"

"He is okay."

She squeezed his chin harder. "Now."

"Of course, Henrietta."

26

CHANCES

"YOUR COUSIN IS GONNA owe us big time," Blaze coughed as he passed the pipe to Robbie. The young Seminole shook his head.

"No, gotta keep a clear head. You smoke so much of that shit it doesn't affect you. Me, I get right messed up."

"Maybe you're right; this stuff is hydroponic. It's, like, molecularly designed by some fucked-up chemist from Amsterdam. Had to try it. Might calm me down a bit. I am too damn hyped."

"Tell me about it."

Both young men sat in the front seat of the Jeep, its side panels open to the elements. They didn't speak for several minutes. Blaze's fingers tapped rhythmically along the barrel of the sawed-off shotgun that sat on his lap. Robbie put his handgun on the dash.

Robbie broke the silence. "I'm not thinking this is such a good idea, bro. We've got to stop anyone who comes out of this place?"

"Yep."

"Supposed to shoot 'em?"

"Guess so. Let's just see."

"Just fucking askin'. Who lives in this shithole?"

"Shhh."

Five minutes later, it was Blaze broke the silence. "When's the last time you saw Jack?"

"Quite a few years, probably at his mom's funeral."

"That whole thing really fucked him up. He beat the crap out of his dad after that."

"It's just not right. People shouldn't have to deal with that kind of shit. It fucks with your head."

Blaze bolted upright in his seat. "Shit, bro. There's a car coming out."

"No shit, you're right. Let's block the driveway."

"Not with my brand new Jeep. No eff'n way. We'll stand in front of the driveway with our guns out. Try to look menacing. I'll do the talking."

* * * *

Jack lay in the trunk of the car, his mind churning. Mercifully, the cord that had bound his feet and hands was gone. His hands were still tied behind his back, but he could move his fingers. His ankles were likewise bound and his mouth was still sewn shut; he could taste the blood that must be seeping out of his cracked and punctured lips. His head and body bounced around as the car buffeted along a rough country road. He took a moment to let his mind clear once the vehicle found a smoother surface.

The Satanist bastards were going to try to frame him in the death of Senator Hunter's family. Buck was taking him to an airplane. *Bastards.* The senator was destined to be gator food unless he found a way out of this mess. James Hunter was his ticket out of jail, the only person who could vouch for his innocence.

The tail lights let Jack see that the lights' metal housing was sharp-looking on one side. *Paydirt!* He moved so that he could rub the plastic cord along the surface. It took him some time, but finally his feet were free. With a little more wiggling, he was able to use the jagged edge to free his hands. The sensation of blood returning to them was one of agony, pins and needles, but it soon passed.

He'd seen a movie once where a captive in the trunk of a car punched out the tail light and stuck his leg out of the hole, hoping that someone would see the leg and report the car. It was worth the try. He twisted around so his head was close to the back seat, hoping to find some leverage. He needed to make sure that his kick was a good one. His captors would hear the impact, and he figured two kicks were all he would get. The fact that he didn't have shoes on was another problem. At first he tried pushing; he did manage to get the housing off, but behind it was the red plastic cover. The hole was too small to fit his hand through, let alone a foot. He sank down into the floor of the trunk in frustration.

As he lay there, he became aware that something was sticking into his left hip. He ran his fingers along its length: a tire iron. His mood picked up. It took him a few minutes to think things through. There was just enough illumination from the rear lights to see the inside of the trunk. He pushed the pointed end of the iron into the gap between the trunk door and its locking mechanism. If it had been a newer model, he wouldn't have had a chance. Buck's old Cadillac offered a fairly large gap. The bar fit into the crack, but his numb hands let him down and the iron slipped out of them and clanged to the floor of the trunk. The car slowed a little bit, and he held his breath hoping it wouldn't stop. He breathed a sigh of relief when the vehicle sped up.

He gathered his energy and steeled himself to do what needed to be done. If he was going to escape, this was the best chance he'd had during his captivity. He took a deep breath and slipped the bar back into the crevice between the lid of the trunk and the frame of the car. He hesitated for a moment, feeling the car accelerate. They had most likely reached Interstate 75. If this was the case, he would not have much time before they reached one of three possible airports. He doubted that they would use Southwest Florida International. His bet was Punta Gorda Airport in Charlotte County, or Pilot Field, out of which many small jets and planes flew.

This time, instead of trying to pull down on the metal bar, he pushed up. To Jack's delight, very little pressure was required and the trunk popped open. He was greeted by a vacuum of air created by the speed of the car. He gasped for breath, the warm South Florida air filling his lungs. He slowly pushed himself up to the edge of the trunk and poked his head up as high as he could. Buck had just passed a black Tahoe, and its lights shone directly into his eyes. The SUV swerved just a little. The sight of a head popping up from the trunk which had just sprung open, not to mention his sewn-up lips and bruised and bloodied face, must have been a shock to the driver. The SUV driver started honking his horn and flashing his lights.

Buck slowed the car and pulled over onto the shoulder. The following vehicle pulled in behind them. Jack breathed a sigh of relief; he would not have done so had he been the SUV driver. There were a lot of crazy people driving around southwest Florida, and you never knew who was packing, never mind having to confront a couple of crazed, murderous Satanists with a prisoner in their trunk.

Just as the car came to a screeching halt, he pushed himself up and over the edge of the trunk. It took nearly all of his energy to finish his roll. His shirt snagged on the locking mechanism. *DAMN!* He gave one more push with his legs on the forward edge of the trunk opening and felt his shirt rip. He fell hard to the ground, landing on his already burning shoulder. The SUV slammed on its brakes, narrowly missing his head as he rolled clear. He kept rolling down into the long grass and brush of the median.

He heard Buck's voice as he rolled away. "Now get back in that car, mister. We don't want any trouble here."

He heard what he guessed to be the voice of the driver. "I know what I saw, mister, I'm calling the police." Silence. "Mister, put the gun down, I don't want any trouble."

Buck spoke. "This is none of your business, put the phone back in your pocket!"

The other door opened and Jack could see the feet of the other man as he walked around behind the car. "Walker is gone!"

Jack saw the flash of light that accompanied the gunshot. He heard the sound of a body hitting the ground. *Jesus.* He was now a good fifty yards away and into the large pine trees that filled the middle of the interstate median.

"Where is he?" yelled Buck.

"I don't know, did he get hit? Look under the cars! He can't go far with his feet tied up." His captors' voices became more distant.

He managed to roll into a ball and then pop up onto his feet. It was a well-practiced move after having been tackled so many times. He hadn't walked in days, and wobbled to the nearest tree and hid behind it. His legs ached; he stretched out a cramp forming in his right calf, the knife wound was a searing pain. He looked back—both men were frantically circling the cars. He crept his way down the pines. Soon he couldn't hear the men's voices at all. They would be onto him in seconds if they spotted the rolled-down grass. His best hope was that Buck and the passenger would need to take time to stow the body of the SUV driver—poor bastard.

Once he was a good hundred yards down the median he ran for the other side of the freeway, stumbling on the uneven ground. He looked back and saw a couple of cars approaching where Buck's car was parked. *More time.* As he reached the road, he saw a construction site on the other side and he ran for it.

As he reached the jumble of parked construction vehicles and debris, he looked back and saw that one of the cars was moving—Buck's Cadillac. It headed north slowly then looked as if it was turning into the median on a turnaround. His heart thumped and he could barely catch his breath with his sewn lips.

The car came back along the highway in his direction very slowly and pulled over to the side of the road. A stream of several cars passed. The car door opened and Buck stepped down from the vehicle, scanned the median, and then looked towards the construction site. He started walking toward it.

He heard Buck's boots as he stomped across some loose gravel. He scanned the area for something he could use in self-defense. The best thing he could find was a long metal bar used for knocking cement off the inside of a mixer. He huddled down behind a steamroller, the bar resting in his sore, swollen hands.

"Walker. I know you're here. I saw your tracks in the grass. Come out and we can work something out."

Jack smiled, nearly ripping his lips off. *Yeah right, like I'm going to work something out with you, asshole.* He tried his best to pick at the stitches that bound his mouth. He was able to pull out a couple on the left side. He could now draw in a partial breath. He gripped and re-gripped the metal bar, his fingers still weak. He picked up a stone and tossed it a distance off to his right. Buck heard the noise and moved toward it, taking steady, measured steps. Within seconds he would pass in front of Jack's hiding place. Jack slowly drew in a breath and pulled back the bar, ready to strike.

Buck stopped. Jack could see the barrel of a gun sticking out past the corner of the machine. Buck began to turn back, but before he could, Jack brought the heavy metal bar down on the large man's forearm, feeling the bone crumble under the blow. Buck doubled over and Jack wasted no time and brought the bar down on the back of his head. Buck's head caved in as the bar embedded into the back of his skull. Jack lifted the bar and slammed it into the back of his head again. He didn't bother trying to retrieve the weapon.

"Sick Satanic fuck. How's that for working something out," he mumbled out of the corner of his mouth. He bent down and took the man's shoes off. They were a bit large but would do. He turned back, looking at Buck's still body, and kicked it in the ribs as hard as he could, three times. He would have kept doing so, but he remembered the other man. He tucked Buck's Magnum in the back of his belt, rolled the body over and searched his blazer and found his wallet and cell phone. "Jackpot," he muttered.

Jack looked toward the old Caddie. It was still running. He shook his head and stumbled towards the vehicle. He contemplated hiding the body but figured it wasn't worth the effort. He slipped into the driver's seat and sat still for a moment, his heart pounding. He flipped down the visor and looked at his face in the mirror. *Christ, I look like shit*, he thought. He pulled out onto the highway, not wanting to get caught by the state troopers stopped at the side of the road, nor to deal with the other Satanist. He couldn't tell if the SUV had moved or not. Where was the other man? *Damn.*

He accelerated to the speed limit and headed south. He made his bearings once he saw an Interstate 75 sign, the digital compass in the car indicating he was heading south. He needed to get the stitches out of his mouth. Knowing there would soon be relief nearly drove him crazy with anticipation. After five minutes he turned off the highway and pulled into a gas station. He took a look at the GPS attached to Buck's dash. There were several recent addresses. The second to last one was an address south of Immokalee. He was willing to bet that this was the McFaddens, but he needed to make sure. He was going to kill Isaac and Jimmy McFadden.

He grabbed an empty coffee cup that was sitting in the dash holder and held it up to his mouth as he walked into the convenience store. The girl at the counter looked at him curiously as he fumbled with Buck's wallet to pay for nail clippers and a bottle of water. He was sure that the cashier saw his stitches and was reaching for her cell phone as he stepped out the door. He jumped back into the vehicle and pulled onto the cross road and headed inland.

With one hand, he clipped the twine with the nail clippers, and with the other, he tried to stay on the road. If a cop had been following him, he would have been pulled over in a second as he swerved from lane to lane. By the time he made it past the interstate, the stitches were out. He should have bought some ointment to disinfect his mouth. What he really needed was a hospital and some good medical care; his leg was still hurting where he'd been stabbed. But he couldn't risk that right now.

He cleared his throat a couple of times, then dialed Gramps; it was one of those numbers burned into his memory from his youth. The old man picked up immediately. "Who is this?"

"Gramps, it's me, Jack."

"Jesus, Joseph and Mary. Are you all right son?"

"I've been better." He took a few calming breaths. "I'll make this quick. You were correct, it's Henrietta LePley behind all of this, and a couple of bastards named McFadden."

"Hmmm. Makes sense. Josh, Nate, and that lawyer's assistant, Janie have gone looking for you."

"Nooo." He remembered Gramps's words days ago: *"We look after each other. We do not leave anyone behind. We do not surrender. We do not get captured. Are we clear?"*

If he had any hesitation about returning to the McFadden estate before, it was gone now.

Gramps interrupted his thought. "They knew it might be the McFaddens, figuring it could be one of three families are behind this. They're a bad bunch, Jack, notorious for doing dirty work for the old families."

"Tell me about it. Fuckers! I gotta go back there." He could feel his face flushing. "Josh won't know what he's in for, and they have Senator Hunter. Can you call them?"

"I've tried, but I'm sure he's turned off the ringer. Jackson, call the police, turn yourself in. If the Senator is involved this has become too big for you."

"Gramps, I will, I promise. I can see the face of that fucking Jimmy McFadden and it will haunt me to my grave if I don't kill the motherfucker. I'm probably gonna rot in a cell for the rest of my life at this point anyway. I got nothing to lose, Gramps. I have to do this. Like you said, there are no coincidences in life. There's gonna be no coincidence when I plant a bullet in the middle of that fucker's face, and his brother's for good measure."

"I have seen this in augury. I feared that you would be like this. Be careful, Jackson. I understand, I was once young and have had my dealings with these people. If you cannot do what you need to do quickly, back off and wait for the police. Remember, they still think you are the bad guy. Don't get yourself killed by a cop's itchy trigger finger."

"This is beyond being fucking careful, Gramps. I let my father beat Mom to death. I will never forgive myself for that. I'll never forgive myself if Josh or the other two get hurt. For once in my life, I'm making a stand. Right or wrong, this is what I am doing." Jack hung up before the old man could talk him out of returning to the McFaddens' house of horrors.

Jack called Perry. His phone rang a number of times before voice mail clicked in. Perry wouldn't answer a strange number at this time of the night. "Perry, pick up your fucking phone. It's me, Jack." He hung up and dialed the number again. This time Perry picked up.

"Perry, It's Jack."

"What the fuck, bro! Where are you?"

"Can't explain in two minutes and that's all I got. I've been abducted by the Satanists, and I've just escaped. I need your help, pal. I need you to look up an address. It'll be in the back country. McFadden."

"You're in a truckload of trouble, my friend. Hang on, give me a few seconds, I'll look that up . . . There's a few of 'em. Pine Island, Naples, here's one on David's road, let me map it . . . Immokalee Road and just keep going thirty miles from the highway, then right. That's Nowheresville, Everglades."

"Perry, I need you to listen and do exactly what I say. It's going to take me thirty minutes or so to get there."

"You're fucking kidding me. You're not going back!"

"Have to, man. My cousin Josh went in there looking for me. I've got to kill the bastards who did this to me before they get him. They've got my boss as well."

"Senator Hunter?"

"Yep, they're going to kill him soon."

"I'm fucking calling the police now, bro, you don't sound right."

"Nope, listen. I want you to call Peter Robertson, got that, of Robertson and Robertson. I'm gonna need a lawyer. I had his number but it's a mushed up ball in my pocket. By the time you get him and explain what's going down, it'll be time to call the police. I just want a little lead time."

"You're one crazy motherfucker, but you're starting to sound like the old Jack."

"Maybe. Prison is too good for these assholes. I've made a mess of this whole thing and my life and I'm willing to risk it. I'm taking a stand no matter what the consequences. This is fourth and goal, Per."

* * * *

Jimmy didn't go far; there was a big hole half a mile away where the gators were thick. Pulling into the small bay, he stopped the engine and panned a flashlight along the grass and mud shoreline. He could see the reflection of reptilian eyes in the beam of light.

He moved to the back of the boat and unfolded the plastic that held Lani Green's body parts. He started with her arms, tossing them toward the shore. It didn't take too long to attract the large predators. Soon there was a swirling of tails and jaws fighting over the fresh flesh. He tossed in the rest, once he had the gators' complete attention. He waited until he saw one of the bigger beasts swim close to the boat before he threw in the head and hands. Ordinarily, he ground them down and dispersed the mess in the river for the catfish, but he hadn't had the luxury of such time. He watched the huge gator crunch the skull in a few savage chomps. “Atta girl,” he said with his puckered grin. The hands went last. He would burn the plastic in a barrel once he returned.

On the way back, he stopped for a look at the spot where he swore he’d seen the outline of a boat. He’d been in too much of a hurry to have a good look on the way out. His instincts had been correct. Hidden in the middle of a stand of tall sawgrass was an airboat—Shark River Airboat Tours.

Jimmy moved his boat toward the shore, shining his flashlight along the bank. He saw a patch where the grass and mud had been disturbed. He frowned. “Fuckers.” He pulled the bass boat up on the embankment, grabbed his hunting rifle and followed the tracks in the mud.

* * * *

Josh put his index finger to his mouth as the sound of a car’s engine roared to life. He pulled himself up on the dock and stealthily worked his way to one of the back windows and looked in. He motioned for Janie and Nate, and whispered: “The building appears to be empty—I want to see where that car was going.” They passed though the strange workshop filled with televisions, chairs, sofas, and stuffed animals. The mortician’s table made Janie shiver.

Janie tugged on Josh’s shirt sleeve. “I think we’ve hit pay dirt.”

The young Seminole nodded in agreement.

Nate put his finger in the air and paused for a second. “I hear that fishin’ boat again.”

Josh nodded. “Shit, you’re right. Get over to the window. Janie, you stay down.”

The sound of a boat could be heard moving toward them from the south. Then the engine cut.

“Holy shit, what now?”

Janie’s cell phone vibrated and she nearly jumped out of her skin. She looked at the screen; it was Peter. She turned off the phone.

* * * *

The driveway through the McFadden property was a quarter of a mile long. Halfway to the exit, Henrietta’s cell rang. She pulled it out of her purse and placed it to her ear. “Henrietta

LePley." She cringed as she heard the French accent on the other end of the line.

"Henrietta, *ma chère*. It's Mason."

"What is it?" she said sharply.

"I have bad news. I will keep it simple. Jackson Walker has escaped. He managed to pry open the trunk of the car and jumped out. I have not seen or heard from Buck. He took off to chase Walker."

"How could this happen?"

"When we pulled over to stop Walker, another car . . . someone who was following us pulled behind us. If it were not for this person, Walker would not have escaped."

"The driver of the car would have seen all of this . . . "

"*Oui, ma chère*. He is dead. He is in the trunk of his car, which I am now driving. I have not been able to get Buck on his phone. Have you heard from him?"

This can't be, said the voice in her head. "Isaac, stop the car."

Isaac followed orders.

"Mason, something must have happened to Buck."

"Where are you?"

"I'm on my way back to the McFadden estate. I will be there soon."

"Isaac, turn the car around."

Isaac hesitated for a moment. "What the heck?" He pointed at the two figures walking toward the car, the slight fog off the river creating a halo effect around their forms. Both appeared to be carrying weapons—one a sawed-off shot gun, the other, some kind of pistol. He stepped out of the car, much to Henrietta's dismay.

He stuck his head out the car window and yelled. "Whoever you are, back up and get the hell off my property."

The men advanced.

Isaac reached into his pocket, pulled out Lani Green's handgun, and fired at the person to the left. He was pretty sure he'd hit his target in the chest, as the man went down quickly in a heap. A second later he was greeted with a shotgun blast and was hit with several pellets, mostly his right arm. It felt as if his ear had been ripped off; touching his lobe, he found a bloody mess. He cursed, seeing the blood on his white jacket.

Another blast from the shotgun took out the front window. Isaac knelt down behind the car door and eyed up his next shot. The shotgun wielder looked as if he was jammed. Isaac braced the gun with two hands on the edge of the open window and squeezed the trigger. He wasn't sure where he'd hit the man, but his target left his feet on impact and then fell to the ground backwards. Isaac hung his arms down for a moment to catch his breath, then walked sternly towards his downed adversaries. He reached the man with the shotgun first; his throat and upper chest were blown apart and there appeared to be no movement in the body. The other man lay convulsing on his side. He'd been hit in the gut, and was trying to hold his innards to keep them from popping out of the wound. The man looked up in fear. Isaac placed the gun on his forehead and pulled the trigger.

He slowly walked back towards the limousine after gathering up the firearms, hesitating before pulling open the door, worried at what he might find. The old matriarch glared at him as he looked down at her.

"Is the situation resolved, Mr. McFadden?"

Isaac took a deep breath. "The two men are dead. They looked to be native."

"Very well. Please take me back to the main house. The smell of the shed is noxious. Mason will be back soon and we will have to devise a suitable response to the mess we now find ourselves in. Walker has escaped, and haven't heard from Buck."

Isaac dropped his head and returned to the driver's seat. His hackles were up. The McFadden family had survived for generations by being wily, knowing their limits, and being in control—a bit psychotic, but always in control. Henrietta's words tipped him over the edge. The control factor was now gone. Jimmy and he would have to look out for their best interests. Those might not include the old woman. If necessary, he would shoot her, too.

* * * *

As Janie slid the phone into her pocket, she heard gunshots from the direction the car had gone. Josh and Nate were watching the back of the building intently. She whispered, "We're cornered. Where did the boat go?"

"That's what I want to know. This guy is a hunter, and I doubt he's going to let his quarry know what direction he's coming from. I don't like it one bit. We can't go out front, either. Time to call the cops."

Out of the corner of her eye, Janie saw headlights coming up the driveway. "Josh, we've got more company. There's a car coming our way."

Nate was the first to move. "Crap, we're out of here. Come, follow me." He went out the back door of the shed and ran along the dock, his heavy boots making loud thumps. "Back to the b—"

There was a flash from the direction they were heading and the crack of a high-powered rifle. Nate's head exploded with the force of the hollow-point bullet that entered through his forehead. Janie heard the sound of a gun reloading with a sharp snap, a cartridge hitting the ground.

Josh stopped in his tracks, searching for their adversary. Both Janie and he saw the man standing on the ground with the gun propped against the edge of the deck, but too late to dodge the next shot. The bullet hit Josh in the thigh; he flew backwards five feet from the impact and landed in the water.

Janie didn't look to see what happened to Josh, but instead became transfixed by the puckered face of the man with the rifle. *Cha-chink*, another round was loaded. Events slowed for Janie, she saw the empty cartridge twirling in the air as it dropped past the edge of the deck. The man leveled the rifle, pointing it directly at her face. It was strange that she could tell where he was aiming. It wasn't her chest, it was right at her goddamned face. *Bastard, I'm not going to die like this*. With all the strength left in her, she dove toward the water. The bullet zipped through the edge of her cheek, but she felt no pain. She saw the puff of smoke from the end of the rifle, and then she felt herself enter the lukewarm water. There was no sound from the splash.

She swam under the dock just as another shot took out a chunk of wood from the piling next to her head. She put the dock between herself and the gunman, then kicked off her shoes. To the left, she could see Josh pulling himself into the reeds. As the man moved up onto the dock, Janie ducked under the water and pushed herself out into the river, using one of the barnacle-encrusted pilings for leverage. She was an excellent swimmer and could make it to the other side in one breath. The water was murky, and there was no way the man would be able to see her in the depths. The bottom of the watercourse was muddy and filled with debris and water plants which grew thick in the deepest section as she passed through. As she neared the far side, something bumped into the side of her leg. It wasn't a bite, it was a heavy bump from something much larger than herself. She refused to panic; if she surfaced, she was sure the gunman would blow her head off. She struggled into the sawgrass embankment, trying not to exhale too loudly as she slowly broke the surface. She carefully pulled herself into the grass. There was a large swirl in front of where she entered. She expected to see a large reptilian tail, but instead swore it was a fin. She scampered back quickly. Another shot . . . a bullet whipped through the grass.

* * * *

"Jimmy, what the hell are you shootin' . . . " Isaac's words died in his mouth as he saw the body lying on the deck.

"Wu-wu-one of the fuckers got away clean. A woman. Jezebel will take care of her. Fresh meat. The other, I don't know. I think he was hit in the leg. He's out in the water somewhere. Won't last long, gators are all over the blood I poured out earlier."

"The old woman is in the house and we're expecting guests." Isaac shook his head, looking at the gore spilled out on the dock. "Get this mess cleaned up."

Jimmy nodded.

27

VENGEANCE

IT TOOK SOME TIME for Perry to get through to Peter after hanging up with Jack. He eventually found his way through an irritating telephone loop to Robertson's answering service, who in turn called Peter directly.

"We're calling the police now!" Peter said in his deep baritone. "What the hell does Walker hope to achieve besides getting himself killed?"

"My thoughts exactly sir, but he didn't seem 'right' on the phone. I tried to talk him out of it. He's hell-bent on vengeance. The tipping point was his cousin Josh possibly being there looking for him. I get the feeling that he really doesn't care if he gets himself killed. He's on a mission, like he used to be before a big game. The blinders are on, and that's that."

"I'm with his aunt. She flew in this afternoon, and she's terribly concerned. Give me the address and I'll call the police. It might be better if I did it; I've been in contact with them throughout this fiasco."

****

Jack was pumped up during the drive, seething with anger. He couldn't get to his destination fast enough. He left the Cadillac at the side of the road a few hundred yards from the McFadden driveway, and steeled himself to the trepidation creeping in. He hopped an old wire fence and nearly fell on his face as he became stuck halfway over. "So much for being sneaky," he mumbled to himself. He brushed himself off and headed toward the McFadden residence. The brush was thick and full of brambles, making it a challenge to move quickly. He decided to stay to the right of the buildings, keeping to the cover of the dense brush.

****

The massive fish swirled the surface of the water with its tail fin, circling in front of where Janie had crawled up the bank. After a time, it appeared to give up and moved away. Janie was relieved as it disappeared into the depths of the muddy river. The gunfire ceased. She could see more people on the deck of the boat house—three people, as best as she could tell in the darkness. She unzipped her jacket pocket; her handgun was still there. She wondered if it worked.

She looked around. She was on a small muddy knoll that looked as if it had been used by gators. Large ones. Behind her was a never-ending sea of grass and reeds. *How do I get out of this?* She calculated that the river was only about fifty feet wide, and the water was moving slowly. She hadn't believed Nate when he mentioned that there might be bull sharks in the river, but she was sure it had been a shark's dorsal and tail fin that broke the water a few minutes back. She was no expert, but it must have been nine to ten feet long, judging from the distance between the two fins. It didn't matter—she wasn't going back in. She held her gun in one hand and a large stick in the other, just in case that big gator came back looking for its bed.

****

Josh couldn't feel his hands and feet, nor could he get the image of Nate's head exploding out of his mind. His leg was starting to hurt. The bullet had hit him just above the knee and had bitten into bone, and below the knee the leg canted off at a funny angle. His attention was pulled toward movement off to his right, and the sound of swishing water. It took him only seconds to pick out the reflection of a large gator's eyes as it moved towards him. His blood must have attracted the creature. He half-stumbled, half-hopped through the grass and thigh-deep water towards their airboat. The gator was getting closer. Josh handled alligators on a near-daily basis, but not in the dark, not in the wild like this, and not with his leg nearly blown off. The creature would stalk him for a time, trying to size up whether he posed a threat.

The boat was another twenty feet away. He moved calmly, and the gator edged closer. He wasn't going to make it to the boat before the huge reptile cut him off. He braced himself against an old stump and pulled out the long hunting knife hanging from his belt. He put one hand under the water, his other up above his head. With one massive flap of its tail, the beast made a powerful strike. Josh sank down low into the water and pushed underneath the gator's jaw as it tried to clamp its toothy mouth down on him. Josh stabbed near its throat, and the beast retreated, making a large splash as it surfaced. Josh took advantage of the opening and hobbled towards the boat. The alligator followed him into the deeper water and looked like it was ready for round two as they converged upon the boat.

Josh grabbed the edge of the craft and attempted to haul himself up. His first effort failed, as he couldn't lift his bad leg over the gunnels. He moved around the craft, putting it between him and the beast, and edged his way around to the cage that protected the large prop at the back. He stuck the knife in his teeth and pulled himself up with brute force. The gator came at him again; he was a sitting duck, hanging off the back of the boat. This time he didn't give the creature room to strike, driving the knife down between its eyes. The gator rolled, pulling Josh with it in its dance with death. Josh released his hand on the knife and hopped gingerly back to the boat. Pain was really starting to set in. He needed help quickly before he went into shock and passed out.

It took him a couple of minutes to roll into the boat. He fumbled around the back seat looking for his cell phone. Thank

God it was still there. He dialed Gramps' number.

The old man answered instantly. "Josh?"

"Yep, it's me, Gramps. I've been shot and my leg's nearly busted in half. I'm losing too much blood. It's the fucking McFaddens. They got Jack, I think . . . and Nate is dead."

"Are you in danger? You need to put pressure on the wound."

"I'm back at the boat. I'm gonna fire it up and get over to the state road."

"The woman?"

"Don't know, she dove into the water. Big gators here."

"Stick cloth in the wound and brace that leg if you can. Upper or lower?"

"Upper, don't look good."

"Damn. I'm calling the Reserve Police, hopefully Benny's near, and I'm calling an ambulance, I'll give them your number so they can find you. I think I know where you are, roughly. Keep calm and head north, you'll run into David's Road. Help is on the way. Jack has escaped, but he's coming back to look for you."

"Christ, tell him not to!"

"I wish I could. He's not answering."

* * * *

Jack moved through the brambles and tall weeds towards the shore of the river. The property was larger than he thought, and it took him several minutes to come within a few hundred yards of the large McFadden manor house. He ducked down as a car came up the driveway from the road, approaching the house. He moved as quickly as he could to the base of an old oak tree dripping with Spanish moss. He watched as a figure exited the vehicle. He instantly recognized the dark-skinned Mason; he whispered under his breath, "I've got a bullet for you as well." The man walked toward the large, well-lit house. He quickly ascended the front steps to the wraparound veranda and entered the house without knocking.

The senator would be in the storage room which had served as Jack's cell for the past three days, if Isaac and Jimmy hadn't already buried him behind the shed. He didn't feel up to taking on Jimmy first; the thought of the ugly man sent a shiver down his spine. Instead, he crept toward the large manor house. He moved between several cars and made his way to the back of the massive house. Inching his way forward, he stood on his toes to look into the window of the large kitchen. The lights were on, but there was no one in that room. He moved slowly to his left, careful not to step on any twigs. He passed a couple of dark rooms and then came to one that was lit. He could hear voices from within. He didn't dare look in the window, but instead listened to the conversation that could be clearly heard through the screened window.

Jack recognized Isaac McFadden's voice. He would remember that polished drawl for the rest of his days. However, for the first time since his incarceration, he could hear tension in it.

"I have followed along, Miss Henrietta, throughout this whole set of circumstances without saying much. If Eric were still alive, he would have none of this. It's time to cut our losses. Jimmy's got Hunter trussed up like a hog. He's ready to bury him in a sinkhole. Now Walker is free. The only thing we have going for us is the fact that the evidence against him is damning. The police are going to be here sooner or later. Walker is either going to get caught or turn himself in. He knows who we are."

Mason spoke. "I think he might yet prove himself to be a thorn in our side. My prayer has told me so."

"As has mine, Mas—" The old woman's words died in her throat.

There was silence for several agonizing moments.

Jack couldn't help himself and poked his head up to have a peek in the window. He reeled—not ten inches from his face was Henrietta LePley, staring directly at him with her perfectly straight-toothed smile. "I was hoping you might come back to us, Jackson."

Through the screen he could smell her honey blossomed breath. He stood transfixed, drawn into the deep green splendor of the old woman's eyes. He felt as if he might want to put his head on her shoulder and give in. He could almost feel her hand running through his hair, her long nails caressing the back of his scalp.

"Now be a good lad and put the gun down," she murmured.

Jack caught a motion out of the corner of his eye, just as Isaac tackled him hard and knocked the gun out of his hand.

The attack cleared his mind, breaking Henrietta's spell. Isaac straddled him, raising his fist and landing the first blow. He broke the ridge of Jack's nose; pain shot through his head, and blood flowed down his shirt. He somehow blocked the second blow with his right arm and tried to twist from under him, but Isaac was wiry and strong.

He tried to land another punch; this time Jack let him throw, except he rolled to the side. Isaac's fist glanced off the side of his head, hitting the ground and throwing him off balance. Jack rolled with him, breaking his attacker's hold. As he rolled, he ended up lying on top of his gun. He fumbled for a moment, but was able to grab the weapon. He rolled back towards Isaac, who scrambled to his feet and looked down at Jack who was now pointing the weapon at him. Their eyes locked on each other and Jack could see Isaac's fear. He pulled the trigger. The bullet ripped a hole in the center of Isaac's throat. His head flopped backwards grotesquely, his lifeless body dropped to the ground, legs quivering. Jack scrambled to his feet and ran back around the house in the same direction from which he had come, not bothering to be careful.

* * * *

Jimmy dropped the senator off his shoulder onto the mortician's table. Hunter was drugged and would not put up a fuss. "Time's up, Mr. Senator." Jimmy walked over to the box of remotes and clicked on each individual television in the shop. He picked up a large blade with wooden handles on each end. "This'll pop that head of yours off in just a few seconds." He placed the blade over the middle of Hunter's throat, but stopped, realizing he hadn't covered the workspace with plastic. "Lucky bugger, you get to live for a few more minutes."

He heard a gunshot, and within seconds his hunting rifle was in his hands. He patted the senator's leg. "You wait here." Jimmy never walked in a straight line, he shuffled from side to side, the gait of a practiced hunter, his eyes darting back and forth. He slipped out the side door, carefully moving to the shadows. There was no use running hell-bent into danger. He stood motionless, watching, waiting.

****

Janie also heard the report of the weapon. *Damn.* She didn't have much time to think. Who was shooting the gun, and at whom? If it involved Jack, he needed her help. She had to move, the place was giving her the creeps; she had a sinking feeling that the owner of her resting place might show at any time. She moved back into the water at the edge of the tall reeds lining the bank. She saw a man run from the boathouse toward the driveway.

She paused for a moment. *Do I dare go back in the water?* Not with that damned shark. She needed to draw the animal back. She splashed the water with the stick, holding her gun in the other. Nothing. She kept doing it, only with more force. A gator moved off the bank ten feet to her right, aroused by the noise. Then a large form surfaced a dozen feet in front of her.

"Damn."

It was a shark. She swore that the thing rolled on its side and had a look at her, its light green eye lifeless and cold. It disappeared for a minute, only to resurface a little closer. The gator kept its distance from the larger creature. It resurfaced again, within five feet of her. She took a step into the water, raised her gun and fired, aiming at the eye. She didn't miss by much, blowing a small hole in the side of its head. The shark went into a wild flurry of spasmodic twists and turns, gradually sinking into the water, a trail of blood following it into the depths. The large gator took off after the dying animal, and she thought she saw a few more of the beasts moving in for the feast. She crept down the shore, as far away from the now churning water as she could get, and slipped into the river quietly. She stuffed the gun into her belt and dove under the murky water, swimming as calmly as she could toward the other side.

****

Jack turned the corner of the house and stopped for a moment checking to see if there was anyone in the front yard and driveway. Things looked clear. He didn't waste another moment and headed towards the boathouse. Just as he reached the large side door, he heard the crack of a twig under someone's shoe. He turned and was greeted by the barrel of a high-powered hunting rifle.

"You're a dead man, Jack Walker." Jimmy moved out from the shadows. "Drop the weapon."

Jack didn't think it wise to try a hero move with Jimmy's gun pointed directly in the middle of his chest. He let the gun drop to the ground, feeling a stab of panic rising in his throat. Jimmy nudged him with the gun and pushed him into the workshop. He walked slowly backwards, watching over his shoulder that he didn't bump into anything. He saw Hunter's form on the table as he reached the middle of the room.

"Sit down." Jimmy pointed at the couch in the middle of the floor.

****

Henrietta made her way down the stairs off the large sweeping porch. Mason followed. They both stopped, Mason putting his hand up demanding silence. They both watched as Jimmy McFadden marched Walker into the boathouse.

Mason addressed the matriarch. "It is time that we left this place. The spirit Satan has told me so. He has never been wrong."

"Fine." Henrietta hesitated as if listening to something. "Get the car running. I won't be long. We cannot leave that half-wit Jimmy McFadden to his own devices. He must be given guidance."

"Be careful, *ma chère*". Mason left her and walked briskly towards the stolen SUV.

Henrietta walked deliberately towards the boathouse. She could hear the sound of the televisions blaring from inside. If she entered, she would not have the benefit of the spirits to guide her. She felt a slight twinge of panic rise in her throat.

Henrietta stepped into the doorway, both men turned their heads to look at her, but only for the briefest of seconds before they reverted their attention back to each other.

"Shoot him now, Jimmy McFadden." Henrietta yelled over the buzz of the televisions.

Jack surprised himself with how calm he felt. "You shoot me, Jimmy, you don't get to hang me on the hooks, let the gators eat me feet first. Remember, an eye for an eye?"

Jimmy hesitated, seeing the reason behind Jack's comment. "He's right, old woman, we need retribution for Eric. Shootin' him in the head just ain't good enough for the bugger."

"Jimmy McFadden, listen to me and put a hole in his goddamned head now!"

A voice rang out from the back of the shop. "Lower your weapon."

Janie's voice was shaky as she stood soaking wet, the light from the dock forming her in silhouette.

"Who in blazes are you? Henrietta exclaimed.

Jack didn't move. Did Janie have the nerve to shoot?

"I said, lower your weapon." Janie's voice was a little louder, urgent.

With the calmness of an expert, Jimmy moved his aim from Jack to Janie and fired, the bullet hitting her square in the shoulder. She was able to squeeze off a shot, but it flew harmlessly high of her target. She fell to the ground, the Glock sliding along the floor towards the old woman. Henrietta moved to pick up the weapon.

Jack heaved himself upwards with all of the strength left in his muscular legs, feeling the burn of the old stab wound. He brought his shoulder up under Jimmy's rifle and drove his other shoulder into his solar plexus. He was surprised at how sturdy the man was, as he didn't budge much and seemed unfazed by the attack, his limited brain process allowing him to remain controlled. Jack could smell the man's foul breath.

Jimmy grabbed the other end of the rifle and hit the back of Jack's head. Jack continued to drive his legs, his head screaming from the pounding he was taking. He reached lower and wrapped his arms around the back of Jimmy's legs. With a spinning motion, he knocked the ugly man off balance and continued to drive. He was able to lift Jimmy and once again drove forward with his legs. The two men flew over the front of the couch, knocking it over onto its back.

They rolled next to the mortician's table near the edge of the water, and Jack grabbed for anything he could find, his hand closing on a long, thin, sharp-ended tube about a quarter of an inch wide. He swung his arm in a big arc, ramming it home into Jimmy's stomach. The pucker faced man howled in pain, sounding like a wounded animal.

Jimmy scrambled on all fours towards Jack, eyes wide,

growling, grabbing Jack's arm and sinking his teeth into him. "Motherfucker!" Jack yelled.

Henrietta fired a shot, the bullet tearing a hole in the wood floor between the men. She fired again, missing wide.

Jack stabbed the thick needle into the side of Jimmy's neck as he lunged forward. Blood shot out of the other end of the tube. Jack rolled away as Jimmy grasped desperately at the tube protruding from him. As Jack scrambled to his feet, Jimmy pulled the tube out. Jack kicked him with all his force in the nose.

Jimmy rolled to the side and Jack pounced, driving the heel of his foot into his mouth; he felt bone breaking. He stomped again and then planted his foot on his chest and pushed him over the edge into the water. It wouldn't be long before the gators had him.

"Die, asshole."

Jack felt the muzzle of the gun on the back of his head. Henrietta's words were ethereal, almost reassuring. "If he isn't already dead, he will be soon enough, Mr. Walker." He turned to face Henrietta, her eyes darker, almost black, her breath no longer sweet but foul. "You have made a mess for me, Jackson, but I will get over it. The devil has his way of rewarding good disciples, and I have been his best."

Over the corner of her shoulder, Jack saw three men in black combat armor silently enter the shed, their assault rifles honed on the gun-wielding woman. He could see the red lines from the laser scopes aiming for her head.

"I disagree. You sold your soul, Henrietta, and isn't the saying 'the devil shall get his due?'"

"Silly boy. I gladly gave my soul and have led an enlightened life. Do you remember our agreement, Jackson? I am the Devil's disciple. I follow his wishes implicitly and your name is in his book." She smiled a tight smile, showing her stained teeth.

"Lower your weapon!" The voice of the SWAT team captain resonated over the blare of the televisions, and Jack dove to the right.

Henrietta raised the gun towards her jaw, but before she could pull the trigger she was riddled with bullets. Jack watched in shock as the projectiles exited the matriarch's back. He didn't feel an ounce of pity for the woman. She fell to the ground, her eyes scanning the room vacantly until her lifeblood slowed its exodus from her thin body. A look of utter shock remained etched on her dead face.

The tracers were now on his head, and he raised his hands in the air.

"Face down on the ground, hands behind your head!"

For all these men knew, he was still the bad guy. He looked over at Janie and was relieved to see that she was still moving. As he put his hands behind his head, Jack shouted, "We have a woman down over by the door. She's been shot. The senator is on the table—for God's sake, someone help him."

Jack was cuffed with a plastic tie and led outside.

* * * *

The property was mobbed with police, ambulances and the press. A man in a pinstriped suit was escorted through the throng of people to the shed, where he was detained by two police officers, one on each elbow. "Jack," said the man. "Peter Robertson. I am glad that you're still with us. Unfortunately, you're going to have to spend some time in jail until we can sort this mess out. Where is Janie?"

"I think she is okay. She saved my life back there."

"She's one tough woman. I'll be in to see you tomorrow, Jack. We'll get the senator to make a statement once he is feeling better. Hopefully we can get you out on bail. Your aunt is willing to pay the bond." Peter patted Jack on the shoulder.

Jack turned as he heard the familiar voice of his grandfather. "You have done well, Jack, but we have lost some of our own. We must mourn their deaths. You can't fight the devil and expect to be unscathed. Be careful, as you have made a dire enemy. Rest now and your fancy lawyer will hopefully get you out on bail."

Jack hugged the old man, then put his hands on his shoulders. "Grandfather. I owe you an apology, I owe our family an apology."

"Stop. There is no need. You needed to be where you were. Remember that I said there are no coincidences in life. You came back when you were needed, just as fate would have it. This has been a painful time, but I am proud of you."

The police officers ushered Jack away from Gramps and the throng of activity and placed him into a detainment van. The door was shut with a loud clank, the locking mechanism engaged.

Sitting across from him was Mason, his hands bound like Jack's. Their eyes met.

"Jackson Walker," said the man in his thick French accent. His eyes were black, and like lasers they seared into the back of his skull. Jack's throat was instantly dry. A wry smile formed on the man's lips. "You have proven very resourceful." His eyes were unrelenting. "You made a deal with the devil, Mr. Walker, a week back. I know you remember."

"The devil? Stop with the bullshit, you Satanic fuck. I made no such deal with any Devil, Satan or whatever else you want to call him!"

"Ahh. Perhaps you thought it was with Henrietta. We both serve a higher being, as agents per se. Mr. Walker. It's time to pay up . . . one way or another. You see, the beauty of being a Devil worshiper is that it's expected of you be dastardly, I take great pleasure in it."

His eyes narrowed and he whispered through pursed lips. "We know where your family lives, we will watch your every move . . . be it as a free man or in a prison cell. This isn't finished."

ACKNOWLEDGMENTS

WRITING YOUR FIRST NOVEL is a daunting task, it's a leap of faith into the unknown. *Devil in the Grass*, thankfully, dragged me along for the ride. If I had been left to my own devices, it would have remained as 2.5 MB on my old laptop's hard drive, thought about every now and then, and eventually forgotten. I met many people along the two year journey and took advantage of their expertise, knowledge and gentle, sometimes not so gentle, prods. I am blessed to have many friends and family who praised my work. If I have learned one thing, your book can never be good enough and I say this with self -deprecation, but you have to stop somewhere. Here it rests.

I would like to thank: the state of Florida, my second home, which inspired me to write my story. Most visitors merely scratch the surface. There is another world there if you look for it.

My wife, Carmen, for her constant love, patience and daily sounding board.

Lori Handelman of Clear Voice Editing, who found some sense in my ramblings and encouraged me to publish the story. *Devil in the Grass* would not exist without her.

My Publisher, Koehler Books; its president, John Koehler; Executive Editor Joe Coccaro; Acquisitions Editor Nora Firestone; Copy Editor T Campbell; and the excellent graphic design staff who gave the book a cool and wonderful face. Thank you for making the process a welcoming and fun experience.

Leticia Gomez, Literary agent, Savvy Literary Agency.

Caughill Legal Services

My readers, friends and family, who encouraged me and gave valuable feedback: Carmen Bowron, Audrey Wright, John Wright, Tamara Schaaf, Kyle Tashjian, Sally Huang, Perry Johnson, Jen Caughill, Bruce Caughill, Phil Bowron, Jim Hunter, Karen Berti, Vicki Bolduc, Bonnie Grimm, Sarah Gleddie, Jewell Betts, Viviane Elltoft, Molly Bowron, Lew Lipsit, Steve Lock, Steve Furley and Graham Heyes.

My Florida fishing brethren.

CPSIA information can be obtained
at www.ICGtesting.com
Printed in the USA
LVOW12s1742080517
533722LV00002B/621/P

9 781633 932067